Captain Rance Knight: the one man Officer Carly Mitchum had made a point to steer clear of. And he was scowling at her as if he'd gladly wring her neck. An empty cup rolled around on the floor, its contents having splattered across the front of his white shirt, staining it a muddy brown.

But the scowl on his face could not detract from the aura of power, the sexual magnetism that surrounded him the way he was stari

Why on earth man, the one with capital le man with dark, silver-flecked hair, deep-set brown eyes and a heavy growth of beard that no matter how often he shaved still looked like he hadn't, had a reputation for being hard-nosed and cynical.

And it was common knowledge he had no use for women officers.

MEN at WORK

✈—MILLIONAIRE'S CLUB   💼—BOARDROOM BOYS   💥—MAGNIFICENT MEN

🔗—TALL, DARK & SMART   🍎—DOCTOR, DOCTOR   🌿—MEN OF THE WEST

🔩—MEN OF STEEL   🔰—MEN IN UNIFORM

MEN *at* WORK
MARY LYNN BAXTER
KNIGHT SPARKS

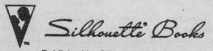

Published by Silhouette Books
America's Publisher of Contemporary Romance

SILHOUETTE BOOKS
300 East 42nd St.,
New York, N.Y. 10017

ISBN 0-373-81033-4

KNIGHT SPARKS

This edition published by arrangement with Harlequin Books S.A.

® and TM are trademarks of Harlequin Books S.A., used under license. Trademarks indicated with ® are registered in the United States Patent and Trademark Office, the Canadian Trade Marks Office and in other countries.

Printed in U.S.A.

Dear Reader,

While I'm definitely fascinated with Texas cowboys, I'm
equally as intrigued with Texas lawmen. In order to serve
and protect, make our justice system work, it takes
courage and daring. I've always been in awe of both.

I've tried to make the hero and heroine of *Knight Sparks*
just such characters. In this particular story, the system
works all right, but they don't.

Although both like their chosen profession, they don't
like each other. Carly Mitchum is a woman in a man's
world. While she's comfortable with that, her immediate
boss, Rance Knight, isn't. He thinks females are not
made to wear badges.

The moment they meet, sparks fly, both on and off the
job. At first, Carly thinks Rance is behind the push to
drive her off the force. Eventually, she learns this is not
true.

Still, it's hard for two headstrong people to swallow their
pride and finally admit that love and being loved is what
makes the system of life work.

When they reach this conclusion, it's the sparks of love
that fly. As a reader, I hope a few of these loving sparks
land on you.

Mary Lynn Baxter

Please address questions and book requests to:
Silhouette Reader Service
U.S.: 3010 Walden Ave., P.O. Box 1325, Buffalo, NY 14269
Canadian: P.O. Box 609, Fort Erie, Ont. L2A 5X3

Prologue

"Well?"

"Well, what?"

Larry Beechum shook his head, drawing attention to his ruddy cheeks that folded into jowls if he let himself put on weight. "Aw, come on, Lanier. You know that dumb act won't wash with me."

Hal Lanier snorted at the same time as he shifted his tall, gangly frame and rested his hand on his holstered pistol.

"You know I'll find out whether you scored with the powder puff, so you might as well come clean," Beechum badgered, a tainted grin thinning his lips.

Lanier couldn't quite look his fellow officer in the face as the two lounged against the wall across from the deserted squad room.

Suddenly Beechum threw back his head and laughed. "I'm right, aren't I? You haven't opened your mouth to her."

Lanier's sheepish grin gave him away even before he spoke. "You're right, I haven't, but I plan to rectify that real soon. In fact, I figured on doing it today."

"Let's hope you'll have better luck than I did." A hard glint appeared in Beechum's eyes. "Carly Mitchum needs to be brought down a peg or two."

"You never did tell me what Timberland P.D.'s only powder puff rookie said to you."

"It's simple. I merely hinted that I wanted to see her off duty, and the high-and-mighty bitch turned me down flat."

Lanier pawed the floor with the sole of his boot. "How the hell did we get *her* on the force, anyway? Police work is not for a woman."

"Beats me," Beechum said. "Hell, a 'split tail' like her should be home warming a man's bed, not out there on the streets dealing with garbage."

"I hear you. So you think I'll fare any better?"

"Let us hope. As I said, I'm depending on you to bring her down a peg or two."

"Then you'll try again, right?"

Beechum's grin held menace. "Right."

Lanier slapped him on the back as both men headed toward the squad room. "Anyone ever tell you that you're a real bastard, Beechum?"

Beechum stopped suddenly. "You complaining?"

"Not in the least." Lanier's tone had dropped to a conspiratorial whisper. "Where would I be without you, partner?"

"Keep that in mind and we'll get along just fine. Forget it and you're in deep trouble, my friend."

Chapter 1

The alarm screeched in her ear. She did not want to open her eyes; she did not want to move. But most of all, she did not want to go to work and face her superior.

The alarm sounded again. It was the most jarring, irritating sound in the world. And it wouldn't quit.

"Great," Carly Mitchum muttered, without looking at the clock radio on the table beside the bed. Instead she reached out fumbling fingers and slammed down the alarm button. She then squirmed deeper under the covers. It couldn't be time to get up, she thought, especially when she'd just gotten to sleep.

Carly allowed herself the luxury of dallying a moment longer, thinking about the hourly visits to the bedroom down the hall. Although it was obvious her uncle was suffering only from a stomach virus, she had nevertheless felt compelled to keep a close check on him.

With a bad heart, one couldn't be too careful, not where Uncle Matt was concerned, anyway. He was more like a father to her than an uncle, and if that wasn't reason enough to forgo a night's sleep, he was her mainstay. He kept her sane in the insane world.

A sudden grimace altered Carly's delicate features. Today was the day she had to give the chief the answer to his "request," and she wasn't looking forward to it, not by a long shot.

Groaning aloud, she tossed back the covers and scrambled out of bed. Ignoring the chill, Carly grabbed her robe, draped over the back of the nearest chair, and padded into the bathroom.

Thirty minutes later she was dressed and ready for a cup of coffee. But just as she was about to flip off the light and walk out, Carly caught her reflection in the mirror. She paused with a lopsided grin. Not bad, she mused. The uniform she wore snugly adhered to her trim, shapely legs—legs developed first by gymnastics and kept in shape with walking and jogging. But nothing, not even the severely tailored long-sleeved navy shirt or matching pants, could disguise the graceful curves underneath.

Not bad at all for a twenty-eight-year-old woman who was still enamored with her chosen profession after four years.

With a sigh, Carly stopped her woolgathering and shifted her gaze to the window. She paused a second longer, caught up in watching the vibrant-colored leaves from the oak and sweetgum trees scatter across the ground.

Ah, the beauty of East Texas. Her home. Although she had spent the past few years in Dallas, her roots were in this small town of Timberland.

Her world was small, consisting of Uncle Matt, Brian Calhoun, a banker friend in Dallas, and her work. She had no complaints. Her life was full; for now she was satisfied, if not content.

Suddenly she gave her head a savage shake and headed toward the kitchen and the invigorating smell of hot brewed coffee. She inhaled deeply and smiled, but then a tiny frown pinched her forehead. Who had made the coffee? Surely her uncle wasn't up and about at this ungodly hour, not after such a terrible night. Still, it was too early for the cleaning lady to be there.

Carly quickly passed through the large family room, her low-heeled black boots sinking into the plush carpet. Reaching the entrance to the brightly lighted kitchen, she paused on the threshold.

Matt Armstrong sat facing the hissing fire that added a cheerful warmth to the room this October morning. Although only in his late sixties, Matt looked older. His thin face was lined and his eyes were sunken, but his chin remained strong, and his hair, although white, was thick.

It was too bad someone like Matt had to have a weak heart. He deserved much better, for underneath his gruff manner was a truly gentle man. In Carly's eyes he was almost a saint. She couldn't bear the thought of anything happening to him. He was the only person who loved her with no strings attached.

"Uncle Matt." Carly spoke softly so as not to startle him.

He jerked his head up. "Morning," he said with a surprising twinkle radiating from his eyes. Even so, there was no hiding the weary droop of his mouth.

"What on earth are you doing out of bed?" Carly couldn't quite keep the censure out of her voice, or the fear.

Matt hunched closer to the flames and held out his hands. "Now, girl, don't start fussing. I'm feeling fine, just fine."

"Yeah, and I'm about to sprout wings and fly," Carly responded flatly, turning her back on her uncle and walking to the counter, where she poured herself a generous cup of coffee.

Matt shook his head and muttered aloud, "My, my, but aren't we sassy this morning. Just goes to show you, young people nowadays don't have any respect for their elders."

"Spare me the lecture, Unc. I know how restless you were last night." However, on closer observation his color did appear to be back to normal, along with his feisty sense of humor.

Matt was eyeing her, as well. "Now how would you know that?"

I sat by your bed the majority of the night watching you, making sure you were breathing, Carly almost said, but didn't, aware he would be doubly upset if he knew she had lost sleep on his account.

Carly spoke with caution. "Remember, I was the one who watched your face turn green before you let me call the doctor and get you some medicine."

"Well, as you can see, I'm none the worse for my experience, though I can't say the same for you. You look like you didn't sleep a wink."

Carly sipped on her coffee, then pulled out the chair next to her uncle and sat down. "Let's say I've had better nights and leave it at that," she said evasively.

"It's the job."

"Uncle Matt, I'd—"

"Things aren't getting any better?" He shook his head. "I was so in hopes that when you transferred from Dallas P.D. you'd be accepted right off."

"Me, too." Her tone was dejected.

"Well, sweetheart, don't let it get you down. Your time's bound to come, especially when they see how good you are. Just remember patience is the key and that you're a—"

"Woman, I know, and the only one on the force. But so what? I'm a good cop, and they're going to have to accept me whether they want to or not."

"Is there one in particular giving you a hard time?"

"Oh, Uncle Matt, there are too many to name." Carly tried to curb the bitterness in her tone, but failed. "One is an officer named Larry Beechum who sometimes rides with me. He's a jerk. I think he has a thing about women in general, even though he stares at me like he plans to jump my bones at any moment. Then there's Lanier, Beechum's sidekick, who also watches me, and Robert Farrell, my shift sergeant. His favorite pastime is aggravating me. Need I say more?"

Matt pinched the bridge of his nose. "I can understand your being concerned about their attitudes. But I'm still convinced that time will take care of most of those problems. When they find out you're serious, they'll back off."

"That's true, but still—"

"It rankles," Matt cut in.

"You'd better know it does, and how."

Her unrelenting frustration threw a pall over the beautiful fall morning. The blatant chauvinism of her fellow officers, from the rookie up to her superiors, was beginning to grate on her nerves.

When she had worked in Dallas, she hadn't encountered this type of treatment, or at least not to this degree. But, then, she hadn't been the only woman on the force, either. Still, that was no excuse.

During her short career as a policewoman, she had never expected to be treated differently, only fairly. And even when she had been treated *unfairly*, as she was now, she'd never said anything. Instead she'd just dug in and worked that much harder, thereby hoping to overcome the prejudices against her. But all her professionalism and hard work was not paying off. As if in punishment for being a female, she was relegated to the lowliest of duties, such as patrolling the school zones and handling dog complaints.

"What if you're going about this all wrong?" her uncle asked suddenly. His voice was low and moderate, while thinning fingers plowed through the full head of white hair. His brown eyes narrowed, making his face appear even more wrinkled and his expression more guarded.

"All wrong?"

"Yeah. Hell, has it ever crossed your mind to loosen up, stop fighting so hard? Have you ever thought about smiling once in a while instead of frowning? A smile might go a long way toward improving relations with your fellow officers. I guess the gist of what I'm saying, sweetheart, is stop denying you're a damned attractive woman and stop trying to be a part of the good ole boy network. Make them respect you for what *you* are—a damn good cop and a female to boot."

Carly's face felt as if it would crack. She sucked in her breath with a harsh sound.

Before she could defend herself, however, Matt sliced the air with a hand. "Believe me, I know how you're feeling right now. You're pretty steamed up. And I can understand that. But I've kept my mouth shut as long as I can. You've blown this discrimination thing way out of proportion. Sure it's okay to want to carve yourself a place in what's always been a man's world, but don't you think it might be more to your advantage to remember you are a female and do it with a little more finesse?"

Suddenly the fight went out of Carly, and there was disappointment in her voice. "Oh, Uncle Matt, not you, too? I can't stand the thought of you deserting me."

"That's hogwash, girl, and you know it. Deserting you is the last thing I'd ever do. I just want you to be happy."

"I know, but that's easier said than done. I can't explain it even to myself, but I feel pressured to prove myself *now*. Today." She paused and gnawed at her lower lip. "That if I don't, I won't ever get the chance again." Her tone sounded desperate even to her.

"That's more hogwash," he snapped, shaking his head in disgust.

"Maybe so, but that's how I feel nonetheless."

His gaze was direct. "There's something else bothering you, something other than the other officers, isn't there?"

Carly sighed and rubbed her temples, suddenly feeling wearier than ever. "It's Chief Crawford. He's pressuring me to transfer to Criminal Investigations under Rance Knight."

"Are you going to make the move?"

"I'd be a fool to. Talk about hard-nosed. Captain Knight's never hidden the fact that he has no use for women officers."

"You have a big decision to make, no doubt about it."

"As far as I'm concerned, it's already made, but still I owe it to Crawford to listen to his sales pitch. It's just that I like working the streets and don't want a desk job."

Matt reached over and patted her hand. "You know whatever you decide, I'll back you one hundred percent."

"Thanks, Unc," Carly whispered, reaching over and giving him a firm hug. "I just wish—"

"You just wish it weren't so hard to be a part of a man's world."

"I guess that's what it all boils down to."

"How does Crawford feel about you—as a cop, I mean?"

She shrugged. "Oh, he's probably just as prejudiced as the next one, but at least he keeps it hidden."

"Hey, break it up, you two."

Startled at the unexpected interruption, both Carly and Matt whipped around.

Carly kept her hand on her palpitating heart, though a smile widened her lips. "Gee, Martha, you scared me half to death."

Martha Ridley, their closest neighbor, was one of Carly's favorite persons. Pleasant-faced rather than pretty, Martha had thick gray hair that framed her broad features and hazel eyes. Filled with boundless energy, she was always warm and friendly, and she doted on Matt Armstrong. That alone endeared her to Carly. It was too bad that her uncle wasn't receptive to Martha's admiration.

"What brings you out this early, woman?" Matt was asking her, his tone surprisingly gruff.

As if completely oblivious to his crankiness, Martha helped herself to a cup of coffee. She then faced Matt with a smile. "I'm going to Tyler today. Thought maybe you might like to ride with me."

"Sounds like fun," Carly chimed in, "but I think Uncle Matt had better pass. He had a touch of virus last night."

"Oh," Martha said anxiously, turning her troubled gaze on Carly as if to say, *why wasn't I told.*

When Carly spoke, her tone was gentle. "He's much better, as you can see. Anyway, you know how he is, independent as hell."

"Will you two stop talking about me as if I weren't here," Matt grumbled, glowering at both women.

Carly merely laughed, and, leaning down, planted a kiss on his right cheek. "I'll leave you two to fight it out. It's time for me to go serve and protect."

The laughter had long ago disappeared from Carly's face. Her mood was once again dark. As she nosed her Firebird in the direction of town and the police station, she rolled down the windows to let in the cool, crisp morning air. She inhaled deeply. It wasn't a long drive, though her uncle's sprawling house on ten acres was not in the city proper.

During the six months she'd been back home, she'd done a lot of thinking during these drives back and forth to work, trying to reconcile the events of her life. When she had graduated from the police academy and signed on with the Dallas P.D., she'd never expected to leave. In reality, her work had become her lifeline as she tried to cope with the unexpected and traumatic death of her husband, Ben.

A shudder passed through her, and for a moment Carly feared her sunglasses would fog up. Though she was long past the tears, there were still times when the senselessness of Ben Mitchum's death threatened to overwhelm her.

"Don't do this to yourself," she muttered aloud, forcing her thoughts out of the past. "The past is dead and buried along with your memories of Ben." Slowly she released her grip on the steering wheel.

The decision to move back to Timberland had not been an easy one. She had dreaded leaving her work, and dreaded leaving her friends, including Brian Calhoun. But her uncle's continual flare-up with his heart had made the move imperative. She owed him too much to turn her back.

Carly's parents had been killed when a drunk driver veered into their lane and struck their car head-on. Her father, also a police officer, had been returning from an association meeting. Her mother had been with him. According to the highway patrolman who had investigated the accident, her parents had never known what hit them.

Matt had been forced to come to the rescue of his brother's child, although his wife had objected fiercely. Ann Armstrong, embittered because she was unable to bear children, had been against taking a child of nine into her home and rearing it as her own.

Consequently Carly's "rearing" had been left to Matt. Though Ann had provided adequately for all Carly's material needs, having come from a monied background, she refused to share herself. Not once did she ever bestow any love on the lonely, confused child. Up until her death from cancer when Carly was in her late teens, Ann had continued to provide only the money, while Matt had furnished the love.

Hence Carly's devotion to Matt. Not only had he surrounded her with love, he had been her inspiration in choosing law enforcement as a career. Like her father, Matt was a cop. Matt had talked to her hour after hour about the challenge his work offered.

She had met Ben at the academy, and he had matched her in determination to be a police officer. They were both in hot pursuit of that lifelong dream, when Ben's life had ended tragically.

Since then, Carly had let nothing interfere with her goal of becoming a policewoman, in spite of close friends having urged her to do something sane and safe, such as modeling or teaching school.

Achieving her goal had been no easy feat. She'd been afraid to care about anyone or anything, afraid that if she did, her dream would be snatched away from her. In the end, however, she had rallied and joined the force.

Yet down deep she still yearned for something other than a career. She yearned for a home and family. No casual affairs, thank you. Her next relationship would be for the rest of her life.

Carly paused in her thoughts and glanced out the window. She wasn't, however, distracted by the view. She scarcely noticed the cars whizzing past her or the uptight drivers behind the wheels. Her thoughts were concentrated on her problems at work. Her stomach felt tied in knots, and a frown marred the normally smooth skin of her forehead.

Was Matt right? Was she overreacting, manufacturing problems where there were none? She drummed her fingers against the steering wheel, paying little attention to the mellow sounds coming from the car stereo.

If Matt was right, and she wasn't saying he was, where had she gone wrong? When had she become so frantic, so intense? Had Ben's death done this to her? She hadn't always felt so driven.

A smile toyed with her lips at the thought of her graduation from the academy; she'd swelled with pride and anticipation. But somewhere along the way that contentment had been replaced with disgust and discontent, especially with the path her professional life seemed to be taking.

From the onset she had vowed to make the most of the change

from Dallas to Timberland, to work extra hard to be accepted, not just as a good female officer, but as a good officer period.

So far, it had been an uphill battle, as the majority on the force remained skeptical of her ability. They never let her forget she was a good-looking woman whom they thought should be home cleaning house and diapering babies.

By the time Carly pulled into the parking lot behind city hall a few minutes later, the frown was back on her face.

"Lighten up, for God's sake," she muttered again, yanking the keys out of the ignition and dropping them into her purse.

When she got out of the car and made her way into the building, her back was straight and her chin set.

Dean Crawford sat relaxed behind the clutter on his desk, his eyes leveled on Carly.

The chief was a beefy, chubby-faced man who was going bald, though he made no effort to hide the fact. What gray hair remained was cut close to his head.

"Well, Mitchum, what's your answer?"

Carly didn't speak for a moment, conscious of the commotion going on around her. Five minutes ago, when she'd entered the squad room, threading her way to Crawford's office in the rear, it had been deserted. Now it was a beehive of activity. Uniformed officers and detectives were standing around drinking coffee and exchanging stories and wondering why she was in Crawford's office. Carly smiled without humor.

"Officer Mitchum."

Carly blinked and forced a smile. "Sorry."

"Don't be sorry," Crawford said briskly, reaching for a half-smoked cigar in the ashtray at his elbow, "just answer my question."

It was all Carly could do to hide her distaste of the foul odor that instantly permeated the room. If this session lasted much longer she would have trouble drawing another breath.

"It's not that simple, sir."

Crawford lifted a brow. "Oh."

"I want to know more about the assignment," Carly said, moving to the edge of her chair.

"What more do you need to know, Mitchum? It's simple. You'll be working under Captain Knight. He'll train you."

"I know," Carly began patiently, "but—"

Crawford flounced a hand through the air. "It's not like I'm ordering you to take the job, Mitchum. I'm merely asking."

I just bet you are, she thought. She knew from past experience that if she didn't accept the transfer, she'd be asking for trouble.

"So, what's it going to be, yea or nay?" Crawford pressed.

Carly refused to be intimidated. "Why me? Why am I being considered?"

"Well, I've been observing you since you joined us. You've conducted yourself like a professional in the field. In addition, I've been reviewing your records from the Dallas P.D. and I like what I see."

Instinct told Carly she must not take his words at face value. He wasn't doing this because she was a good cop; he was doing this to needle Rance Knight. Their ongoing feud was no secret. Knight wanted Crawford's job and didn't care who he told. And knowing how Knight felt about women cops... "But would there be an advantage in making the move? I'm happy where I am."

"If you're asking if there would be more money, the answer is no. If you're asking if there's a promotion in it for you, the answer is no. And if you're asking if the hours would be shorter and the work less grueling, the answer is no. But as I've already said, you're a good cop and as a woman you would be an asset to C.I.D."

Carly was quiet for another moment, still doubting the sincerity of his motive. Then she stood and said, "Under the circumstances, Chief Crawford, I think I'll pass. As I've already said, I'm perfectly content with my present assignment." Her tone was as cool as the morning air.

Crawford stood, as well, actively inhaling on the cigar dangling from one side of his mouth, his puffy cheeks red. "Sure you won't change your mind?"

Carly knew he was angry, even if the expression on his face belied the fact. The hostility in the air said otherwise.

"I'm sure," she said quietly. "But thank you for considering me."

After another moment of awkward silence, Carly turned and walked to the door. Once she'd closed it behind her, she released her pent-up breath and began hurrying down the hall.

So intent was she in replaying her conversation with Crawford that she didn't pay attention to where she was going. With her head bent in an effort not to notice her fellow officers' stares, she bumped headlong into something big and solid.

"What the hell!" a voice exploded.

Chapter 2

Gripping her by the forearms was none other than Captain Rance Knight, the one man Carly had made a point to steer clear of, and he was scowling at her as if he'd gladly wring her neck. An empty cup rolled around on the floor, its contents having splattered across the front of his white shirt, staining it a muddy brown.

But the scowl on his face could not detract from the aura of power, the sexual magnetism that surrounded him, heightened by the way he was staring at her.

Carly swallowed hard, trying to saturate her dry mouth so that she could speak. However, Knight was the first to recover.

"Dammit, Mitchum, why the hell don't you watch where you're going?"

"Sorry...sir," Carly stammered when she got her breath back. "I...I didn't see you."

His tone reeked with sarcasm. "That's rather obvious."

Why on earth did she have to run into this man, the one man who was trouble spelled with capital letters? This tall, rugged-faced man with dark, silver-flecked hair, deep-set brown eyes and a heavy growth of beard that no matter how often he shaved still looked like he hadn't, had a reputation for being hard-nosed and cynical. And it was common knowledge he had no use for women officers. Rumor had it that his dislike of them stemmed from an ex-partner, a female ex-partner, whose negligence had almost gotten him killed.

Shortly after Carly had joined the force, Knight's comment to another female officer, no longer there, was passed on to her. "If the Lord had wanted a woman to be a cop, He'd have given her something besides a pistol." In Carly's opinion, the quote more than summed up this man's chauvinistic attitude.

And if that wasn't reason enough to keep her distance, Rance Knight was serving his stint as head of Internal Affairs, the department that investigated fellow officers for possible wrongdoing. No one wanted to be associated with that division, least of all Carly.

Still, up close he was damned attractive, Carly thought. Too bad he had such an unhealthy disposition and was off-limits. Under other circumstances she just might be interested....

Realizing that he was still holding her, not only with his hands but with his eyes, as well, Carly swallowed again, suddenly frightened.

"Please...I..."

At her stammered words, he released her arms quickly, reacting as though he'd been burned. The expression on his face was one of surprise and distrust.

Feeling her face flame with color, Carly tried to gather her scattered senses. "I...I told you I was sorry."

A muscle in Rance's prominent cheekbone stood out. "So you did, Mitchum, so you did."

Once again their eyes met and held, and suddenly the seconds seemed to limp past.

"Er...I'll be glad to take your shirt and wash it," Carly said at last, thinking that this was a fair offer. After all, why hadn't *he* been watching where *he* was going. At the thought of taking the defensive again, her cheeks grew hotter. There was something about the proximity of this man that totally unnerved her.

He continued to stare at her, only differently this time, as if he were documenting everything about her—her mouth, her breasts, her stomach, and lower....

She almost gasped aloud as her heart slowed, then lurched into a heavy rhythm that made her whole body throb. Still their eyes held, his dark and unreadable, hers wide and inquiring, watching a muscle tick in his left cheek.

"That's won't be necessary, Mitchum," Rance said, a sudden smirk disfiguring his thin lips.

Damn him! she thought, but merely shrugged and said, "Suit yourself." Then, feeling as if she might have gone too far, she rushed on to say, "I mean, yes, sir. Whatever you say."

"Where were you going in such an all-fired hurry, anyway?" Carly licked her lips. "To...get some coffee."

He rolled his eyes heavenward. "If that isn't just like a woman to—"

"To what, sir?" Carly cut in.

"Forget it, Mitchum," he said tightly. "It wasn't important."

"Still, I'd like to hear it, sir," she said, her tone full of sweetness and light.

He raised thick eyebrows. "All right. It's just like a woman to go off half cocked—"

Red-hot anger boiled inside Carly. "I resent that, sir." She ached to slap his smug face.

"Let it go, officer, while you're still ahead."

Carly would never know if she would have let it go or not. Before she could make a decision, a detective working under Knight strolled up and effectively shattered the tense moment.

Wade Grisham was chuckling openly. "Hey, you two, if I'm not mistaken, the bell for round one just sounded." Suddenly his eyes landed on the front of Rance's shirt, and he grinned widely. "Ah, now I get it."

Carly purposely ignored him.

Rance drawled, "Grisham, if I were you, I wouldn't let my mouth overload my rear."

Unabashed, the tall redheaded detective focused his attention on Carly, his lips still twitching. "Mornin' Mitchum," he said, shoving his glasses closer to the bridge of his nose.

It was all Carly could do to respond in a normal voice. "Good morning."

Grisham turned back to his boss. "Hey, Captain, you out of clean shirts?" His deep-bellied laugh echoed down the hallway. "Or better yet, maybe you just forgot to pay your laundry lady?"

Rance's tone was threatening. "Knock it off, Grisham. You're about to talk yourself into early retirement."

"Sorry, sir." Although the grin was no longer in evidence, Grisham's eyes were alive with merriment. "Seriously, if I interrupted anything, I'm—"

"You didn't," Carly said.

Following those tersely spoken words, Carly turned her back on them both and strode down the hall. Instead of going to the lounge for coffee as planned, she ducked into the nearest ladies' room.

Closing the door behind her, she looked around and, seeing she was alone, slumped against the hard surface. Her eyes dipped to her hands, which were clasped tightly together in front of her.

To her dismay, they were trembling.

Several hours later, when Rance made it back to his office, he still had one thing on his mind and one thing only—Carly Mitchum.

Her personnel folder was open on his desk.

"Hell, Knight," he muttered aloud, "when you screw up, you screw up royally. No, sir, there's no halfway point with you."

He couldn't put the morning's fiasco to rest. Disgusted with himself, he stood at his office window and stared outside with unseeing eyes. What had driven him to antagonize her?

Granted, he didn't like women officers, didn't think they had a place on a police force. But whether he wanted to admit it or not, his bizarre actions had been brought about by more than his disapproval.

It was Carly Mitchum herself.

Stunning. That was the word that came to mind. Feature for feature she approached perfection. She was endowed with a peaches-and-cream complexion that went hand in hand with her curly chestnut hair, blue eyes and a mouth men would die to kiss. Not only was she tall and slender to the point of fragility, but there was something proud in the way she held her head, high yet slightly tilted.

Sure, when she'd joined the force, he'd noticed her right off. How could he not? Especially as she continually strutted around the station? But his baser instincts hadn't been affected. And still wouldn't be, if she hadn't smacked into him, and he hadn't felt those soft breasts against his chest.

And that's what stuck in his throat. She was too damned beautiful to work around nothing but men. It was bound to cause trouble.

Who was he kidding? Her presence had already caused trouble. He could testify to that. Not only was she playing havoc with the system, but with others, as well. Why it was only yesterday that he'd heard her being discussed in the squad room in less than complimentary terms. In fact, he'd called the officers down on the spot.

"Can it, Knight!" he spit aloud now. So she'd felt good in his arms, *felt right*, been so soft against him, smelled so good. And so she'd looked up at him with hauntingly lovely blue eyes. So damned what?

He wasn't interested in her. Even if she weren't off-limits to him, which she was, he still wouldn't be interested. For one thing, she was too young and he was too old, too jaded. For another, she'd been reared with a silver spoon in her mouth, while he'd been reared with practically nothing but a roof over his head.

Oil and water don't mix. And to think that idiot Crawford was trying to force her into transferring to his department.

Bracing his hand against the window jamb, he rested his forehead against his arm. At forty, work was the dominating force in his life. Always an overachiever, Rance had excelled in his studies in law enforcement at Sam Houston University, and after slaving to graduate, he'd gone to work for Houston P.D. But it hadn't taken long to get fed up and burned out with big city politics. That was when he'd decided to return to his hometown of Timberland, where he hoped to work himself up through the ranks. He had done just that, and in record time, too.

But now he had his eyes on a bigger job. He wanted to be chief of police, and was determined that nothing would stop him, least of all a woman, any woman, no matter how much he might be attracted to her. Women who wanted long-term relationships had no place in his life.

Besides, he'd already traveled that road. One marriage was enough for him. The only female he catered to was his sixteen-year-old daughter. He doted on her. Between his daughter and his work, his life was complete. He didn't need anything or anyone else.

The buzz of the intercom brought Rance up short. He blinked several times as if to clear his head, before whipping around and crossing to his desk.

"Yeah?"

"Captain, the chief wants to see you in his office."

"Okay."

When Rance walked out the door a few minutes later, his mind was free of Carly Mitchum for the first time that day.

"Well, how was your day, Carly?"

Carly's smile was weak. "Oh, all right."

"That bad, huh?"

This time Carly laughed and plopped down on the couch in the lounge next to one of the department's dispatchers, whom she now considered a good friend.

Angie Glenn was blessed with petite features as well as a petite body. Though only about five feet, she was remarkably endowed in the right places.

To make her more enticing, Angie had short blond hair and a bubbly personality. But she was very much engaged to the local football coach, which kept her from being "hit on" by the officers in the department. Her fiancé was known for his boxing skills, or so Angie had told her with a laugh.

At the moment they were the only ones in the room, much to Carly's relief. She immediately propped her feet on the glass coffee table, strewn with the morning paper, and eased her head back against the leather cushion.

"It's scary sometimes—the way you can read my mind, Angie."

Angie smiled. "It's no big deal, believe me. There are times when everything you're feeling shows on that beautiful face of yours. And this is one of those times."

Carly wrinkled her nose. "I guess that's a backhanded compliment, so I'll say thanks."

"Don't worry about the thanks, just tell me about your day. Why the disgusted look?"

"No reason, really," Carly hedged. "Farrell ought to be proud of me, though. I issued more than my share of speeding tickets today."

Angie flicked a blond curl off her cheek. "And you'd rather do anything but that."

"That's an understatement. But that only goes to show you how little I rate around here."

Angie's eyes filled with sympathy. "Don't give up. You're time's coming. One of these days you'll get their respect, you wait and see."

"Only problem is I may be too old to care."

"I doubt that."

A silence fell between them while Carly pressed a finger against her temple, feeling a headache coming on.

"By the way, how did your session with Crawford go?" Angie asked, breaking into the silence.

"It didn't. I turned him down flat."

Angie frowned. "Was that wise?"

"Probably not," Carly said, opening her eyes and sitting up. "But C.I.D. is the last place I want to work. You know how those bunch of detectives are. Most of them are divorced, and the ones that aren't are just looking for a reason to be. If I entered their world, I'd merely be fair game." She shook her head. "That's not the way I see my career developing."

"But what about those slimeballs you work for now? Beechum and Lanier, for instance. They're two jerks if I ever saw any."

Angie's assessment of her fellow officers brought a lopsided smile to Carly's lips, making her suddenly appear vulnerable. "True, but so far I've managed to get my bluff in on them." She paused. "Or at least I hope so."

Angie wasn't smiling. "Don't be too sure of that, especially with Beechum. I've seen the way he looks at you. That's why I find it hard to believe he hasn't made a pass at you."

Carly's face turned red. "Now that you mention it—" she began.

"Ah, so I was right," Angie interrupted, her eyes flashing. "He has made a move."

"Well, sort of, but it's nothing I can't handle."

Angie gave an unladylike snort. "You'll let me know if you want Josh to teach him some manners, won't you?"

Carly laughed and shook her head. "I don't know what I'd do without you."

"Me, either. Someone needs to keep you in line."

Carly stood and stretched. "Oh, you don't have to worry about that. Uncle Matt hovers as much over me as I do over him. And speaking of Uncle Matt, I guess I'd better get home and see how the ornery old codger made the day."

Angie grinned. "Well, have a good evening. And do me a favor, will ya? Forget about this place for a while."

"Yes, ma'am," Carly said with a grin, crossing to the door.

"Oh, by the way," Angie said to Carly's back, "was your assault on Rance Knight planned?"

Carly swung around, her eyes wide. "How did—"

"Hey, come on, you know nothing is sacred around here. I kept waiting for you to tell me about it, but since you obviously weren't going to, I couldn't keep quiet."

"Somehow that doesn't surprise me."

"So?"

"So what?"

"So tell me."

Carly's face was a mask. "I'm sure you've already heard all the juicy details."

"Sure did." Angie grinned. "But not from you."

"And you're not going to, either. Goodbye."

Although Carly was quick to slam the door behind her, she wasn't quick enough to drown out Angie's "Chicken."

Rance had come to the conclusion long ago that Chief Dean Crawford was a weak-kneed bastard who took great pride in straddling the fence until the fence started to shake beneath him. Then and only then did he resort to action. By Rance's standards, it was usually too late.

Through the glass window of Crawford's office door, Rance watched as the chief sat back in his chair, the phone receiver cradled between his left ear and shoulder. Rance had to hand it to Crawford. Even though he'd been anchored behind a desk for more years than Rance cared to count, he hadn't allowed himself to grow flabby. Through vigorous exercise at the gym, he'd kept himself in tip-top shape.

Too bad that commitment didn't spill over into his work. The cops in the department didn't necessarily like him, nor did they respect him. Apparently Crawford was either blind to this fact or didn't gave a damn. He just seemed to rock along, comfortable with things the way they were and making no effort to change them. But the department suffered from his neglect and lack of leadership. Morale was at an all-time low, something that Rance, if he ever became chief, would rectify.

Glancing up, Crawford signaled for him to enter.

Instead of taking a seat in one of the chairs, Rance eased down on the corner of the chief's desk and immediately picked up a pencil and began toying with it.

Crawford didn't mince any words. "Two things, Knight. First, even though Mitchum turned thumbs down on the transfer to your department, I want you to know I haven't given up."

"Why?" Rance asked, keeping hold of his temper by a mere thread.

"Why what?"

"Why are you determined to move her?"

Crawford ran a hand over the bald spot on the top of his head. "Because, as I've already told you, I think she'll make you a good hand."

Rance almost swore, but didn't. He wasn't about to rise to

the bait, give Crawford the satisfaction of knowing that he was furious. He knew exactly why Crawford was trying to force this issue—the chief wanted to get back at him. Crawford knew Rance was after his job, and every time Crawford got a chance to nettle him, he took it.

Rance's voice was cool. "Well, for the record, I haven't changed my mind. I'm still against it." Then, changing the subject, Rance asked, "What else did you want to see me about?"

"The robberies, of course. We're in trouble up to our elbows over that last burglary, Knight, especially since that clerk showed up at the wrong time and was wounded."

"I have to tell you that he's barely hanging on to life."

Crawford slammed a beefy fist into the palm of his other hand, stood and began pacing behind his desk. "Dammit, what a mess."

"But it could be worse, especially if that fellow dies." This time Rance's tone was as cold and hard as the glint in his eyes.

"You've got to get on this one quick, or the press will have a field day tearing us apart. This is just the type of stuff they love to exploit. I can just see the headline in the paper now: FATHER OF TWO DIES AFTER SURPRISING A BURGLAR."

"And the follow-up, which won't be in print, of course, but will be hinted at: what are the police going to do about it?"

The color in Crawford's face was mounting by the second. "Exactly. That's why we have to move on this thing now."

"Right. I'll see Winston and get all the particulars on the burglaries, go over them with a fine-tooth comb, try to come up with something, anything."

"In other words, we've got nothing."

"We've got nothing."

"Dammit," Crawford said again, more to himself than to Rance. "If only that poor fellow hadn't chosen to return to the pharmacy to get Lord knows what that he'd left behind, he wouldn't be lying flat on his back, fighting for his life."

"And the department wouldn't be under the gun," Rance said sarcastically.

If Crawford took umbrage at Rance's sarcastic bluntness, he

didn't show it outwardly, but when he spoke, his tone bordered on the defensive. "It's a senseless waste of a life, that's all."

Rance lifted an eyebrow, thinking that his ears were playing tricks on him. Crawford caring about anything or anybody but himself? Rance couldn't believe it.

"I couldn't agree more," Rance said at length, "and if we don't catch the one or ones responsible, there'll be more bloodshed."

"What does your gut instinct tell you, Knight?"

"It tells me that it's more than one man. For one thing, the work is too professional, too smooth. Not only have they hit pharmacies here in Timberland, but Nacogdoches, Lufkin and Tyler as well."

"So far, we are the only one to claim a near fatality."

Rance stood. "So far, but if we don't shut the operation down soon, I'm sure that'll change."

"Let's stop it before it does."

"Don't worry," Rance promised, "we'll get the bastards, and when we do, the charge will stick."

A few minutes later Rance was in his office, about to send for his ranking detective, Bud May, when the phone rang. Reaching for it, he barked into the receiver, "Knight."

"Dad?"

Instantly his face changed, the lines around his mouth eased and his eyes lighted. "Hi, Stacy, honey."

"Hi, Dad," she said, laughing softly at the other end of the line. "For a minute, I wasn't sure it was you. You sound so...oh, I don't know...mad at the world."

"Sorry, honey, I've just got a lot on my mind."

"Bad day, huh?"

"No more than usual." Then, switching the subject, he asked, "To what do I owe the honor of this call?"

Rance could picture his daughter, more than likely lounging in the center of her bed, trim as a pencil with her shoulder-length brown hair a mass of tangles on the pillow and her green eyes shadowed by thick lashes and gazing up at the ceiling. The thought brought a grin to his face. This woman-child was the only good thing that had come out of his marriage.

"Actually, I wasn't sure I'd catch you at the station this late," Stacy was saying.

"Well, I'm glad you did. What's up?"

"Oh, Daddy, does something have to 'be up' for me to call you?"

"'Course it doesn't, honey. It's just that you don't do it often enough for me to take it for granted."

She chuckled. "Actually, the reason I'm calling is that I'm coming to stay with you this weekend, if it's all right."

Rance didn't hesitate. "Fine. I'll look forward to it."

"Mom's going out of town."

"I suspected as much," Rance responded evenly.

"And with James, too. I wish—"

"Don't say it, Stacy," Rance cut in.

"Oh, Dad," she whined, "I wish you and Mom..." Again she faltered.

Rance strove to hang on to his patience. "Stacy, you know that's a dead issue. Your mother and I are finished. We'll never get back together." His tone softened. "You're going to have to accept that."

He could hear her sigh. "I hear you, Dad, only I don't have to like it, do I? Nor do I have to stop hoping."

"No, I guess you don't." He almost smiled at her reasoning. Teenagers. He guessed that if he lived to be an old man, he'd never understand how their minds worked.

"Dad."

"Huh?"

"Mom's real...mad at me."

"What have you done this time?"

Stacy's tone turned petulant. "Nothing. But she says I've been running around too much. All she does is gripe about my friends. I'm sure she's going to call and tell you I'm getting out of hand."

"Are you, Stacy? Are you getting out of hand?"

"Oh, Dad," Stacy wailed, "I knew you'd take her side."

"Dammit, I'm not taking sides. Anyway, that's not the point.... Oh, hell, we'll discuss this when I see you."

"All right," Stacy said, sounding suddenly forlorn.

He hung up the receiver, feeling much older than his actual years, then leaned back in his chair, a grim expression on his face. He feared his daughter was getting out of hand, far too rebellious, and it was clear that Denise couldn't handle her.

Then again, he wasn't sure he could, either. When it came to dealing with a hardened criminal, he knew exactly what to do. But when it came to his own kid, he felt lost.

On top of that, Stacy couldn't have picked a worse time to come. But somehow he'd cope. He always had, though merely coping didn't seem good enough anymore.

The house was unusually quiet.

"Uncle Matt," Carly called, a twinge of fear in her heart, "where are you?"

No answer.

As she quickened her steps toward the den, her heartbeat started to race. Although a fire was smoldering in the hearth and a lamp burned beside his chair, there were no signs of her uncle.

Carly's next stop was the kitchen; she saw the note immediately. It was propped against the fruit bowl in the middle of the solid oak table. As she read it, a smile crossed her lips. Matt had gone with Martha to Tyler, after all.

"A lot of good my preaching did," Carly mused aloud, but she knew that Matt was in good hands. If he hadn't been up to it, Martha wouldn't have taken him with her.

Anyway, as Matt had so often reminded her, he wasn't an invalid and hated being treated like one. In defense of herself, Carly knew she couldn't be too careful; that last heart attack had inflicted permanent damage.

Still, she was glad he had gone. She saw his willingness to go with Martha a good sign. If anyone needed and deserved a good woman, it was Matt Armstrong. Martha Ridley was just such a woman, only Matt was too stubborn to see that she adored the ground he walked on and always had.

Living with Ann had been hell on earth, as Carly well knew. Maybe that was why Matt was reluctant to get involved with another woman. Even now, Carly didn't like to think of those early years when she had been at her aunt's mercy.

"So don't think about it," she muttered, disposing of her uniform in haste and slipping into a jogging outfit. Then, taking a quick look out the window, she concluded that it wouldn't get dark for at least another thirty minutes. If she went through a short warm-up, she would have time to run a couple of miles.

A short time later, stretching exercises behind her, Carly hurried outside and began jogging down the country road that ran alongside her uncle's property. She inhaled, pulling the cool air deep into her lungs, at the same time trying to blank everything out of her mind.

She wasn't successful. Thoughts of Rance Knight seemed destined to haunt her.

The encounter with the head of investigations had shaken her more than she cared to admit. Especially since she had committed the unpardonable—she'd loved the way his hard body felt against her.

Her breathing now came in short, rapid spurts.

Was she losing her mind? Not only had she heard Rance's famous quote, but gossip had been flying around the station about his personal life, as well. Carly had learned that while there were many women in city hall who would have liked to share his bed, he stayed clear of them. Gossip also had it that he'd been involved in a messy divorce, with a daughter caught in the middle, a daughter who was the apple of his eye.

While his troubles were unfortunate, Carly was not sympathetic. From the first day she had met Rance, she had been uncomfortable around him and had made a conscientious effort to avoid him.

Forget him! she cried silently, but much to her chagrin, she couldn't, conceding that Rance Knight intrigued her, in spite of the fact that he was too sure of himself, too ambitious, too...too everything to suit her. But when those brown eyes had seemed to strip her bare, something had happened inside her, something she still couldn't understand, much less explain.

Fifteen minutes later, she opened the door into the den and immediately saw the roar of the fire.

"Is that you, Carly?"

The warmth of her uncle's voice suddenly melted the coldness around her heart.

Chapter 3

Matt casually strolled into the den, only to pull up short. Carly was sprawled on the couch, looking comfortable but tired, and tired not just from jogging, either. Something else was bothering her. He could see it in her expression. Her face was a study in misery and self-disgust. Every few moments she ran splayed fingers through her thick curls.

Lord knows there had been enough times in her life when she'd been upset or hurt. When the young man she had married had had his life so cruelly snuffed out, for one. She had been dealt a severe blow, but even during that emotional tempest she had rallied, had kept her equilibrium. Her fierce pride and the inherited Armstrong temper had come to her rescue.

Suddenly those traits seemed to have deserted her. She obviously hadn't listened to a word he'd said that morning. Why couldn't she see that she was already one helluva good cop and didn't have anything to prove? She reminded him so much of his brother, the same rich-colored hair, the same high cheekbones. But more than that, the same integrity and the same courage.

That courage and self-discipline had gotten her through the

trying years with Ann, who on her better days was a hard woman. Ann had never ceased to resent Carly from the moment she had come through the door, clutching a doll to her chest and trying to control her trembling lower lip. His heart had gone out to her, but not his wife's.

While Matt had no proof, he was certain Carly had taken much more abuse from her aunt then she ever let on. But no matter how cruel Ann had been to her, Carly had always made excuses for her. However, when he'd come home from the station at night, Carly had never failed to come running out the door, straight into his arms.

Matt allowed himself a deep sigh, thinking of all the verbal slinging matches he and Ann had had over Carly. And not once had Matt regretted his decision to stick by Carly then. Nor did he now. He had always been and still was her greatest fan.

Now, as his eyes narrowed on her once again, he thought she looked so dejected and vulnerable, yet so beautiful. Apparently she'd had another rough day.

Carly sensed she was no longer alone. Her eyes widened as her uncle strolled deeper into the room. "Hey, if you don't snap out of it, your chin's gonna be dragging the ground any minute now."

Carly attempted a smile. "I am a sad case, aren't I? To tell you the truth, I don't know what's wrong with me." But she did, and she hated herself for lying.

"Did anything out of the ordinary happen today?" Matt asked, as though making casual conversation.

Carly's face turned ashen. "As a matter of fact it did."

"Oh."

Matt had crossed to the fireplace and was now jabbing at the logs with the poker. Momentarily the flames blazed, again casting a warm glow in the room.

Carly refrained from answering for a moment, her gaze centering on the sizzling fire as if she were mesmerized by it.

"You're not in any real trouble, are you, honey?" Matt asked, breaking into the silence.

Carly shook her head and focused her attention on Matt. "I may be."

"You might as well spit it out. What have you done now?"

"I careened into Rance Knight this morning and caused him to spill coffee all over the front of his immaculate white shirt."

A smile flirted with Matt's lips. "I bet the big fellow didn't know what hit him."

"It's not funny, Uncle Matt," Carly snapped, but a smile threatened her lips.

"What'd he say?"

"What do you think he said?"

"Something foul, I imagine."

"And a few choice words to boot."

"To which you didn't respond, of course."

A hot flush crept up Carly's neck. "Well, you know me."

"Do I ever," Matt responded, shaking his head vigorously.

"Anyway, as I've already told you, Rance Knight is without a doubt the most prejudiced officer on the force."

"That's too bad."

"I couldn't agree more." And more's the pity, too, she thought, simply because he was such a hunk. "Can't you see me working under Knight?"

Matt pinned her gaze. "No, I can't. But, then again, you do have trouble keeping your mouth shut."

"I know, Uncle Matt, but it's so hard. Damn, I didn't mean to run into him, for heaven's sake. It was an accident, pure and simple. But did he look at it that way? Of course not. He made a big deal out of it, as if he enjoyed watching me squirm."

"And did you squirm?"

A sheepish smile brightened Carly's features. "Well, for a minute, I'll have to admit he had me going."

"How 'bout a cup of hot chocolate?" Matt asked suddenly with a grin. "Maybe it'll calm you down."

"I'd love a cup," Carly said, struggling into a sitting position. "But let me get it."

"Nope. You just keep your seat. It's gonna be a cold day in hell before I let you or that woman next door make an invalid out of me."

Carly shrugged. "Whatever you say."

A minute later, Matt shuffled back into the room, carrying two cups of steaming cocoa topped with ice cream.

They sipped in companionable silence for a while, then Carly, hoping to steer the subject off her once and for all, asked, "Speaking of Martha, how was your day?"

Matt snorted. "Every time I let her drag me off somewhere, I swear it's going to be the last time. Why, she wants to finger every item in every damn store."

Carly grinned. "Of course you saw Barbara."

"You don't think Martha would miss seeing that daughter of hers and those grandchildren, do you?"

"No. And she shouldn't."

"Uncle Matt, why don't you just give up and marry her?"

Matt glared at her. "Have you taken leave of your senses, girl?"

"That depends on who you talk to," Carly responded with an indulgent smile.

Matt flapped his free hand in the air. "Well, you might as well put that notion out of your head, because it's not about to happen."

"Why?"

"Because I went through hell with your aunt, that's why."

The smile disappeared from Carly's lips. "I know that," she said softly, "but Martha's nothing like Aunt Ann."

Matt sipped on his coffee while he stared into the distance, a thin white line forming around his mouth.

Carly pursed her lips. "Sorry, didn't mean to upset you."

"You didn't. It's just that—"

"You wish I'd mind my own business."

He grinned. "Well, that thought did cross my mind."

Carly reached over and began unlacing her jogging shoes. When she looked up, Matt was staring at her.

"You know there are rumors flying around town that when and if Crawford retires, Knight will get his job."

Carly stood suddenly. "Oh, please, let's not get off on the subject of *that* man again."

"Well, I just thought you ought to think about that in your dealings with Rance."

"Oh, so it's 'Rance' to you, huh," she said, crossing to the fireplace.

"What'd you expect? I've known him since he was a boy."

Carly stuck her hands over the flames. "And you approve of him?"

Matt lifted his shoulders in a shrug. "Never thought about it one way or the other. All I know is that he's a damn good cop."

"I'm sure he is, but he still has the personality of a barbarian."

Matt chuckled. "As I remember, he was a little headstrong."

"A little?"

"Well, at least you don't have to work with him."

"Thank God for small favors."

Matt was quiet for a moment. Then, after draining the last of his hot chocolate from the cup, he said, "You aren't sorry you came back home, are you? I mean...I know you were happy in Dallas with your job...and with Brian..." He let his words trail off as his bushy white brows drew together. "I didn't want you to come back here, but you insisted, and being the selfish old man I am, I couldn't resist."

Carly leaned down and picked up her shoes, then scooted closer to her uncle. "I wouldn't have it any other way," she whispered, kissing him softly on the cheek.

"You're a fine, decent girl, Carly Mitchum." His voice was a trifle unsteady. "And I'm proud of you."

Fighting back the tears, Carly leaned over and planted a kiss on the top of her uncle's head. "Now, I'm going to bed and I suggest you do the same. Good night."

"'Night."

Carly paused at the door a moment and looked at her uncle's bent head, feeling another tug at her heartstrings. Swallowing a sigh, she walked out of the room.

Carly eased farther down into the scented bath water and felt the heat seep into her flesh, all the way to her bones. God, it felt good to relax, she thought.

This was her time to indulge herself, and she aimed to make the most of it. Having found a comfortable niche for her head at the back of the tub, she closed her eyes, feeling suddenly and deliciously drowsy. She let her mind drift, not wanting to dwell on anything. Not work. Not her uncle. Certainly not Rance Knight. And, most of all, she didn't want to think about the phone call she owed Brian Calhoun.

The weekly conversations were becoming unpleasant at best. He never failed to end them with "Carly, when are you going to leave that godforsaken one-horse town and come back to where you belong? You know how much I miss you...."

She flicked a damp curl off her forehead. Would that other man, the man of her dreams, ever come along? The one who would love and cherish her as Ben once had?

Brian Calhoun certainly could not offer her that, in spite of his insistence that he could. Therein lay the problem. He resented her keeping him at arm's length. He wanted to be her lover as well as her friend, but so far she could handle only the latter. Since Ben's death, she hadn't let another man get beyond the wall she'd erected around herself.

Still, Brian was a fine man, and she could do worse, she had told herself time and time again. He was smooth and cultured and interesting and knew exactly where he was going. His goal was to be the president of one of the largest banks in Dallas, and no doubt he would accomplish that with fanfare. But life as a banker's wife held no appeal for her.

Carly scrubbed her skin that much harder. Even the idea of being Brian's wife repulsed her. He was a charming, stable man, but his way of life was not for her. It was only a matter of time, she knew, before he went his way and she went hers. Yet she would miss him; she considered him a good friend. He had filled a void in her life when she'd needed it most.

Though she felt she hadn't abused his strength, she was aware that he had read more into their relationship than was there, even with her being honest about her feelings from the start. However, he wouldn't take no for an answer and wanted her to marry him.

Rinsing off, Carly stood and patted her skin dry with a thick towel. Minutes later she was in bed. Alone, as always. Moonlight danced across the ceiling, creating odd shapes, while tears wet her face. She wished that Ben were beside her. There were times like now when she yearned for the arms of a strong man, someone who loved her, who would gladly share her joys as well as her sorrows.

Kicking aside the covers, Carly sat up on the side of the bed, trying to curb her hammering heart. She had to get her head back on straight and stop playing mental games. Still her mind continued to play its treacherous tricks, teasing her with images of rowdy kisses and hot caresses that led to that final frenzy of sexual gratification.

Suddenly feeling drained, she lay back down and once again closed her eyes. She felt herself drifting into a tumultuous sleep. Seemingly unconnected images cycled through her mind. Beechum. Lanier. Farrell. Brian.

But haunting her more vividly than any was Rance Knight.

Over the next few days Carly worked harder than she had since joining the force. Eight hours often stretched to ten- and twelve-hour days.

When she wasn't answering calls for domestic disturbances or working school zones, she was a prisoner in the station bent over massive amounts of paperwork. More the rule than the exception, she was given the unwanted tasks of filling out Uniformed Crime Reports for the FBI. It was clerical work that none of the men wanted to do. So the duty sergeants invariably gave it to her.

Carly despised doing it, and today was no different. Instead of working her regular day shift, she was pulling the second shift, two till ten. Still, the majority of her time had been spent in the report room, sitting on her backside.

But fifteen minutes ago, she had completed and turned in the last report. Now she was on patrol. The night was quiet as she sped down Highway 65 on the outskirts of the city. She took a deep breath and forced herself to relax. Another hour and she would be off-duty. It couldn't come soon enough to suit her, either. She was mentally exhausted.

It was after she had exited from the highway and was headed back toward town that she saw the vehicle ahead of her ignore the stop sign and keep on going. Immediately Carly sped up and activated the red light atop the car. Minutes later the Trans Am pulled off the road onto the gravel shoulder. Carly followed suit.

Leaving her headlights shining, she unbuckled her seat belt and reached for her clipboard. She then got out of her car and approached the vehicle, noticing on first cursory glance that the Trans Am was occupied by teenagers.

The driver had the window down and was staring at her. Fear shone from his eyes.

"Hello, I'm Officer Carly Mitchum."

"Hello, Officer," he responded.

Carly could see him clearly now and guessed him to be sixteen or seventeen years old. His eyes were wide, and the hand on the steering wheel was trembling. But it was his breath that concerned her; the smell of beer almost knocked her down. It looked like she had a 10-55 on her hands—driving while intoxicated.

"May I see your license?" Carly asked.

"Sure...er...okay, Officer."

"Also your proof of liability insurance."

"I have...that, too."

Using her flashlight, Carly looked at the documents. The young man's name was Thomas Hooper. His age, seventeen.

"One moment, Mr. Hooper," Carly said, then turned and went back to her car and radioed the station. "Two-oh-five."

"Go ahead 205."

"I have a carload of teenagers and a 10-55."

"Ten-four," the dispatcher responded.

"Also run a check on license number 309 Charles, Mary, Paul."

"Ten-four."

"Request backup," Carly added, giving her location.

When she walked back to the window, there were no sounds coming from inside the car. The group sat in stoic silence.

"Mr. Hooper, the reason I pulled you over is that you failed to stop at the stop sign."

He gulped. "Er...I did?"

"Did you see the stop sign?"

"Uh, no, sir...I mean no, ma'am."

His slip of the tongue brought uneasy chuckles from the back seat.

Ignoring them, Carly continued, "Please step out of the car."

"Me?" His voice had risen an octave.

"Yes, you, Mr. Hooper."

After finally lumbering out of the low-slung seat and standing, the youngster towered over Carly's five feet seven inches.

"How much have you had to drink?"

He licked his lips. "Just a few beers, Officer, that's all."

"I want you to do as I tell you."

"Yes...ma'am."

"Stand on one leg, please, with the other one extended in front. Do that for five seconds."

He tried, but was unsuccessful.

"This time," Carly added, "stand with arms extended—"

"Oh, please, ma'am," he interrupted, shaking his head.

"Stand with your arms extended," Carly repeated, her tone firm.

He did as he was told.

"Now," Carly added, "turn your palms up and tip your head back."

"Oh, please..." His tone was pleading now.

Carly said, "Please touch the tip of your nose with your forefinger."

Thomas Hooper failed that test, as well.

While he slumped against the side of the car, chin on his chest, Carly turned her attention to the other occupants of the car.

"All of you, out please."

One by one, the teenagers filed out. Besides the driver, there were four others—two boys and two girls. It was only after both girls had climbed out and were standing by the side of the vehicle that Carly gasped.

For a moment, Carly could do nothing but stare dumbfounded at the pretty brown-haired girl. Then, recovering, she said, "Stacy?"

"Oh, please, Officer Mitchum, promise you won't call my dad."

Chapter 4

Detective Bud May, blond and blue eyed, shifted back in his recliner and looked at his boss Rance Knight. "Even if I do say so, my Terri fixed one helluva good meal," he said, breaking a long moment of friendly silence. "And speaking of good meals, why didn't you bring Stacy?"

"She wanted to come, but a friend was coming over and they were going to listen to tapes or whatever the hell kids do nowadays. She'd rather do that than eat, especially if it means seeing her friends. She's still so closely tied to the kids here."

Bud unconsciously rubbed his protruding stomach. "Well, all I got to say is she missed some good groceries."

Rance nodded, following May's lead and plopping his large frame down on the den couch, then sinking back into the cushions. "That she did, and if I'd eaten another helping of that broccoli-and-cheese casserole, my stomach would be protruding just like yours."

After getting up from the table and helping Terri May clean up the kitchen, they had drifted into the den to relax.

A small fire sizzling in the Franklin stove gave the high-ceilinged room a cozy effect, adding to the tranquillity.

Bud switched his attention to his mustache and was now fingering it. "My stomach is kinda gettin' out there a little too far, isn't it?"

Rance grinned. "You said it, I didn't."

"All right, all right. I get the point. With both you and Terri on my case, I guess I'll be forced to go on a diet."

"Maybe you won't have to resort to such an extreme."

The detective's face lighted. "Oh, you got something in mind?"

"Yeah, work."

"You mean it?" May grimaced as if the mere thought were distasteful.

"Just like I said."

"I take it you're referring to the pharmacy heists."

"Yep." Rance's tone was clipped.

"But we still don't have anything yet, do we?"

Rance stretched and yawned. "No, but I aim to correct that real soon, or know the reason why." The challenge of discovering who was hitting those drugstores gleamed like a piece of forbidden fruit.

Bud wasn't fooled by Rance's level drawl. He scrutinized his superior even closer, while grooming the other side of his mustache.

"Let's have it," May said.

Rance picked up a throw pillow and tossed it to the opposite end of the sofa, then reached for it again. "I don't know what you're talking about."

Bud snorted. "Hey, Knight, remember me. I used to be your partner before you got promoted. I know when there's something tickling in that brain of yours. So how 'bout coming clean?"

"What's tickling my brain, as you so aptly put it, has nothing to do with the burglaries, or at least I don't think so."

"Mmm, that's interesting," Bud said.

Rance reached in his pocket for a cigarette and lighted it.

"I thought you gave those nasty things up," Bud said, his tone tainted with disgust.

"I did. But only for a while. What can I say? I'm hooked. It's just that simple."

"Well, do me a favor and don't deal me any more grief about my weight, okay? At least I'm not gonna die of lung cancer."

"Oh, so you think a heart attack is a more pleasant way to go."

"Well, it's quicker, anyway."

"Hell, May, you're sick."

Bud laughed. "To paraphrase my wife—it goes with the job."

"Don't I know that," Rance agreed, his expression once again serious.

"So what's on your mind?"

When Rance didn't reply, Bud sighed impatiently.

Rance bowed his head and looked away. "Okay. Dirty cops, that's what's on my mind."

Bud stared at him. "Damn, Rance, that's heavy-duty stuff."

"Don't you think I know that?" Rance's response was harsh.

"Do you have names, proof?"

"Nope. I've heard the rumors. Apparently you haven't."

"That's right, I haven't."

"Well, now you know, so keep your eyes and ears open, okay?"

"Whatever you say."

"You don't sound surprised."

May shook his head. "I'm not, especially in light of what's been happening in the department lately."

"Yeah, and we both know whose fault that is."

"Speaking of our fearless leader—" Bud's smile was anything but humorous "—does he know of your suspicions?"

"No, and even if he did, he wouldn't believe me."

Bud got up, ambled across to the stove and shoved another log inside, then he turned to face Rance. "You're right. Anyone who thinks transferring Carly Mitchum to C.I.D. is a good idea would definitely not believe you."

Rance's eyes turned cold. "Let's not open up that can of worms. Anyway, you know how I feel about Officer Mitchum—"

"Especially after she christened your shirt with coffee." A wide grin was plastered across Bud's lips.

"I wouldn't push it if I were you, friend." Although Rance's tone was soft, Bud recognized the steel underlying each word. Rance's feeling about women cops was no secret.

Bud merely threw back his head and laughed.

In spite of himself, Rance grinned. "One thing for sure, it scared the hell out of her."

"But only for a moment. I understand she got right back at you."

"Don't say it, Bud," Rance began, only to suddenly stop in midstream. Terri May was standing in the doorway. "Hey, come join us," Rance added, standing.

Terri smiled. "How about some homemade cheesecake and coffee?"

Both men groaned simultaneously.

"I'll take those groans to means yes. I'll be right back."

True to her word, she returned minutes later, but not with any food. She again paused in the doorway.

"What's up, honey?" Bud asked.

"Phone call for Rance."

"Thanks," Rance said with a smile. He then got up and walked to the other side of the room, where a yellow phone sat on the desk.

A moment later, when Rance placed the receiver back on the hook, his face was pale.

"What's wrong?" Bud asked, not bothering to mask his concern. "You look like you've just seen a ghost."

"It's Stacy," Rance said in a deadly calm voice. "She's in trouble."

Carly sat alone with the distraught girl in the patrol car. The backup had already come and picked up the other teenagers and was now en route to the station.

Although the heater was no longer running, the air inside Carly's patrol car was warm. Still, Carly and Stacy both shivered, steaming up the windshield with their breath. Carly knew that Stacy dreaded her father's imminent arrival. As to why she was shivering—well, maybe for the same reason.

Carly cast a sidelong glance at the hunched-over teenager, dreading with each moment that passed the appearance of Rance Knight.

After recovering from the shock of finding Stacy in the car, Carly had gone back to the radio and patched a message through to headquarters asking that they call Rance. His whereabouts, however, had not been easy to come by. Stacy had clammed up and refused to answer her, but her girlfriend had been more cooperative. She had overheard Stacy and Rance talking about his plans for dinner and had relayed that information to Carly.

Stacy's sudden, pitiful whimper drew Carly's attention once again. She had met Stacy Knight at the station shortly after she had gone to work there. One afternoon Stacy had been waiting for her father to get out of a meeting. At loose ends, she had wandered into the lounge; Carly had been there alone, checking through a report. Stacy introduced herself and she and Carly had struck up a conversation. From then on, Stacy had made it a point to say hi to Carly every time she came to the station.

Carly had sensed immediately that buried underneath Stacy's bubbly personality was a lonely and troubled girl. For that reason, Carly wasn't surprised that Stacy was sitting beside her now.

"Would it help if I turned the heater back on?" Carly asked when Stacy's shoulders continued to quiver.

Ignoring her question, Stacy cried, instead, "Why, oh, why did you have to call my dad?"

"You know I had no choice," Carly answered with more calm than she was feeling.

Stacy's shoulders shook that much harder.

Carly took a deep breath and let it out. "You're going to make yourself sick if you don't stop crying."

Stacy raised tear-stained cheeks and glared at Carly. "How would you know?" she snapped. "I...I thought you were my friend."

Carly held on to her patience with difficulty. What a mess, she thought despairingly. She couldn't believe this was happening to her. Stacy Knight of all people. What had she done to deserve this twist of fate?

"Believe me, I am your friend," Carly said, her tone soft and even. "And in spite of what you think, I do know how you feel. But you were doing something you weren't supposed to be doing and now you'll have to answer for it."

Stacy clutched at Carly's arm. "He's...he's going to be so mad at me," she whimpered, letting go of Carly and rocking in the seat, bent over like a question mark.

Carly reached out to touch the long, silky hair, only to suddenly draw her hand back. "Don't you think he'll listen to your side of the story?"

"If...if only I hadn't listened...to Beverly," Stacy wailed.

Instantly alert, Carly turned in the seat and eased her head back against the glass. Although she had asked, Stacy had been mum concerning the facts. At least she hadn't been drinking, Carly reminded herself. That would definitely be in her favor when Rance arrived.

"Was it your friend's idea to go with them?" Carly's question seemed to cut suddenly into the soft, silent night.

Stacy's face was clear in the moonlight. "Yes," she whispered.

Unexpectedly, Carly shivered at the same time that Stacy pulled her lightweight jacket closer around her.

"Go on," Carly prodded.

Stacy swiped at the tears running down her cheeks, only to then hiccup. "Dad...took me out to get a hamburger, then dropped me back by the house. I was supposed to stay there, not go anywhere, but—"

"But your friend called and changed your mind."

Stacy had stopped crying now and was staring at Carly. "Well, sort of. Actually, Bev came over, and then Thomas, her boyfriend, came by with another friend and talked us into—"

"Riding around."

"How...how did you know?" Stacy asked, wide-eyed.

Carly hid a smile. "Well, even though you might find that hard to accept, I *was* young once, too."

For a long moment, there was silence in the car as Stacy

seemed to be considering what to say next. Her forehead was creased in a frown, and she was chewing on her bottom lip. Carly didn't press her, hoping she'd keep talking of her own free will.

"Bev...Bev said we wouldn't be gone long, that this guy with Thomas was really neat and that I should get to know him."

"Did you know they were drinking when they picked you up?"

Stacy looked as though she were about to start crying again. It was all Carly could do to keep from reaching out and touching her.

"They weren't, or at least I don't think they were. Anyway, we hadn't been driving around long until Jeff, that's his name, reached down into a paper sack and pulled out a beer."

"And he handed it to Thomas."

Stacy nodded.

"Then what happened?"

"Thomas...he...he didn't just drink it like Dad does—he guzzled it down like he was dying of thirst."

Carly drew a deep breath and let it out slowly. "What did you do then?"

"I asked them to take me home, but they all just laughed at me, called me chicken."

Kids! At this moment, Carly was inclined to side with her uncle. "Didn't it make a difference to them that your father's a cop?"

"Yeah. They laughed and said if we got stopped he could take care of things." Stacy paused and brushed a lock of limp brown hair out of her eyes.

When properly groomed, Stacy would be a knockout, Carly thought. Now, however, she looked like a bedraggled puppy. Her high cheekbones were splotched with mascara, and her eyes were puffy from crying, while her faded denim skirt and long T-shirt were askew on her slender body.

"Officer Mitchum, Dad's going to kill me," she cried again, hysterical.

At the sudden beam of lights from behind her, Carly lifted

her eyes to the rearview mirror. She started to tremble. "Speaking of your...dad, he just drove up."

"Oh, damn, oh, damn," Stacy whispered. "I've had it. I know I have."

"You stay here," Carly said. "I'll talk to him."

Stacy grabbed Carly's arm just as she opened the door. "Oh, please help me." Stacy's eyes were frantic. "He'll listen to you. I know he will."

Carly knew better, but she refrained from voicing her thoughts, positive Stacy would find out soon enough. If anything, her presence would make things worse. Still, she had to try.

She got out of the car and stood self-consciously against the door. Within seconds Rance was in front of her, looming over her. A shiver tore through Carly, but not from the cold night air. Carly could hear her own heartbeat.

It was obvious Rance was seething. Without mincing any words, he came straight to the point. "What happened, Officer?"

Carly slanted him a look and stepped aside. He smelled fresh, as though he'd just gotten out of the shower.

"Dammit, Mitchum, I asked you a question."

Refusing to let him intimidate her, Carly squared her shoulders and, tipping her head back, looked him in the eye. "Sir...your daughter's upset."

In the far distance, a streak of lightning illuminated the countryside for a second, outlining the leafless black trees.

"Mitchum, that's not what I asked you."

Carly licked her dry lips. "I know—"

Rance waved a hand through the air, cutting her off. "I'm not interested in your opinion. Just tell me what the hell this is all about."

Without batting an eye and without changing the polite but frigid tone of her voice, Carly told him everything, beginning with when she had stopped the car and ending with everything Stacy had told her.

"Dammit," he swore, then strode around the hood to the other side of the car and yanked open the door.

It was all Carly could do to hold her tongue as she followed him. Never had she met a more insensitive, insufferable man.

Beneath a nearby streetlight Stacy's tortured face was clear through the glass. Rolling down the window, she lifted widened eyes to her father.

"Get out of the car, Stacy," Rance ordered shortly.

"Oh, Daddy," Stacy pleaded, despair in her voice.

Rance swore again.

"Oh, please don't, don't be mad at me. It wasn't my fault...they wouldn't listen to me." Stacy talked breathlessly, running the words together almost incoherently.

"Get out of the car, Stacy," Rance repeated.

This time Rance's tone brooked no argument, and Stacy had no choice but to do as she was told.

Carly stood by with her top teeth sunk into her bottom lip, unable to decide who was the more pitiful of the two, Stacy or her father. Mingled with the fury on Rance's face was a deep-seated pain and uncertainty. It was clear, for all his outer macho toughness, that Rance Knight was out of his league when it came to his daughter.

"Get in the Bronco," Rance was saying to Stacy. "I'll be there in a minute. I want a word with Officer Mitchum."

Stacy stood still while her eyes bounced back and forth between Carly and her daddy.

"Stacy..." Though Rance never raised his voice, the effect was the same as if he'd shouted the girl's name.

Carly fidgeted, wishing she were anywhere other than here.

Stacy was the definition of misery. Her features were drawn and her eyes were squeezed tightly shut, as if she couldn't bear what she would see if she opened them.

"No," Stacy finally whispered.

She was really scared of her father, Carly thought. Yet gut instinct told Carly that in spite of Rance's anger, stemming partly from embarrassment and partly from fear, he would not hurt a hair on her head. But, then, a verbal skirmish with Rance would be tantamount to the harshest physical punishment, especially to a youngster who wanted his approval more than she wanted anything else.

"What the hell do you mean, no?"

"You don't care about what I think or feel." Despair deepened Stacy's voice. "You never have, or you wouldn't have gone...away, wouldn't have left me with Mom. All you care about, have ever cared about, is your work."

Rance's sharp breath ripped through the silence like a bullet. "Stacy, for God's sake, will you just get in the Bronco? We'll settle this when we get home."

Stacy's fear seemed to have lessened. "No, we won't. We never do. When I do something you don't like, all you do is yell at me."

"I've never once yelled at you, young lady, but that doesn't mean I'm not going to this time."

It was obvious that Rance was struggling with his temper, determined not to lose it.

Embarrassed, Carly looked away and tried not to listen to the bitter exchange between father and daughter.

Then suddenly Stacy turned a frantic gaze on Carly. "Please, Officer Mitchum, can I go home with you?"

Carly turned to Rance. She opened her mouth to speak, but no words could get past her throat. It was as if her vocal cords were frozen.

Rance's mouth gaped as he stared at his daughter. It was apparent that he, too, was at a loss for words.

The eerie shadows around them added to the hostile silence.

Rance was the first to recover. "That's ridiculous. Officer Mitchum doesn't want to be bothered. You're going with me and that's final."

Stacy's shoulders sagged, and deep sobs tore through her lips.

Without thinking, Carly crossed to her and placed an arm around her shoulders, drawing her trembling body into her side. "It's no bother, Captain."

"Officer Mitchum..."

Carly ignored the warning. "Really, it's all right if she comes home with me. It's past time for me to go off duty and—"

"Dammit to hell," Rance muttered, a murderous glint in his eye.

Carly went on as though he hadn't interrupted. "I'm willing for Stacy to spend the night with me."

For the longest moment, Rance stared at her, his features completely devoid of expression.

"All right," Rance said, his words harsh. Then he turned to Stacy. "Running away from the problem won't make it go away. Remember there's tomorrow." He paused. "Think about that."

"Uncle Matt," Carly said, "this is Stacy Knight. She's going to be our guest for the night."

Carly and Stacy had just walked into the den, where Matt sat in front of a smoldering fire. Carly had hoped he would already be in bed so she wouldn't have to explain Stacy's presence until the following morning. No such luck.

The wrecker had arrived to tow off the Trans Am while Rance had waited for her and Stacy to get in the squad car; then Rance had driven off, heading in the opposite direction. Carly, of course, had had to go back to the station and wrap things up before she was free to leave with Stacy. Once there, she'd kept Stacy waiting longer than she'd intended, as there was the DWI to take care of, plus three more minor consuming counts, all of which had involved endless paperwork.

When she'd finally gotten away from the station, the ride to the Armstrongs' rambling brick home had been accomplished in virtual silence. Carly had been content to let Stacy wallow in her self-pity, knowing that anything she said wouldn't do any good. Anyway, there wasn't much she could say.

Now, as Carly watched her uncle struggle to an upright position in the chair, obviously having been dozing, she wanted to get the explanations over and done with as quickly as possible. Stacy needed to be in bed, and so did she.

"A pleasure, young lady," Matt said, standing and holding out his hand.

Stacy took a tentative step forward and placed an unsteady hand in his. "Me...er...too."

Then his eyes peered over Stacy's bent head and focused on Carly. His eyebrows were raised in question.

Carly sighed. "Stacy is Captain Knight's daughter."

"I see."

He didn't, of course, but Carly wasn't about to open that can of worms again, at least not in front of the girl. On closer perusal, Stacy looked like she was about to fall on her face. Her features were pinched, and dark shadows circled her eyes.

"Uncle Matt, if you'll excuse us, I'll show Stacy to the guest room and get her settled."

"What about you, are you going to bed, as well?"

Carly couldn't quite meet his eyes. "I think so. I'm pooped. I'll see you in the morning."

Matt smiled, but it was apparent he was none too happy with the way Carly had refused to confide in him. Well, he'd just have to wait till morning, Carly thought, her shoulders rounded with fatigue.

"Good night, then," Matt said. "I might as well turn in, too."

"That sounds like a good idea. You look tired yourself."

Thirty minutes later Stacy was showered and snug in the bed in the guest bedroom. Carly was perched on the edge of a dusky rose-upholstered chair she had dragged up to the bed.

"Feel better?" she asked softly, noting that even if Stacy didn't feel better, she certainly looked better. If nothing else, the shower had restored color to her cheeks.

Stacy nodded.

"Are you sure you won't take me up on that offer of hot chocolate and muffins?" Carly's tone was gentle.

The moment Stacy had come out of the bathroom, dressed in one of Carly's long granny gowns, Carly had urged her to eat something. Now she was asking again, certain the girl was hungry.

"I'm sure," Stacy said, tears welling up in her eyes once again.

"Oh, Stacy, please, don't cry."

"I'm sorry, Officer Mitchum—"

"Under the circumstances, I think it's all right if you call me 'Carly,' don't you?"

"All right, 'Carly,'" she said. "I'm sorry you got caught in the middle of this mess with Dad and me. It's...it's a no-win situation," she added with a sudden burst of maturity far beyond her years.

"Your father loves you, Stacy. It's just that..." Carly faltered, not knowing what else to say. After all, who was she to give advice. She didn't know the relationship those two shared, other than through gossip. But one thing she did know, Stacy was hurting and Carly was powerless to help her.

"I know." Stacy smiled wanly. "He just doesn't understand me."

Carly's gaze was intense. "Is that what he tells you?"

"All the time. He and Mom, both."

"Why didn't you want to go with him? It wasn't because you were really afraid of him, was it?"

Stacy rolled over on her side and faced Carly. Tears stuck to her eyelashes. "No," she whispered. "I was...am so ashamed. I've never really disobeyed him like I did tonight."

"Why did you?"

Stacy's chin jutted. "I guess I was still upset with Mom. She was going with...that man again this weekend, and I hate him. He's nothing like Dad."

Oh, boy, Carly thought. "Maybe...maybe you shouldn't compare them."

"I can't help it." Stacy's tone had turned mutinous. "Since she and Dad got divorced, she's been acting really weird."

Carly squirmed in her seat. Stacy was telling her things she didn't want to hear. Besides, Rance Knight would have a heart attack if he knew his daughter was discussing his business with her.

Carly was determined to change the subject. "I'm sure when you talk to your dad and tell him that you're sorry, things will work out."

Stacy shook her head. "The only thing that'll make me feel better is for Dad to come back home." She paused and sniffed. Carly handed her a tissue from the box beside the table. "But I know that's never going to happen."

"I'm sorry," Carly whispered as she stood and leaned over the girl. "I wish I could wave a magic wand so all your troubles would be settled.'' She brushed away the tears on the girl's cheek. "Because I like you, Stacy Knight." A genuine smile broke through Carly's lips. "For a sixteen-year-old kid, you're not bad.''

Stacy grinned. "For a lady cop, you're not bad, either.''

"Good night.''

"Thanks...Carly.''

Carly paused at the door. "I'll see you in the morning.''

Although Carly went straight to her room, she didn't go to bed. Pushing unwanted thoughts aside, she discarded her uniform and slipped into a long cotton caftan. Shortly afterwards she padded into the kitchen, where she poured herself a cup of milk and stuck it in the microwave. She was counting on the hot chocolate that Stacy turned down to work its magic on her, force her to relax. If not, she was in for another long, sleepless night.

She had just sat down in the den in front of the fire and was sipping on the hot liquid, when she heard a soft rap on the door.

Her brows furrowed as she stood and made her way across the room. "Yes?" she said.

No answer.

Reaching up, she pulled back the night latch and opened the door. Suddenly Carly felt as though she had swallowed a lump of ice.

Rance Knight stood facing her.

"Can I come in?" he asked.

Chapter 5

"Of...of course." Those three words came out so softly that Carly barely heard them herself. She simply stood there, her palms moist, her tongue clinging to the roof of her mouth.

Rance frowned and stayed where he was, the sight of her stopping him. He knew he shouldn't have come as soon as his eyes focused on the expanse of white throat made accessible to him by the low-cut garment.

With fingers that were definitely unsteady, Carly stepped aside and motioned for him to come in, all the while keenly aware of her appearance. Should she flee to her bedroom and change clothes? The caftan was not transparent, but her nakedness underneath seemed to make it so. Anyway, she *felt* naked.

"It's...late, I know," he said, feeling overheated. *What am I doing?* he asked silently, inhaling the scent of her body and imagining the small circumference of her waist underneath the caftan.

She didn't move. Instead her eyes tracked his jerky gait to the center of the den. Suddenly he stopped and twisted around, returning her stare with equal intensity.

They studied each other in awkward silence. The air inside

the room was warm, too warm. Carly forced her eyes to remain steady on him, suddenly having the crazy feeling that her fate was being decided at this precise moment.

Rance cleared his throat. Although the sound filled the silence, it did nothing to lessen the mounting tension.

Carly raised her hand and caught a thick strand of hair, consciously thrusting it behind her ear. She knew she looked a mess.

She glanced away, but not before her cheeks flushed with color and her throat went dry as parchment. If only he wouldn't stare at her like that....

"Can...may I get you a cup of coffee?" she stammered, when the silence became interminable.

His eyes remained on her a bit longer, moving over the curves of her breasts. "Not...right now," he said hoarsely. "Maybe later."

Another awkward silence fell between them, though Carly's blue eyes never strayed from his dark, sober face, which was lined with fatigue. His hair scraping his collar was mussed, as though he'd been running his fingers through it. His lips were drawn together in a tight line, a smile nowhere in sight.

"How about a drink, then?" she asked almost desperately. "A beer?"

"No, but thanks."

She shrugged as if to say, *What do you want, then?*

He shoved a hand down into his jeans pocket. "Look, do you mind if I sit down?" His voice was light, but had a steely undertone.

Carly's flush deepened as she strove to get a firm hold on her scattered emotions. "I'm sorry, I didn't mean to be rude. It's just that I'm not used—"

"To having company pop in on you at bedtime," he finished for her.

"Right," she murmured, "especially not my superior officer."

He looked at Carly with a quiet, calculating intensity. "Not even if his daughter happens to be spending the night with her?"

"Not even then." She smiled in spite of herself.

Something dangerous flickered in his eyes, then it was gone

just as quickly, and he turned away. "I wish to hell you hadn't gotten involved in this."

"It's a little late to worry about that, don't you think?" Carly was holding her voice steady, but her hands were balled into fists at her side. She sensed a restlessness in him, as well as a deep-seated anger. She could understand why.

He was upset and floundering, and for once was not in control of a situation. He was having trouble handling that. However, she refused to let him intimidate her any longer and by no means would she be his whipping post for his frustrations. Yet by bringing Stacy home with her, she certainly had put herself in a precarious situation.

While her thoughts had gone off on a tangent, Rance had sat down on the sofa near the fireplace. Eager to get this charade behind her, Carly sat down next to him and reached for her cup of hot chocolate.

He was so close that she could smell the tobacco scent that mingled with his cologne. She was aware of the warmth exuding from his body, the quiet threat of his masculinity.

"Is...she all right?" Rance asked at last. His voice was strained.

"She's fine," Carly answered, keeping her voice low and soft.

Rance's chin lifted. "She was so damned upset. Hell, from the way she was acting, you'd think I beat her or...worse."

For a moment Carly didn't know how to respond, because under the anger, she heard grief. "When we got here, she took a shower and went straight to bed," she said, feeling an unwanted twinge of sympathy for this man.

"Did...did she say anything?"

Carly averted her gaze. "No...not really," she lied.

His dark eyes searched hers with a new kind of curiosity before dropping to her mouth. "I...guess what I was trying to say a few minutes ago was that I apologize for Stacy's involving you in our personal business."

Carly buried her back into the cushions, his proximity continuing to send turbulent sensations through her body. She couldn't even breathe correctly. Would he notice? She just wished he'd say what he came to say and leave. She was becoming more rattled and ill at ease by the second.

"She...didn't—involve me, I mean," Carly finally said. "I'm the one who—"

"We both know better than that." He sighed with massive disgust, but Carly didn't take umbrage; she sensed it was directed more at himself than at her.

"It doesn't matter now, anyway," she murmured, forcing herself not to look at him, especially not at the way the muscles in his legs filled out his jeans. She couldn't seem to stop the gooseflesh rippling up and down her spine.

"Most of the time I get along great with my kid," Rance was saying, "but then sometimes, like now—" He broke off, lunged to his feet and crossed to the fireplace. He leaned down and picked up a log off the hearth and laid it on the fire. Once the fire was rejuvenated, he turned around. There was pain in his eyes. "Hell, who am I kidding? Most of the time I manage to screw up royally when it comes to my daughter."

"She's sixteen, Captain," Carly pointed out softly, having totally recovered her equilibrium and her sound judgment.

His grin was broad and mocking. "And that makes everything all right, huh?"

"No, that's not what I'm saying." She kept her tone even, not about to let him fluster her. "It's...it's just that Stacy's more sensitive, especially now," she finished lamely.

"Why do I get the feeling you're just offering lip service?" Rance paused. "Why don't you just say what's on your mind?"

Carly flushed, unsure if he was serious and actually wanted her opinion, or if he was mocking her again. She didn't like being off balance. "All right, Captain—"

He interrupted. "Don't you think we can dispense with the 'captain' business?"

His unorthodox request caught Carly completely off guard, rendering her speechless for a moment. Under no circumstances could she call him by his given name.

As if realizing her confusion, a shadow of a smile crossed his lips. "You were saying?"

"I was saying," Carly continued with as much dignity as she

could muster, "that yes, I think you handled the situation all wrong."

"Go on. I'm listening."

"More than anything else, I think Stacy wants your approval and can't stand the thought of disappointing you."

He sighed heavily. "Maybe I do expect too much out of her. I don't know. And as you say, she's only sixteen. But dammit, she could have been killed." His voice was again as hard as steel, but unsteady. "What if that idiot boy had crashed? Stacy, as well as the whole lot of them, could have become statistics."

"I agree, but still you could have been more gentle with her."

"Gentle, hell! It was all I could do to keep from throttling her. That's one of the things I made her promise me long ago—that she would never get in a car with anyone who was drinking."

Carly rushed to Stacy's defense. "I'm not sure she knew it—until it was too late, that is."

"No excuse."

"See, you're doing it again."

"What?" His eyes were steady on her moist, parted lips.

"Being unreasonable." Carly couldn't believe she was talking to him like this and that he was actually listening.

"Is the offer for that coffee still open?" he asked abruptly.

Carly blinked, then stood. "Of course. I'll...I'll be right back."

"Need any help?"

"No...I can handle it."

Hurriedly refilling her cup and one for Rance, Carly ignored the fact that her hands were trembling. But when she almost spilled both cups placing them on a tray, she forced herself to pause and breathe deeply.

Rance met her halfway, and she handed him his cup. Their hands brushed, but neither acknowledged the brief physical contact.

"Thanks," Rance muttered tersely.

Carly felt his eyes on her as she walked to her chair and sat back down. He remained standing, using the mantel as support for his back.

A silence fell between them as they both looked elsewhere, making a big deal out of sipping their hot drinks.

"So you think I'm too hard on her?" Rance asked at length, the lines around his mouth more pronounced than ever.

Carly set her cup down on the table beside her and looked up at him. "Yes, I do. She feels pulled in two right now."

His eyes narrowed. "You're referring to the divorce, right?"

Carly nodded.

"I thought you said Stacy didn't confide in you?"

Carly started to turn red, feeling suddenly defensive under his steady, unsmiling gaze. "She didn't, not really. She just said that since you and her...mother parted, things hadn't been all that great, that she doesn't get to see you very much."

"She's right." Rance's tone was bitter. "Her mother and I both are too damned busy—me with my work, and Denise...well, she's too busy with her men."

Again Carly was at a loss for words. "I'm...sorry," she said, for lack of anything better to say.

"Yeah, so am I. But as God is my witness, I hope to do better."

Carly fidgeted in her seat, fighting the urge to fling her arms around him, promise him that everything was going to be all right. Both confused and appalled by her thoughts, she bit down on her lower lip. Still, she was unable to turn away from his pain.

The moments ticked by.

Suddenly Rance took slow, deep breaths and muttered, "I should get the hell out of here."

"Don't...worry about Stacy. She'll be all right." Carly focused her gaze on the flames now leaping up the chimney, all the while trying to stifle her sympathy for him. She didn't want to feel sorry for Rance Knight. She didn't want to feel anything for this man.

"Do you mind if I look in on Stacy before I go?" he asked, drawing her back to the reality of the moment.

"No, go right ahead. She's in the first room on the right."

He nodded and then walked out of the room, his shoulders slumped in dejection.

When he returned a few minutes later, Carly was standing in front of the fire, warming herself.

He paused in the middle of the room, and their eyes held.

"She's sleeping," he said, but there was a gruffness in his voice that hadn't been there before. And if she wasn't mistaken, his thick eyelashes were wet with tears. Of course, she could be wrong about that, as the only light in the room other than the fire was an obscure lamp in one corner.

"I'll drop her by your apartment on my way to work in the morning."

"I'd appreciate that."

His tone again had a rough edge to it, reiterating the point that Rance did not want to be beholden to anyone, least of all her. Carly sensed this with every fiber of her being.

They were at the door now, and the second Rance wrapped his big hand around the knob, the tension in the air became almost palpable.

His eyes searched hers for another long, static moment. Then his breath turned harsh.

"Look," he began, "while I'm grateful for what you did tonight, I don't want you to think..." He paused. "I guess what I'm trying to say is that it doesn't change things."

"I never thought it would." Carly's tone was crisp and cool.

Rance's brows lowered. "It's just that I'm not in the habit of leaving my dirty work to a woman, especially when—"

"She's a woman *cop*," Carly finished for him, stiffening. He just had to say it; he just had to make a reference to her gender. The fragile truce that had developed between them was gone. They were back to square one.

His lips curved a little, but his eyes still focused beyond her. "For the record, I guess that's the bottom line."

The tension was so thick between them now, it was suffocating in its intensity.

Suddenly Carly gave in to the red-hot fury boiling inside her and felt the words spill from her lips before she could stop them. "Off the record, and just between you and me, Captain Knight, you're a bastard."

Rance didn't move so much as a muscle. He merely stared

at her for a threatening moment that seemed to have no end. The shadows kept their expressions private from each other.

Then he opened the door.

"Good night, Officer Mitchum," he said.

When the door closed with a finality behind him, she was not sorry in the least for her outburst. He'd had it coming.

A shadow fell across Rance's desk, and he looked up to see Bud leaning over his shoulder. Bud's eyes were scanning the report. He finished and then shuddered.

"Whoever shot the drugstore clerk must've gotten up on the wrong side of the bed. Getting peppered four times had to hurt like hell. I can't believe the unlucky guy is still alive."

Rance gave Bud a scorching glance and slammed the folder shut. "How many times have I told you not to sneak up on me and read over my shoulder?"

"My, my but aren't we in a foul mood this morning."

Rance glared at him.

Bud lifted an eyebrow. "Tough night, huh?"

"You could say that."

Bud was silent as he stared at his superior and his friend, his frown matching Rance's. "I read Mitchum's report on the kids last night. Mess, isn't it? It was lucky she pulled them over before anyone got hurt."

"Yeah."

"Did you and Stace...er...get things ironed out between you?"

Rance sighed and leaned back in his chair, causing the aging springs to suddenly groan. For a moment there was silence.

"Well?" Bud pressed.

"We had a long talk this morning, and for now things are okay." Rance's lips thinned. "But it all still boils down to the fact that she's never accepted the divorce."

"How long's it been now since you and Denise split?"

"Two years."

Bud scratched his head. "That's a helluva long time for her to stay upset."

"Tell me about it."

Another silence.

"Look, if you'd rather not talk about it, just say so."

"All right. I don't want to talk about it."

Bud held up his hands. "I understand. No offense."

For the first time in a long while, Rance smiled. "Get the hell out of here, May. I *know* you have work to do."

"I'm glad you mentioned that."

"What?"

"Work," Bud said.

"What's up?"

"We think we may have a witness, someone who saw a man tear out the side door of the pharmacy and jump into a late-model sedan."

Rance became instantly alert. "Since when?"

"First thing this morning, actually. That's what I came in to tell you, only you bit my head off, instead. Boggs is getting his statement now."

"Let me know the minute you have anything."

"Will do."

When Rance was alone again, he tipped his chair and folded his hands behind his head. What else was going to go wrong? he wondered, staring up at the ceiling, his eyes mesmerized by a tiny spider spinning its web in a far corner of the room.

One thing was for sure, today was not turning out to be a great one. In fact, it hadn't been one of his better weeks. He guessed he was suffering from a case of the blahs.

And yet he had much to be thankful for. He had told Bud the truth when he'd said he and Stacy had straightened things out. He had been standing at the window this morning when Carly had pulled her car up in front of his condo.

When Stacy had walked through the door, they had looked at each other for what seemed like a long time. Then Stacy had thrown herself at him and cried, "Oh, Daddy, I'm sorry, so sorry. Please don't be mad at me. I love you."

"I'm sorry too, baby," he said, "and I love you more than you'll ever know. That's why I can't stand the thought of anything happening to you. You're all I have."

She pulled back and peered up at him. "Only because you prefer it that way, Daddy," she pointed out gently.

He laughed, realizing more and more how little he understood his teenage daughter. One minute she was an innocent child, the next a young woman with insight far beyond her years.

Looking down at his desk now, he ran a finger over the framed photograph of Stacy that he kept on his desk, trying to imagine what his life would be like without her. Drearier and lonelier than it already was, he told himself with cynical amusement.

He knew, however, that she still blamed him for the breakup of their home, though she had never come out and said it. While he was no more to blame than Denise, he felt he could not make Stacy understand that, no matter what he said. So he hadn't said anything. He was counting on time to heal the hurt that festered inside his daughter.

Hadn't that been what Carly...

Ah, Carly again. Couldn't he think of anything else? Why did his every thought have to revolve around her?

From the moment he had walked out of her house last night, he had thought of little else. Even the trouble with his daughter hadn't been able to distract him.

The minute she'd opened the door, he'd known he was in trouble. He'd almost groaned aloud, feeling suddenly wanting, excited...damn pleased with the sight of her. He'd felt alive for the first time in years.

Her hair had been slightly mussed and looked as soft as silk as it formed a halo of curls around her face. He'd longed to run his hands through it.

And her outfit. It had been more suggestive than concealing. It was the same color blue as her eyes, and the hint of her nipples under the fabric had drawn his eyes like a magnet.

Even now, twelve hours later, he could still feel the effects of those moments. She had made him ache. Sweat broke out on Rance's forehead, and he cursed again.

He knew what would happen if he gave in to this uncontrollable hunger for her. The lesser of the evils would be the loss of the promotion he wanted, because the unspoken, yet unbroken rule was that you *never* get your pleasure and your paycheck in the same place.

And the worst would be another long-term commitment.

He despised women like Carly Mitchum, and not because she was infiltrating a man's world, either. Though Lord knows, that was reason enough. He could not get it out of his mind that she was merely a spoiled little rich girl playing cops and robbers.

He smashed a fist down onto the desk. He had to stop thinking about her, he told himself. She was definitely a risk he couldn't handle.

Yet he still wanted her.

Chapter 6

The shift meeting had just broken up, and Carly was outside about to step into her car, when a prickly sensation crawled up her neck. She sensed she was not alone. Her heart gave an unexpected lurch. Then, suddenly angry, she whipped around. Hal Lanier stood behind her. "Don't you know it's rude to creep up on someone?"

"Hey, simmer down, sugar," Lanier said, flashing her a leering grin.

Ice dripped from her voice. "First, I won't simmer down, and second, I'm not your sugar."

"We could change that in a matter of seconds. All you have to do is say the word."

"What do you want?" Carly asked, her patience wearing thin. Out of the corner of her eye, she saw his sidekick, Larry Beechum, standing by his car in the distance, though not so far away that he couldn't hear the exchange between her and Lanier. Beechum, too, had a leering grin on his face. They were up to something.

Lanier's grin widened, though his beady eyes had shifted as

if uncomfortable with the sudden turn of events. He pawed the concrete with his right foot.

"Spit it out, or get out of my way," Carly snapped, while staring boldly at the gangly, sandy-headed officer. "I have work to do even if you don't."

"Oh, I have work to do, all right," Lanier drawled, looking her full in the face now, his confidence seemingly restored. He took a step closer and lowered his tone. "How 'bout you and me gettin' together, say tonight? We could start with a few drinks, then..." He paused with a knowing shrug and leaned even closer, his gaze dropping to her chest, where the rise and fall of her breasts was evident.

Carly felt his warm, unpleasant breath on her face and stepped back, her legs brushing against the side of the car seat.

Before she could say a word, Lanier went on, "Then we could go to my place..."

"Dream on, Lanier." Her lips twisted sarcastically. "Because that's all it is—a dream. As I said before, I've got work to do, so get the hell out of my way and stay out."

Lanier's features turned dark and ugly. "Why you little b—"

He never got the rest of the word past his lips. Carly gave the door an outward shove, striking Lanier at the knees. Even she heard the crunch as the metal made contact with his kneecaps.

"Damn you," he said through clenched teeth while he bent over and rubbed his knees. "I'll get you for this!" He was shouting now. "You can count on it!"

Carly turned a deaf ear to his threats and merely got behind the wheel and started the engine. Subbing on the midnight shift was bad enough without being harassed. Seconds later she glanced in the rearview mirror and saw that Beechum was standing next to Lanier and they were both staring at her car, their features cold and menacing. She knew that while they had been enemies before, they were now *bitter* enemies.

Well, it couldn't be helped, and by no means was she surprised. That type of behavior seemed to go along with the territory. When she'd been in Dallas, there was an officer who thought she should be honored to warm his bed, and from the moment she'd turned him down, he'd been hell-bent on causing her trouble.

Only this time, there were two. Monkey see, monkey do—that was Beechum and Lanier. They were vindictive and dangerous, and she'd be smart to keep that in mind.

Suddenly she felt stifled. Wasting no time, she rolled down the window. Cool, invigorating air, heavy with the sharp aroma of pine, hit her in the face. She took a deep breath and let it out slowly.

However, her anxiety wasn't all job related. Since the episode with Stacy Knight several days before, she'd been walking an emotional tightrope.

With a savage shake of her head, Carly fiddled with the button on the radio, steering the Ford around a sharp curve.

She guessed what she feared the most was that Crawford would force her to transfer to Rance's division. If so, then what?

The last thing she wanted or needed was to get involved with that man, and she wished she could put him out of her mind.

"Two-oh-five. Two-oh-five."

Angie's voice came loud and clear over the radio.

Instantly alert, Carly reached for the microphone. "Two-oh-five. Go ahead."

"Check out grocery on Front and Elm."

"Ten-four."

"Active alarm. Suspected burglary in process. Code 2."

"Ten-four. En route."

Carly ground her foot down on the accelerator and felt the car lurch under her. Moments later she pulled up alongside the convenience store, instantly turning the car's motor and lights off. Her eyes quickly scanned the area. There were no other cars in front, which was in her favor.

Going on the assumption that the burglar was still in the building, Carly reached beside her for her shotgun, unsnapping it from its mount. With adrenaline pumping through her body, she reached for the door handle.

The piercing scream froze her hand, but only for an instant. By the time the next scream rent the stillness, she was out of the car, gun leveled. However, before Carly could so much as take a step, an overweight, gray-haired woman was running toward her, still screaming hysterically, her face a mask of terror.

The woman stopped abruptly in front of Carly and tried to speak. "Oh, God, oh, God, you've got to help me!"

One clear thought rushed through Carly's mind: the woman was going to get shot in the back.

Even though the woman doubled Carly's weight, Carly nevertheless grabbed her by the shoulders and tried to pull her to the ground.

The woman fought her. "No!"

"Get down and stay there," Carly demanded sharply, digging her hands deeper into the woman's shoulder blades.

"No, no. You...don't understand, Officer. There's—" She stopped, as if struggling for her next breath.

By now Carly had managed to wrestle her to the ground. They were face to face on their knees.

"You've got to get...get in there right now," the woman went on. "It's...it's the worst thing that's ever happened to me." Catching Carly off guard, she scrambled to her feet and headed back toward the store.

Carly lunged and tore after her.

"Go inside," the woman screamed, coming to a halt outside the door. She moved then to the right of it, all the while wringing her hands and jumping up and down. "Please, oh, please go inside."

"Have you been robbed?" Carly shouted in order to make herself heard over the woman's fit of hysteria.

Having now reached the entrance herself, Carly dropped to the ground, certain the burglar was still on the premises, but telling the woman to get down was impossible. So, gripping the gun tightly and holding it up, she crawled on her hands and knees until she had wedged herself inside.

She saw nothing. Heard nothing. The interior was as quiet as a tomb.

The woman came in behind her. "Get down, for God's sake!" Carly hollered.

The woman looked down at her and blinked. "Why?"

"Have you been robbed?" Carly asked again, becoming more perplexed by the second.

"No."

Carly slowly got to her feet. "What do you mean, no?"

The woman crossed her hands under her heavy bosom and sneaked a look to her left before turning back to Carly. "I ain't never mentioned being robbed, Officer."

"What is it, then, Ms...?" Carly took a deep breath.

"Mrs. Braden," she supplied absently, then added, "please, will you just go look?"

"Look at what?" Carly's tone was cold.

"I...don't know," Mrs. Braden whispered, starting to wheeze again.

"What do you mean, you don't know?"

"I don't, that's all," Mrs. Braden responded tightly. "All I know is it's something cold and wet."

"Where?"

"Under the cabinet."

"Show me."

Mrs. Braden sniffled. "All...right."

They walked to the back of the store into a makeshift kitchen. Mrs. Braden crossed to the cabinet against one wall and stopped. After pointing to the door on the right, she faced Carly.

"Go ahead, show me," Carly said.

Mrs. Braden violently shook her head.

Hanging on to her patience by a mere thread, Carly stepped forward and yanked open the door.

She saw it immediately. Mrs. Braden was right. It was cold and dark and wet. And black.

"Oh, no," Carly whimpered, just as the huge snake moved, curling tighter around the large bag of flour.

"See, see, I knew it was something awful!" the woman cried, jumping up and down again.

"Stop it!" Carly was barely able to get the words through her stiff lips, especially as her stomach was turning upside down. She was afraid she was going to be sick any second.

"You've got to do something." Mrs. Braden was screaming

again. "I've got to get breakfast started. Them truck drivers'll be here before long, expecting me to have their biscuits ready."

Carly was backing up.

"Where you goin', Officer?" The woman's voice had risen an octave higher. "You can't leave me."

"Watch me," Carly said, pivoting on her heel.

"You're a cop. You've got to get that thing out of there."

"Not me! There're two things I don't do, lady. I don't do snakes and I don't pick up dead dogs, but here's the number of someone who does." Carly reached into her pocket, pulled out a stray piece of paper and jotted down the information with rapid, jerky movements.

After slapping the paper down on the table, Carly hit the door and never looked back.

Carly was looking forward to some days off, but with her crazy schedule of late, she wasn't sure when any would be forthcoming. It seemed that the older she got, the harder it was to attune her body to the change in shifts.

Today was one of those days. Even though she'd just come off the midnight shift, she was due back on evenings. It was twelve o'clock now, and she'd been up only long enough to shower and slip into a robe. Carly's stomach growled, reminding her she hadn't eaten in a while.

When she walked into the kitchen, her uncle was hunched over the table, scribbling something on a piece of paper.

She smiled. "Good morning."

Matt looked up and shook his head. "Good morning, my eye. It's after twelve, girl."

Carly smiled. "Well, it's morning to me."

"Worked mids, huh?"

"Yep."

"Going back to bed?"

"I wish. I have to go in at two. Our schedules are all messed up. Maybe next week I'll get back on days."

Matt's gaze softened. "I hope so, too, because you're looking a little bedraggled."

"Thanks, Unc. You sure know how to make a person feel better."

He chuckled. "Can't fault a person for speaking the truth."

Carly walked over and planted a kiss on the top of his head. "One of these days your smart mouth is gonna get *you* in a heap of trouble."

"That's what Martha keeps telling me."

Carly turned to the refrigerator and opened it. "Speaking of Martha, how is she?"

"Fine. In fact, that's where I was heading. I was leaving you a note."

Carly turned around. "Oh?"

Matt's tone was defensive. "Now don't go gettin' your hopes up, girl. She's had a flare-up with her arthritis, and I'm going to drive her to the grocery store. That's all."

Carly had difficulty keeping a straight face. "Whatever you say."

"Well—" he coughed "—I did promise that I'd take her to one of her Autumn Club's get-togethers tonight," he added.

Carly's grin widened. "Mmm. Sounds good to me."

"What about you?" Matt asked, abruptly changing the subject. "Are things any better?"

Carly decided against a sandwich and instead took out a small bowl of leftover spaghetti and placed it in the microwave. "I guess so, or at least I'm too busy to worry about it."

"Good." He paused at the door. "I'll see you later. Have a good evening."

"You, too," she said, blowing him a kiss.

After pouring herself a glass of iced tea, Carly sat down and started to eat the Italian food with relish, taking advantage of the quiet. She smiled, thinking about her uncle and Martha. In spite of his blustering protests, Matt cared about Martha. Carly would give anything if he'd have enough sense to marry her.

Her smile growing at the thought, Carly got up and poured herself a cup of coffee. She had just sat back down, when the phone rang.

Groaning, she picked up the cup and crossed to the buffet. It was on its fifth ring by the time she lifted the receiver to her ear.

"Hello."

"Carly."

It was Brian Calhoun.

"Are you there?" he asked when she didn't respond immediately.

"I'm here. Sorry, I took a sip of my coffee."

"Mmm. Wish I were there drinking some with you."

"That'd be nice," she lied, only to then feel a pang of unwanted guilt.

"Yeah, wouldn't it, though." His tone had a low, intimate ring to it.

"Are you at the office?" she asked, calmly switching the subject to something less personal.

"Yes, and my desk is a mess."

"I find that hard to believe." And she did. Nothing about Brian's work was ever a mess. Tall and thin with curly blond hair, his features were perfect—too perfect. In her mind she could see him clearly now, sitting at his desk, impeccably dressed in a pin-striped suit and a tie.

"Well, you're right," he said with confidence, "it's nothing I can't handle."

Carly glanced down at her watch. "I'm going to have something I can't handle if I don't get off this phone and get dressed."

"Speaking of work, I expected you to be at the station."

"My schedule is messed up this week."

His tone changed. "Look, when am I going to see you?"

Carly sighed. "Oh, Brian, I don't know."

"Dammit, Carly, why don't you just say you'll marry me, and then we won't have all these troubles."

"Please, Brian, not now. Anyway, we've been over this before. You know how I feel."

"Yeah, I know. Unfortunately I don't feel the same way. I want to marry you."

"Please, can we talk about this later?" Carly pleaded softly. "I really have to go."

"Promise you'll call me later?"

"I promise."

Men! Carly thought thirty minutes later when she breezed into the station. Brian couldn't have chosen a worse time to start harping on the subject of marriage again.

"Hi, Carly," Angie called from her glassed-in cubicle.

"I'll talk to you later, okay? I'm running late."

Without waiting for Angie's reply, Carly entered the squad room and, after nodding to the officers seated around the tables, went to check her box. Not expecting to have a message, she was perplexed when she saw the piece of white paper.

When she read it, her heart almost stopped beating.

Captain Knight wants to see you in his office.

Chapter 7

Rance drew on a cigarette and watched Bud May pull on his mustache. They had been discussing the latest pharmacy burglary, which had just occurred. In Timberland alone, last night's heist upped the total to four.

"Dammit, there's got to be a pattern, and we're missing it," Rance pointed out.

"You're right," Bud agreed, "but as you say, so far we haven't been able to pick up on it."

"Since the eyewitness proved to be of little help, we're still dancing in square one, right?"

"Well, not entirely," Bud replied. "He did give us a description, though a vague one."

"'Vague' is an understatement." Rance took another drag, then ground the cigarette down into the ashtray at his elbow.

May shrugged. "It was dark, after all."

"Yeah, I know."

"Crawford's uptight."

Rance grimaced. "Yeah, and he's after my hide, of course. We don't even have a suspect."

"From the looks of you, he's close to getting it."

Rance's face hardened. "What the hell's that supposed to mean?"

"Looks to me like you're losing weight and haven't slept in weeks."

"Well, I haven't, but that's none of your business, either."

Bud was quiet for a moment, as if realizing that maybe he'd overstepped his bounds. Friend or no friend, Rance was still his boss. "Have you heard the rumors?"

Rance's eyes narrowed. "What rumors?"

"Rumors are flying around now that it's the police who are involved in the pharmacy robberies."

"Damn," Rance muttered, standing and coming from behind his desk. "That's all the hell we need."

"I couldn't agree more."

"Do you believe it?" Rance asked, leaning against the front of his desk.

Bud pushed out his lower lip. "Wouldn't be surprised."

"Damn!"

"My sentiments exactly."

"Keep your nose and ears to the ground."

"Will do," Bud said, getting up and crossing to the door. Once there, he turned around. "Oh, I almost forgot, Arley Bishop's wife is definitely going to have that heart transplant. What d'you think about the department doing something?"

Rance sighed. "I've already thought about that. I talked to Arley yesterday, told him we'd do what we could to help. But even at that, it's going to take a miracle for him to pull it off financially."

"Especially on a patrolman's salary."

Rance's answer was another sigh.

"How do we go about organizing a fund-raiser? Should I talk to Terri?"

"That wouldn't hurt. In the meantime I'll see what I can do from this end." Rance paused thoughtfully. "I've been toying with an idea."

"Talk to you later."

"Later," Rance said to the detective's retreating back.

The last thing Carly wanted to do was go to Rance's office. It had been thirty minutes since she'd gotten the note out of her box, and still she hadn't headed that way. But the shift meeting was over now, and she had no choice.

"Hey, Mitchum, you gonna stand there and daydream all day?"

Robert Farrell's low, grinding voice brought her head up with a start. "No, Sergeant, I'm not," she answered patiently.

"Then get the lead out and hit the streets. And remember to make a pass by all the drugstores at least once. Orders from the captain."

"Thank you for reminding me—again," she said with false sweetness.

"Just wanted to make sure you were paying attention," he said airily.

Carly swallowed a sharp retort and said, "Always, Sergeant."

She then turned and headed down the hall toward Rance's office, noticing, to her dismay, that her hands were trembling slightly. Robert Farrell she could handle, but Rance was a different matter altogether.

She paused outside Rance's closed door before taking a deep breath and knocking.

Rance's brusque "Come in" did little to relieve her mounting anxieties.

The moment Carly opened the door and crossed the threshold, she blurted, "You wanted to see me?" To her credit, she actually smiled.

At the sound of her voice, Rance's head came up sharply, as if caught off guard by her appearance. But it wasn't her appearance that shook him; it was her smile. Fleeting though it was, it transformed her face, making her more beautiful than ever, yet somehow vulnerable.

Grappling with his inner turmoil, Rance spoke in a curt tone. "Yeah." He then turned abruptly and stalked to the window behind his desk.

Carly slowly inched into the room, trying to ignore the erratic beat of her heart, while pretending not to notice the way the muscles bunched in his shoulders as he lifted his right hand and rubbed the back of his neck with long, shapely fingers.

When he turned back around and walked toward his desk, he caught her eye. Carly paused in midstride, feeling suddenly light-headed. Each time she saw him, her response was more and more physical. He attracted her and frightened her all at once.

"Please, sit down," he said, his voice sounding as if his throat had suffered an injury.

"If you don't mind, I'd rather stand," Carly responded, trying to disregard her jittery nerves.

"Fine by me." Rance wasn't looking at her now. His gaze was again focused out the window. "There are two reasons I wanted to see you."

"And they are?" She held her breath.

He turned, and his gaze fell to her mouth. "First off, I have a letter from Stacy."

"For me?" Her uneasiness forgotten, she smiled.

In spite of himself, Rance returned the smile. "She asked me to give it to you."

"I've been wondering about her," Carly said truthfully, and she had been, wondering if she and Rance had found a common ground. Unrealistically she had come to care for the girl.

As if he could read her mind, Rance said, "At the moment, things are cool between us." His lips twitched. "That's my daughter's terminology, you understand."

"I'm...glad," she said, knowing she must sound strange. But God, how else could she act when he was actually behaving like a human being? She was seeing a side of Rance Knight she didn't know existed.

"Uh, here's the letter."

Carly stepped closer and took it from his outstretched hand, careful not to touch him. She slipped it into her pocket, planning to read it in private.

"When Stacy comes back to visit, she'd like to see you again. You made quite an impression on her."

Carly's eyes lighted. "I'd like that."

"Would you really?"

"Of course. Why wouldn't I?"

He shrugged. "No reason, except my ex can't wait to get rid of her."

Carly didn't know what to say, so she didn't say anything.

"But, then, you're nothing like my ex-wife."

"I'm...not?" she stammered again, jolted by the comparison.

"No," he said harshly, averting his gaze, but not before Carly saw his lips tighten.

They both lapsed into silence then, a silence so intense that Carly could hear her own pulse beating.

"What else, Captain?" Carly asked at length.

Rance wore a deceptively bland expression, but he was thinking how her features seemed to change from moment to moment.

"Do you mind if I smoke?" he asked unexpectedly, shocking himself. Damn, since when did he have to ask a rookie if he could smoke in his own office?

Carly shrugged. "If you must."

"Good God!" He threw up his hands in mock surrender, while his mind swung in two directions at once. He wanted to hold on to his irritation, but on the other hand, he couldn't help but admire her spunk. Even more, he liked the way her nose wrinkled when she was agitated, as she was now. He wanted to find something wrong with her, but couldn't, no more than he could stay angry.

Carly ran her tongue across her lip. "You were about to tell me the other reason...."

His features tensed up again. "Ah, so I was. It has to do with Arley Bishop's wife."

"Did she—"

"No, she didn't die, but I'm afraid she will if she doesn't have the heart transplant."

"I'm sorry," Carly said, then fell silent a moment, her thoughts swinging to Officer Arley Bishop, whom she admired and enjoyed working with. Maybe it was because he felt the same about her, never failing to treat her as an equal. While she'd known his wife was suffering from heart trouble, she'd never been given the details.

"I'm going to organize a fund-raiser." Rance lifted his shoulders. "Although I don't know how much good we can do."

"I think that's a great idea."

"Would you like to help?"

"Help or take charge?" Her tone held an edge. She knew what he was thinking—things of this sort were woman's work.

"Help."

"Help whom?"

"Me."

"*You?*"

Rance's bland expression gave nothing away. "Do you have a problem with that, Officer Mitchum?"

"Er...sorry, of course not," she said. "It's just—"

"It's just what?"

He was in touching distance of her now. She was afraid to move, knew it would be visibly rude if she did. But again she found his proximity threatening. He was so big, so overpowering...so everything. "All...right," she said softly.

"Does that mean you'll help?"

He gave her that rare, lopsided smile she was learning to like and hate all at the same time. "How could I refuse? Under the circumstances," she added hastily.

"Good, then it's settled."

Carly looked at him carefully, the tilt of his head, the way his eyes seemed to bore through her, and wondered why she kept getting mixed signals from him.

Her inability to understand Rance made her not only uneasy, but nervous, as well, because she didn't understand herself and her reaction to him.

"Is that all, Captain?" She knew her voice had grown curt and cool.

"For now, Officer Mitchum, for now."

Two days later, Carly's head was still reeling from that encounter with Rance. Although she hadn't see him, not even in passing in the halls, she had nevertheless nearly driven herself crazy thinking about him and their strange conversation. Several times she'd even wondered if she'd dreamed it.

"Hey, what's with you, friend? This is the second time in a matter of minutes that you've zonked out on me."

Carly released a pent-up breath at the same time as she reached over and turned the volume down on her walkie-talkie. "Sorry, Ang."

Although Carly was on duty, she had stopped by Angie's apartment to check on her after Angie had called in sick with a stomach virus. Carly was perched on the edge of a chair in the living area; Angie was curled up on the sofa in her robe and gown.

"Well," Angie asked.

"Well what?" Carly feigned innocence.

Angie reached for the glass of Coke sitting on the coffee table in front of her and took a healthy gulp. "Ha, you're not kidding anybody, least of all me. So I want to know what's on your mind. Level with me." Angie looked solemn. "Something's bothering you, isn't it?"

"Oh, Angie, I just wish it were that simple."

Angie shrugged. "Sometimes talking about it helps."

"Not this time."

"Why do I get the impression your despondency doesn't have anything to do with work?"

Carly could not bring herself to look her friend in the eye. "Because it doesn't, not really," Carly answered, but not without reservation. She simply could not discuss her crazy and unfounded attraction to Rance, certainly not with someone who worked in the department. Anyway, it was something she had to settle within herself. Some things were just too personal to talk about.

Angie suddenly uncurled her legs and scooted to the edge of the sofa. "I'm glad. I was hoping that sooner or later those idiots you work with would get their act together and see how hard you work."

Carly grinned. "Those 'idiots' as you call them will never get their act together, not where I'm concerned, that is."

"Oh, I don't know so much about that. Even Crawford, as dense as he is, sees your potential. Hey, speaking of Crawford, has he pressured you any more about going over to C.I.D.?"

"No, he hasn't. But there's no guarantee he won't later."

"Oh." Angie's brows were furrowed. "You mean he might force you to take the transfer after all?"

"I hope not, but I wouldn't put it past him. Would you?"

"Are you kidding? I wouldn't put anything past that man. As my dad used to say, 'he couldn't find his tail with a search party.'" Her expression changed. "If only Crawford had enough sense to step down while he's ahead and let Rance Knight take over. He's just what the department—"

A squawk from the walkie-talkie interrupted her.

"Two-oh-five."

Carly put the walkie-talkie to her lips. "Two-oh-five. Go ahead."

"Lady phoned in, said husband was lying on the floor bleeding. Address is 726 Wiley Street."

"Ten-four. En route."

"Thanks for stopping by."

"I'll talk to you later," Carly said over her shoulder, heading out the door at breakneck speed.

The houses on Wiley Street were jammed together on small lots. You could barely tell where one lot began and another ended. The neighborhood was a quiet middle-class one, 726 was at the end of a block of brick homes.

As Carly maneuvered the car close to the curb, she reached for the microphone and reported her location.

Two women were standing in the yard, sobbing. The second they saw Carly get out of the car, they ran to her.

"Oh, please, Officer," the older of the two cried. "Hurry, hurry, help my husband and my daughter!"

Carly started toward the front door. "I'll do what I can."

"No," the woman screamed from behind her, stopping Carly in her tracks. "Go around to the back door."

"Stay here," Carly ordered, before dashing around the side of the house.

Not knowing what or *whom* she might be facing, Carly drew her .38 revolver from her holster and approached the door. It was standing wide open.

At this stage, she could almost taste the danger, and it was something she thought about often. Nothing could be taken for granted.

Quickly but cautiously, her mind clear and her steps sure, Carly walked up to the door and peered inside. For a heartbeat, her breath caught somewhere deep in her throat.

The sight immobilized her, turned her stomach. Blood was everywhere. It was smeared across the carpet and on the wall nearest her.

Forcing her uncooperative limbs to move, Carly stepped around the man's body that lay facedown just inside the entrance to the kitchen. Cocking her pistol, she walked farther into the house and into the den.

Another body lay on the floor, that of a young girl lying on her back, a gaping hole in her chest.

"Oh, God," Carly groaned, again forcing her body to move. Cautiously she inspected the rest of the house, but it was empty. She reached for her walkie-talkie and said, "Two-oh-five."

"Go ahead 205."

"Request backup, ambulance, JP and detectives. Two bodies down, one a male Caucasian, the other a female Caucasian."

"Ten-four 205."

Then, turning, Carly ran back outside to her car, all the while sucking air into her lungs. The reporting party sat huddled together on the front porch, quietly sobbing.

Ignoring them for a moment, Carly reached through the window, grabbed a clipboard and small tape recorder off the seat and dashed back to the two women who appeared to be mother and daughter. They were standing and waiting, holding on to each other.

The older woman raised dazed eyes to Carly. "Are...they all right?"

"I'm sorry," Carly said gently. "They are both dead. They've been shot."

"Oh, no," she cried. "Oh, no."

The girl by her side, whom Carly judged to be a teenager, had yet to say a word. She simply looked confused and overwhelmed.

"I'm afraid I have to ask you some questions, Mrs.—?"

"Mrs. Dies," the woman whispered, her shoulders quivering. "Joan...Dies."

"Can you tell me what happened, Mrs. Dies?" Carly inquired, keeping her tone low and soft.

Carly slipped the recorder in her pocket and turned it on. She didn't intend to lose a word of this interview.

"He...my husband," Mrs. Dies was saying, "was sick. He...came home from work early, and I went to collect the money." She started crying again; wracking sobs shook her body.

The young girl hugged her mother closer.

Carly turned to the girl, giving Mrs. Dies time to collect herself. "What's your name?"

"Tammie," she whispered.

"Tammie Dies?"

"Yes, ma'am."

Carly turned her attention back to Mrs. Dies. "You were saying that you collected money."

Mrs. Dies picked at the soggy tissue in one hand. "Paul manages three...local fast-food restaurants and since he...he was too sick this afternoon to collect the money, I did it for him. A little while later I went to the grocery store—Tammie here went with me—so I could fix Paul some soup. He and Jan—my eldest daughter—stayed behind."

She paused while her shoulders shook in grief. "When...when we came home, we...we found them. It...it was horrible."

Carly placed a comforting hand on her shoulder.

"Do you have any idea who would want to harm your husband and daughter?"

"No...no." She stared up at Carly with horror-filled eyes. "Who...who could do a thing like this?"

"That's what we have to find out. Would you like for me to call someone for you?" Out of the corner of her eye, Carly noticed the neighbors on both sides were standing in their yards, gawking.

"No," she whispered. "Not right now, anyway."

"I want you and your daughter to sit in my car. Help is on the way."

Once Carly sealed off the area, still clutching her clipboard, she walked across the yard and began questioning the neighbors, asking if they had seen or heard anything. One told her that he'd heard gunshots, but by the time he'd gotten to his door and looked out, there'd been no one in sight.

Carly thanked him and was making her way back toward the house, when a young man charged across the street. He didn't stop until he had leaped the curb into the yard.

"Stop. That's far enough," Carly shouted, when the young man blatantly disregarded the taped-off area.

He halted and turned around.

He looked like a leftover from the hippie era of the sixties, Carly thought, raking her eyes over him. His hair was dirty and scraggly, and he was wearing cutoffs, a tank top and had bare feet even though the temperature was in the forties.

And he had blood on one of his pants legs.

"Hold it right there," Carly said.

He ignored her, and while weaving unsteadily on his feet, he began yanking at the rope.

"Shove it, lady!" he shouted. "That's my father in there. You can't stop me from going in."

Though she was stunned at the news, Carly didn't show it. Instead she pulled out her stick and continued to walk toward him. When she was close enough to smell his breath, Carly realized he was drunk out of his mind and didn't know what he was saying or doing. Still, she couldn't let him inside the house.

Her eyes dropped to his ripped cutoffs. "Where did that blood on your pants come from?" she asked.

"It ain't none of your business," he slurred, "but I cut myself shaving."

Carly didn't believe a word he said, but she didn't let on. "Look, your mother and sister are in my car," she said calmly, trying to reason with him. "Come on, I'll take you to them."

"Kiss off, lady," he spit, and turned around.

That was his first mistake. Carly raised her stick and cracked him across the back of his knees, sending him crashing face first into the hard, cold ground.

"Bitch!" he screamed, eating dirt.

Because she had caught him unawares and because he was so drunk, Carly had the edge. Placing her booted foot square in the middle of his back, she leaned down and snapped handcuffs on him.

Just as she forced him to his feet, her backup arrived. It was Arley Bishop.

"Here, Arley, put this creep in your car."

"Be happy to, Mitchum."

It was then that she heard the screech of more tires. Two vehicles followed by an ambulance pulled up in front of the house. Several car doors opened, then slammed at the same time.

The first one to appear was Rance. Following close on his heels was Detective Bud May and two other men. The justice of the peace got out of the other car.

Carly met Rance halfway.

"Let's go inside, Officer," he said briskly, his trained eyes going beyond Carly, circling, assessing the situation. "You can fill me in on the details later."

"Yes, sir," Carly said.

The moment Carly walked back inside the house, the room began to spin. *Oh, Lord, please,* she prayed silently but fervently, *don't let me get sick in front of these men.* Somehow it was easier to think about her physical discomfort and possible embarrassment than the stark reality of death that was all around her.

The detectives, taking instructions from Bud, were scrutinizing the floor, while another was busy snapping photographs and another fingerprinting. Two ambulance attendants stood nearby, talking quietly, waiting.

Rance's muttered "Damn!" suddenly drew Carly's attention. His gaze was on the body of the young girl.

Carly, unable to stand idle another second, approached him. "Captain?" Her tone was tentative.

His was impatient. "What is it, Mitchum?"

"The kid I just arrested for interference is the deceased man's son."

"So?"

Carly quelled the urge to slap him. "So, there was blood on his pants legs, and when I ask him where he got it, he said shaving."

"What's your point, Officer?"

"I think he had something to do with the murders. I think he should be questioned further."

Rance looked around him a moment, then back at Carly. "Who are those two people in your car?"

Carly blinked. "What...I mean, Mrs. Dies and her other daughter."

"Why don't you make yourself useful and see if you can help them?"

At first Carly couldn't believe her ears. Was his tone that condescending, as if he were speaking to an imbecile or a child? Of course it was. The bastard didn't believe a word she said.

"Well, Officer, what are you waiting for?"

"Not a thing, Captain," she said with icy politeness. "Not a thing."

As she was leaving the room, she heard the justice of the peace say, "Captain, this ain't no suicide or accident. That leaves murder."

"Damn!" Rance exploded again. "It's going to be a long night."

And it was. Carly walked into the house at one o'clock the next morning. She didn't pause until she reached her bathroom.

Once there she knelt over the commode and lost the entire contents of her stomach.

Chapter 8

Carly had just finished washing her face with cold water and brushing her teeth, when she heard a soft tap on her bedroom door, followed by the knob being turned.

Grabbing a towel, she peered around the corner. Her uncle stood just inside her room, dressed in his robe and house shoes, a deep frown wrinkling his forehead.

"Are you all right?" he asked, his eyes dark with concern.

Hearing the sympathy in Matt's voice was almost Carly's undoing. She feared another onslaught of tears. The whole time she'd been throwing up, she'd been crying.

"I'm...fine now," she lied, not wanting to upset him any more than she already had.

"Well, you don't look it."

Carly tried to smile, but failed miserably. "I guess I earned it. I had a terrible night, but that's no excuse," she said, rushing her words, "for waking you up. I'm sorry."

"You didn't," he replied gruffly.

"Then what—"

Matt didn't let her finish. "The doorbell woke me up."

"The doorbell," Carly mimicked, looking blank. "But I didn't hear it."

Matt ran a hand through his thick hair, which made it stand on end more than it already was. It was obvious he'd been asleep, but his eyes were sharp and penetrating. "You have a visitor."

"A visitor?" Her frown was dark. "At this time of night?"

"At this time of morning, you mean," Matt corrected crossly.

"Who...who is it?"

"Rance Knight. He wants to see you."

A surprise gasp escaped her, and her knees suddenly wanted to give way. *Rance—here!* She groped to find an order to her thoughts.

When she didn't respond right off, Matt asked, "What do you want me to tell him? If you ask me, you don't look fit to see anyone, especially not at this hour." He made no effort to hide his disapproval.

Carly drew a troubled breath. "I have to, though—see him, I mean."

"Why don't I tell him that you'll—"

"No," Carly cut in, anticipating what her uncle was going to say. "Just...tell him I'll be there shortly." She paused. "It's probably something to do with the case we just investigated," she added lamely.

Matt didn't look convinced. "If you're sure."

Carly forced a smile. "I'm sure."

Her uncle continued to look at her strangely, as if he wanted to say something else but didn't quite know what.

"I'm fine, I promise," she said, when he still hadn't moved.

His expression told her he didn't believe a word, nevertheless he turned and headed toward the door, muttering to himself.

"Good night, Uncle Matt. And thanks."

His loud snort was the last thing she heard before the door closed behind him.

Several minutes later, still in her uniform, though minus her gun belt and boots, Carly stood uncertainly outside the door into the den, wishing for a second that she could run away. But that would be cowardly, and while she might be foolish, cowardly she was not.

As to why he had come to see her at this ungodly hour, she refused to speculate, but if she were to hazard a guess, she'd guess it would be to fault her for her performance this evening. But, then, that didn't make sense, because he could do that as easily tomorrow.

For the moment, it was enough that he had come. *Carly, would you just listen to yourself?* She caught a sudden breath at the implication of her thoughts. How could she feel this way after he'd insulted her ability and her intelligence? Where was her pride? She didn't know. When it came to Rance, she didn't know anything anymore.

Rance was leaning against the mantel, his shirt collar unbuttoned and his tie hanging loosely below it. He looked beat, and the fatigue that dominated his strong features made him appear older than he was. She wet her lips.

"Captain," Carly said softly, suddenly and overwhelmingly conscious of her own haggard appearance. But she'd known no amount of makeup could hide her exhaustion, so she hadn't even bothered with repairing it.

Rance looked at her across the space between them, his eyes dark and disturbing, but for once he didn't hold her gaze. He looked away, saying, "I guess you think I make it a habit of ringing women's doorbells at ungodly hours."

His attempt at humor fell flat. It didn't bring a smile to either of their faces, nor did it relieve the mounting tension.

"Do you?" she asked lightly, for lack of anything better to say.

Rance ran a hand around the back of his neck and strode to the middle of the room. "No, believe it or not, I don't."

Alarmed, she sensed a feeling of déjà vu. "Well, now that you're here, would you like something to drink?"

"No, thanks."

He reminded her of a lighted fuse. Though his thick lashes hid the expression in his eyes, the tousled hair, the lines beside his mouth and his jerky movements gave him away. This was another side of the cool, aloof Captain Knight she had never seen.

Rance cleared his throat. "Would you apologize to Matt again in the morning for my waking him up?"

Her breathing had turned ragged. "It's all right. He...didn't mind."

He smiled, but it was a rather twisted sort of smile. "Yeah, I bet."

Carly looked away. His deep, husky voice was like a caress.

"You look like hell," he said bluntly, unexpectedly, his voice now sounding thick, unnatural.

How much more did she have to endure? She felt the sting of tears behind her eyelids and hated herself for being weak. Wasn't it enough that she'd seen two bullet-riddled bodies, lost everything in her stomach and dreaded going to bed because of the nightmares that would follow?

"Why...did you come?" she whispered, her lips quivering slightly. She felt like a fool.

Rance didn't respond, though his eyes never strayed from her face. Rarely did he despise himself as he did at this moment. Yet he couldn't tell her the truth, that the honest-to-God reason he was here was that he couldn't stay away, that his desire for her had become a constant ache inside him.

Since he couldn't say all that, he didn't say anything.

Carly straightened slowly, having recovered some of her anger. "Did you come to tell me that I'm in trouble, that I did something wrong this afternoon?"

She was unknowingly provocative as she glared at him, her hair wild about her face, her blue eyes made more luminous by her emotions. The blouse, taut across her breasts, drew his attention to their swelling fullness.

"Is that what you think?"

Carly felt herself crumbling under his devastating stare. "Well, isn't it?" she asked weakly.

He was standing so close to her now that she could see the dark shadow of his beard, feel his warm breath on her face....

"No, dammit, it isn't."

"Then, why..."

Rance's expression was tormented. "Because I was worried about you, that's why."

She sucked in her breath and stared into his eyes for a long moment.

His hollow laugh failed to mask his pain. "I bet you find that amusing, don't you?"

"No," she whispered, shaken.

Rance, too, was shaken. "If you don't stop looking at me like that," he muttered, "I'm not going to be able to——"

"What?" The word came out in a breathy gust.

"Stop myself from doing this," he said in a strangled note.

Suddenly there was no barrier between them. His hand plunged into her silky hair, and his dark eyes burned with hunger before he brought her mouth to his. The sensation was electric. Her hands pressed against his chest for a split second, then she sagged against him.

Their lips clung, hot and desperate, while his tongue invaded her mouth, warm and wet. No man had ever touched her with such ruthless force, sending the blood charging out of control through her system. And still they clung. Mouth to mouth. Belly to belly. Kissing in wild, hot, desperate need.

Rance had lost control. Raw passion that had nothing to do with love reduced his will to nothing. He was crushing her, wanting to get into her skin.

He was rock hard against her. Instinctively she arched closer, wanting, demanding more.

Then it was over. He jerked his head back and thrust her to arm's length, leaving her mouth parted and aching for more.

"No!" he rasped, his eyes dazed. "This is insane. I'm insane!"

Carly's heart sank like lead. Then it rebelled. Just who did he think he was? Did he think he could come on to her, take carte blanche with her body, then cast her aside at the slightest whim? How dared he!

She shot him a scalding look. "I think you'd better go."

Rance took a step forward and muttered savagely, "I didn't mean to— Oh, hell, I don't know what I meant."

Carly turned away, her lungs aching from the effort of breathing. "Please...just go away."

In the space of a heartbeat, he wrenched open the door and went out, slamming it behind him.

Rance stared up at the notes in front of him with unseeing eyes. He was supposed to give every shift a briefing on the pharmacy heists beginning tomorrow. Although he had prepared a list of what he thought were the pertinent points that needed to be covered, he still wasn't satisfied.

Following a guttural oath, he flung the scratch pad to the floor. Then, locking his hands behind his head, he stared at the ceiling. It was after twelve o'clock and he was lying prone on his bed, but sleep was the farthest thing from his mind.

Maybe if he tried counting sheep, he'd finally coast into never-never land.

He laughed harshly, flung his arm out and switched off the lamp on the bedside table. Still the room swam in light. There was a full moon; he could see it through the half-closed mini-blinds.

He was furious with himself for giving in to his carnal desires and for breaking every rule he considered unbreakable. His downfall twisted in his gut like bitter acid. *You just had to do it, didn't you? You just had to touch her.* But oh, was he paying for it, paying dearly. He was in pain, and no amount of cold showers could relieve his stiff discomfort. He had wrestled the bed until he was worn out. His overtaxed muscles continued to rebel, as did his throbbing manhood.

Again he turned over, searching for a comfortable position. There was none. He was too keyed up. His entire body throbbed, courtesy of erotic images of Carly filling his mind.

"Sonofabitch," he grunted. *Don't do this to yourself. Think about something else.*

He couldn't. Even now the fire in his groin was out of control. He could think of nothing except his raw desire to possess her, driving wildly and hotly into her softness until they were both wrung out.

He should never have touched her. That was his first mistake.

He should have kept his damned hands to himself. But, then, he'd been certain that to kiss her would be to erase her from his mind. Ha! Was the joke ever on him.

When she'd walked into the den and he'd looked at her pale face and haunted eyes, he'd been lost. For a moment he'd thought she might be close to the breaking point—he was certain she'd been crying or sick. Or both.

He'd told her she looked like hell, and at the same time he'd reminded himself that she was a cop. Death was part of the job, he'd also reminded himself. She'd have to sink or swim on her own. She'd even stood up to him about the Dies kid, even though he didn't think her theory was valid. Yes, she'd hung in there; he'd have to give her that.

Still, the moment she'd followed him back to the crime scene, he'd had an almost irresistible urge to put himself between her and the gruesome sight sprawled before them.

She wouldn't have appreciated that. In fact, she would have been furious if he'd questioned her ability. Yet he knew it got to her, and not because she was a woman, either. It was because she was human with feelings and...

Hell, why was he tormenting himself? He knew he could never touch her again, though he ached with the thought of doing just that, of touching one of those full breasts... But if he wanted to advance his career, then she was off-limits. He'd already blown it once. It was time to get his act together, time to get some sleep.

He closed his eyes and did in fact end up counting sheep.

"Anyone have any questions about what I've just been over?"

Although Carly had hung on to Rance's every word, she had refrained from looking at him. He had been talking to the evening shift for fifteen minutes, and the entire time she had kept her head down as she took notes.

She would never forgive him for humiliating her, for making her night intolerable and her day dreary. If she never saw him again, it would be too soon.

Two officers asked questions, to which Rance readily responded, and then he dismissed them.

"Good luck," he said, finally ending the session.

There was the immediate shuffling of chairs as everyone stood, duty bound.

"Well, I guess it's off to the races," Arley Bishop said to her with a smile. The officer had sat down next to her and had thoughtfully brought her a cup of coffee, which she'd scarcely touched.

"Guess so," Carly answered with a short-lived smile. "How's Ruth, Arley?"

He shook his head. "Not good, I'm afraid, though we sure have high hopes for the transplant."

"I'm keeping my fingers crossed."

"Everyone's been so nice, especially Captain Knight."

"Is she on a restricted diet of any kind?" Carly asked, changing the subject.

Arley scratched his head. "Not really. Why?"

"I know someone who bakes the best buttermilk pies you've ever put in your mouth."

"I'm sure she can handle that." Arley grinned. "If not, I sure as hell can."

"Hey, what you two so chummy about?"

Arley stared beyond Carly's shoulder and made a face. "Get lost, Beechum."

"Ah, now, is that any way to talk to a fellow officer?" Beechum asked in a mocking whine.

Carly kept her back to Beechum, and in doing so caught Rance's movement out of the corner of her eye. She watched as he scooped up his notes with one hand while trying to balance a cup of coffee in the other.

As if knowing he was being scrutinized, Rance paused in his actions and looked up. Their eyes met, but for only a moment. Feeling her face flush, Carly quickly collected her dignity and turned away. Even so, she could not control her heart; it was beating double time.

"Beechum, has anyone ever told you that you're a royal pain in the butt?" Arley was saying.

Beechum's eyes lost their humor. "How 'bout if *you* get lost, Bishop? This little lady and I—well, we have some unfinished business...." His voice trailed off as his eyes fastened, unblinking, on Carly. "Don't we, sugar?"

"I'm warning you," Bishop began, his nostrils flaring.

Carly placed a hand on Arley's arm. "It's okay, Arley, I can handle it." Her gaze swung back to Beechum. "Now *I'm* warning you, Larry!" Fury curled around every word she uttered.

"Lord, but I love it, sugar, when you get all hot and bothered," Beechum said with a grin.

Behind her Carly heard snickers from the few officers who were still in the room, but she paid little attention to them as her cheeks turned bloodred and anger boiled inside her. It was time she put Beechum in his place once and for all.

No one saw Rance move toward them, or paid much attention as he approached the nearby pot and refilled his mug with steaming hot coffee.

Beechum continued to leer at Carly, whispering conspiratorially, "What do you say to dumping your sidekick here and strolling out with me? I got some heavy plans for us."

Arley grabbed him by the arm and shoved him back. "Shut your filthy mouth."

"What the hell!" Beechum cried, grabbing his nape as scalding coffee soaked through his uniform.

"Sonofa—" he yelled, spinning around, a murderous expression on his face.

The remainder of the word came out as nothing but a whimper.

Rance smiled pleasantly, though his eyes were cold. "Didn't mean to drown you, Beechum. But you just moved at the wrong time." Rance reached into the back of his pocket, pulled out a clean, white handkerchief and handed it to him. "I'll try to be more careful."

Beechum gulped and began backing up. "Huh, that's...all right, Captain. Accidents will happen. Er...it'll dry, and no one will be the wiser. Trust me, it's no big deal." Beechum then turned and marched toward the door, but not before he shot Carly a venomous look. For what seemed like an interminable length of time, no one moved or said a word, not even the ogling bystanders.

Only Rance seemed unaffected as he poured himself another cup of coffee and ambled to the back of the room, where Bud May stood waiting for him. Carly knew better, though; Rance was furious. She had seen it in his eyes and in the rigid set of his shoulders.

But more than that, she had seen the twisted smile on his lips. There was no doubt in her mind that Rance had noticed Arley shoving Beechum and had chosen that precise moment to make his move.

Arley was looking at her with a strange light in his eyes. "Reckon what possessed the captain to put it to Beechum?"

"I couldn't say," Carly snapped, feeling a sudden urge to get out of the room before she did something stupid like walking up and thanking Rance for his act of chivalry.

Placing distance between Rance and her did little to wipe him from her mind, much to her disgust.

She had been patrolling now for hours, with part of her mind tuned to the radio and part of her mind on Rance. The evening shift had been uneventful, which, unfortunately, allowed her too much time to think.

She had no choice but to accept that there was indeed a chemistry between Rance and her that was as undeniable as it was rare.

By giving in they were both asking for trouble. She had wondered about how his mouth would feel against hers. Now she knew and now she wanted him with a hunger that had no beginning and no end.

Suddenly the radio squawked, and all thoughts of Rance left her. She was all business.

"All units in the area between Loop 6 and downtown, possible 10-55 driving recklessly—green Chevy, unknown year and license plate."

Carly lifted the microphone to her lips. "Two-oh-five. I'm in the area."

"Ten-four, 205."

Carly sped around the next curve so that she was heading in a southbound direction on the loop, all the while thinking that she should have known the quiet was too good to be true. It was ten-thirty, nearly time for her to head back to the station. It never failed.

She spotted the car immediately. Not only was it directly in front of her on the deserted stretch of highway, but it was traveling at a high rate of speed and swerving radically from one side of the road to the other.

"Two-oh-five."

"Go ahead 205."

"Spotted vehicle traveling at high rate of speed southbound on the loop. License number 624 Adam, Charles, Edward," she reported in standard police code.

"Ten-four."

Carly turned on her red lights and siren and upped her speed. But when she got close and shone her spotlight, the vehicle didn't yield. It sped up.

"Damn," she muttered, jamming down harder on the accelerator and continuing to follow.

The dispatcher came on again. "Vehicle is a 1975 Oldsmobile Cutlass registered to a Frank Tatum."

"Two-oh-five—have him in sight. He won't stop."

The automobile was traveling and weaving at such speed that a chase would result in an accident. Carly hoped to avoid that at all costs. The windows were down, which increased the chance for fatalities in the event of a crash.

Suddenly, without warning, her worst fears were realized.

The car spun off the highway onto the median, where it struck a sign. After mowing the sign down, it kept going. Then the driver yanked the wheel to the right, sending the vehicle zooming across both lanes. Still the car did not stop.

With a dry mouth and clammy hand, Carly radioed for an ambulance and backup. By the time she replaced the microphone, the vehicle had left the highway, slammed into a guardrail and finally stopped halfway up the grassy embankment. A woman sailed out the window and landed on her neck, just as

Carly hit the brakes and brought her own car to a screeching halt.

"Oh, no!" Carly cried in disbelief as the woman began to roll down the slope. She jumped out of her car and ran at breakneck speed, her breath rattling in her throat. "Oh, God, oh, God," she chanted, scrambling up the embankment. Just as she got within touching distance, the woman's legs spread apart.

Within seconds a baby lay nestled between them.

Chapter 9

A baby! A baby still tied to the mother by the umbilical cord.

For a moment Carly thought she was dreaming, but the full horror of the situation became quickly apparent. Her heartbeat exploded, and her breathing grew very rapid. She could almost feel the adrenaline rushing through her system.

Carly pulled off her jacket and, lifting the baby as though it were a piece of fragile glass, wrapped the coat around it. Then, twisting toward the mother, she checked for a pulse. At first Carly felt nothing. Frantic, she checked again, forcing herself to take deep breaths to steady herself.

The second time around she thought she felt a flutter. Hope made her giddy. She checked the pulse still a third time, but this time there was nothing, not even a flutter. Swallowing the hot bile that had risen in the back of her throat, she pushed her jellied legs into an upright position. She then dashed to the car for a blanket and the oxygen tank stored in the trunk.

After racing back to the victims but before covering the woman with the blanket, she carefully placed the mask on the baby's tiny, puckered face, all the while battling back the fear that the baby wouldn't make it.

"Oh, please, keep breathing," she begged. "Oh, please."

The next task she did without thinking. She lifted the infant and placed it on the mother's stomach with the cord still attached, once again fighting down the hot bile that surged up her throat.

The night was cold and clear, the stars proudly displaying their beauty as if in a contest to see which could outshine the other. But Carly was not aware of the majesty of the sky or the numbing chill of the night.

What concerned her now were the other victims of the mishap. From her position on the ground beside the baby, she whipped around and surveyed the damage behind her. But just as she got up and headed toward the two men on the ground beyond her, her backup, followed by an ambulance, arrived.

Arley Bishop and Robert Farrell spilled out of the patrol car. Directly behind them were two med techs carting a stretcher.

"Thank God," Carly whispered fervently before running toward them, shaking a fist at the bundle. "Hurry. Please hurry!" she shouted. "There's a newborn baby. It's wrapped in my jacket."

"A baby?" Farrell echoed as he pushed past Carly.

Carly had barely knelt beside another victim and was feeling for a pulse, when Arley bent over still another man and administered to him. "Did you say a newborn baby?" His tone still held amazement.

Carly nodded. "Yes...and the mother's dead."

"Damn, Mitchum," he ground out. "What the hell happened? It looks like Armageddon was fought here. And the fumes. God, they're potent enough to knock you down. They must've been drunk out of their minds."

Carly's teeth were chattering so much she couldn't answer. But she could feel Arley's gaze on her as she took the man's pulse.

"Are you all right?" Arley asked.

"Hell, no, I'm not all right," she cried, jumping up and making room for the med tech.

"Whatever you say," Arley mumbled, moving out of the way, as well.

"Mitchum," Sergeant Farrell hollered, "get over here."

"Yes, sir." On legs still not steady Carly did as she was told.

From that moment on the evening passed in a blur, which later Carly deemed as a blessing in disguise. Although she knew she functioned with a clear head, her insides remained a tangled mass of raw nerves.

There had been two male passengers besides the woman and the driver. Everyone was drunk with the exception of the dead woman. None of the others was injured, though the driver had been pinned in the upside-down car. The two male passengers had been thrown clear.

But Arley had been right in his assessment of the damage. Broken glass was strewn all over the grass and the highway. Debris—broken guardrails and crushed highway signs—was scattered everywhere.

While the sheriff's department helped with roadblocks and sealed off the area, Carly and Bishop went to the hospital with the three men and the baby. There the three adults were turned over to another patrol officer.

Before they returned to the scene of the accident, Carly and Bishop stopped back by the emergency room to check on the baby.

They were met in the hallway by the doctor attending the infant.

"How...er...is...it?" Carly asked with fear in her heart.

The doctor's expression softened as if he understood what Carly was feeling. He smiled. "*It* is a baby girl. And she's going to be just fine."

"Hallelujah," Carly whispered, her eyes filling with tears.

Bishop grinned. "All right!"

"I hear the praise goes to you, Officer," the doctor added.

Carly shook her head. "I only did what I was trained to do. I'm just sorry the mother didn't make it."

The doctor sighed. "So am I. Because of your quick actions though, a life was saved. You should be proud."

The doctor's words of praise warmed Carly's cold heart more than once throughout the remainder of the evening, during the long, grueling hours of doing skid tests, taking measurements, estimating the damage done to the highway and working up the detailed accident report.

"Way to go," Arley said hours later, as they made their way out of the station.

Every bone in her body groaned with fatigue, and she had to force herself to pay attention. Nevertheless a smile transformed her taut features. "Thanks, Arley. I guess it's those rare times of saving a life that keep us going."

"In the thankless task of preserving the peace," Arley finished with a wave of his hand.

That thought was still with Carly when, a short time later, she crawled into bed. She smiled. Then, before she fell into an exhausted sleep, something else crossed her mind—she hadn't thought of Rance Knight in hours.

"Should I bow now or later?" Angie asked the next afternoon when Carly walked through the door of the station.

Carly paused at the dispatcher's window and grinned back at her friend. "I guess later will be all right."

One more day of subbing on the three-to-eleven shift and Carly would have two wonderful days off, Sunday and Monday. She planned to do nothing during that time but sleep, and sleep some more.

"As soon as you have a minute, I want a blow-by-blow account of what happened." Angie was all eyes as she rolled back the glass that separated her from Carly.

"It'd be simpler if you just read my report."

"But not nearly as exciting."

"Whatever," Carly said. "Maybe we can get together on one of my days off."

"Good." Angie grinned again. "Never hurts to be in the company of a celebrity."

"Don't use that ridiculous word. Anyway, I was just doing my job."

"That may be, but the entire station's buzzing about you." Angie leaned closer and added in a conspiratorial whisper, "Even Farrell for once was singing your praises."

"I find that hard to believe." Carly failed to keep the censure out of her voice.

"Well, believe it. And you'll never guess who he was talking to." Angie paused and rolled her eyes. "None other than the station's hunk, Rance Knight."

Carly's heart skipped a beat, but her voice stayed cool. "Oh, really."

"Is that all you have to say?" Angie sounded indignant. "Here's your one chance to shine, and you're acting like it's no big deal."

"It isn't," Carly said, finding the subject tiresome. "I'm too zonked right now to even think, much less care what the fellows are saying. Anyway, you know how it is around here—hero one day, goat the next."

Angie raised her eyes as if seeking divine guidance. "Get outta here before I lose control and throttle you."

Carly laughed and, turning, walked down the hall toward the squad room.

Thirty minutes later the meeting was over, and she was on her way back outside to her car, her ears still ringing with words of congratulations. But she knew it wouldn't last. Today they were tolerant of her; tomorrow they would treat her like the powder puff they thought she was.

Suddenly Carly had the feeling someone was watching her. Suspecting that Beechum was once again the culprit, she wheeled around. A wave of color flooded her cheeks.

Rance was leaning negligently against the side of his car, which was parked a short distance from hers. He had obviously followed her outside.

After what seemed like an eternity, he straightened and walked toward her. He didn't stop until he was only inches from her, leaning his large frame against the side of the car.

She wanted to turn away, but she simply stood there looking at him, her heart stranded in a ridiculous storm of hope.

His eyes were broodingly intense and searched hers. He didn't speak for a long, static moment.

She moved uncomfortably, their last encounter suddenly leaping to the forefront of her thoughts.

"I understand you're the hero—or should I say the heroine—of the moment," Rance said, his voice low. She was so near, her fragrance scented the air around him. He felt a distinct lack of oxygen.

Carly looked up at him, feeling a chill course along her spine, a chill that had nothing to do with the weather. Then, afraid that he was making fun of her in an underhanded way, she said the first thing that came to mind. "If you have a point, I wish you'd make it."

His eyes sparked dangerously. "I was paying you a compliment, only..."

A tiny frown creased her brow. "Only what?"

"For heaven's sake," he burst out, exasperated. "I don't want to fight with you."

"What do you want?"

His eyes seared her skin.

Carly felt the situation getting out of control. "What...are you doing here? In the parking lot, I meant to say."

His mouth lifted in a surprising half smile. "I work here, remember?"

He was enjoying this, damn him. "But not on weekends," she said innocently. She was not about to let him know to what extent he had unnerved her.

"Point taken," he said, holding her gaze.

They lapsed into a prolonged silence while Rance reached into his pocket for a cigarette. He lighted it, then took what Carly thought were quick, angry puffs. Good, she thought. He wasn't as immune to her as he appeared.

As the seconds lapsed into minutes, Carly studied him covertly, intensely conscious of how attractive he was in a light brown sport coat and dark brown slacks. She couldn't take her eyes off him as he continued to drag on the cigarette. She saw that his eyelashes were extremely long and thick. Why hadn't she noticed that before?

Rance lifted his glance from the cigarette to Carly, a reluctant smile on his lips. "Apparently you aren't accepting any accolades."

She didn't pretend to misunderstand him, though she was reluctant to reopen the subject of the accident. "Not really."

"You should, you know."

"Why?"

"You earned them."

"I was just doing my job."

"That's what I mean."

Carly's tone held regret. "I won, but lost one."

"That's better than losing two."

"True."

Another silence fell between them, an awkward one as they both realized they were actually conversing like normal people.

She still looked fatigued, he thought, but there was a sparkle in her eyes that turned them darker, as dark as bluebonnets. And her hair, curly and sweet smelling as if she'd just shampooed it, was brushed severely back from her face. Maybe she thought it was a professional look, but it made him want to touch it.

Carly's voice, when she finally spoke, was breathless. "Well, if there's...nothing else, I need to be on my way." When he looked at her like that, it was hard for her to breathe, much less keep her mind on work.

"Actually, there is something else." He rocked back on his heels.

"Oh?" Her tone held suspicion, while her eyes held his.

"Stacy wants to see you," he said heavily.

Carly blinked. "Stacy?"

"Yeah. Stacy, my daughter. Remember?"

"Of course I remember," Carly snapped. "It's...it's just that I'm surprised, that's all."

She was looking at him warily. "Don't you remember my telling you that the next time she came, she wanted to see you?"

Still confused, Carly weighed each word carefully. "I'd love to see her, too."

His face changed, softening magically. "Every time I talk to her, she sings your praises."

"I'm...glad. I read her note—it was sweet."

Another silence followed, deeper than the one before.

Rance fished in his pocket and drew out another cigarette.

After lighting it and taking a healthy draw, he asked, "Will you ride with me to take Stacy to her grandmother's?" Ignoring the way her mouth fell open, he went on, "I thought maybe we could have breakfast first, give you and Stacy a chance to visit—" He broke off with a muttered curse, seeing the stunned look on her face.

Carly's mind churned. "Captain, are you—"

"Call me Rance," he muttered harshly.

"All right...Rance, then," she whispered, having completely forgotten what she was about to say.

"Look, if I promise there won't be a repeat performance of the other night, will you come?" He watched her face closely.

It was on the tip of her tongue to refuse. The game he was playing was wearing a bit thin. But it was too late for them to quit. She knew it. He knew it. The kiss had taken care of that.

"Yes," she whispered at last, her senses tingling.

"This...us...could backfire, you know," Rance managed to say after a few seconds, his voice deep and soft.

"I know." Carly swallowed and raked her fingers through her hair, letting the thick strands fall where they may.

"I'll see you in the morning about ten."

In what she thought was a calm move, Carly got behind the wheel, only to then miss the keyhole by inches. She cursed silently, then glanced sideways.

He was smiling. "By the way, I thought you did a damn good job last night—handled yourself like a pro."

Following that announcement, he pulled back from the car.

Carly could only nod, suddenly unable to speak. She didn't look back until she was turning into the street. He was still standing there, watching her.

When Carly got home shortly after eleven and walked into the den, Matt was still up. Or partially up, she thought, peering down at him with an indulgent smile. He was snoozing in his favorite chair; a fire crackled in the hearth. She was certain he'd waited up in order to talk to her. With her crazy schedule of late, they hadn't spent any time together. She knew he was champing to quiz her about the accident; without a doubt, he had read about it in the *Timberland Gazette*.

She tiptoed to the couch and, after tossing her purse down, went into the kitchen and fixed two cups of hot chocolate. Placing them on a tray, she headed back to the den. Unwilling to disturb her uncle as yet, she fell into her favorite chair.

Although her shift had been uneventful, she still felt dragged out from yesterday. She gazed into the fire, letting its warmth mesmerize her. Then with a sigh she laid her head back and closed her eyes, thinking that ten o'clock in the morning was looming closer by the second.

She had rehearsed over and over in her mind how she'd stop at the nearest pay phone, call Rance and tell him she'd changed her mind, that something had come up and she couldn't go with him...and Stacy.

When it came down to it, she simply could not make the call. No other man had ever filled her with such mindless sexual excitement. Anyway, Stacy was going with them. Who could ask for a better chaperon?

"Why didn't you wake me up, girl?"

At the sound of her uncle's gruff voice, Carly's head shot up. "I didn't have the heart to, that's why." She smiled. "You looked so comfortable and peaceful."

"Huh," he said with a snort. "That's what's wrong now. It's too peaceful around here."

Carly laughed. At the same time she bent down and slipped off her boots. Immediately her face mirrored her relief. "Ah, now I feel human."

Matt chuckled. "I know the feeling. First thing I used to do when I got in. Always thought wearing boots was like having your feet cramped down in a hole all day."

Carly smiled and shook her head. A comfortable silence fell between them while Carly unbuckled her belt.

"Seems like your life's anything but dull," Matt pointed out when Carly's task was done and she was again sitting. "From the way the paper reads, you're almost a celebrity."

Carly leaned forward and stirred the hot chocolate.

Grinning, Matt watched her a minute, then said, "If you're

GET A FREE TEDDY BEAR...

You'll love this plush, cuddly Teddy Bear, an adorable accessory for your dressing table, bookcase or desk. Measuring 5 ½" tall, he's soft and brown and has a bright red ribbon around his neck – he's completely captivating! And he's yours *absolutely free*, when you accept this no-risk offer!

▼ CLAIM YOUR FREE BOOKS AND FREE GIFT! RETURN THIS CARD TODAY! ▼

NO OBLIGATION TO BUY!

THE SILHOUETTE READER SERVICE™: HERE'S HOW IT WORKS

Accepting free books places you under no obligation to buy anything. You may keep the books and gift and return the shipping statement marked "cancel". If you do not cancel, about a month later we'll send you 6 additional novels, and bill you just $3.96 each, plus 25¢ delivery per book and GST.* That's the complete price — and compared to cover prices of $4.75 each — quite a bargain indeed! You may cancel at any time, but if you choose to continue, every month we'll send you 6 more books, which you may either purchase at the discount price...or return to us and cancel your subscription.

* Terms and prices subject to change without notice.
Canadian residents will be charged applicable provincial taxes and GST.

0195619199-L2A5X3-BR01

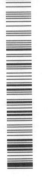

SILHOUETTE READER SERVICE
PO BOX 609
FORT ERIE ONT
L2A 9Z9

Canada Post Corporation/Société canadienne des postes

Postage paid | **Port payé**
If mailed in Canada | si posté au Canada

Business | **Réponse**
Reply | **d'affaires**

0195619199   01

MAIL▶POSTE

If offer card is missing write to: Silhouette Reader Service, P.O. Box 609, Fort Erie, Ontario L2A 5X3 not careful, you're going to grind the bottom outta both those cups.''

Carly's hand froze, and she looked at him with anger flashing in her eyes. "I didn't do anything any other cop wouldn't have done. It's because I'm a woman that there's such a big flap about it."

"If I didn't know better," Matt said, "I'd think you were wearing your feelings on your sleeve again." His tone was disapproving, but his eyes were warm.

Carly reached for her cup of chocolate and sipped on it. "Maybe you're right."

"Suppose you tell me what happened."

"Sure you're not too tired?" Carly asked, trying her best to mask the weariness in her voice.

Matt's eyes narrowed. "I'm not, but I bet you are."

"No, I'm fine," Carly lied. "But I will make it quick."

Matt listened intently as she gave him a detailed account of the accident and events that followed. Even though Matt had been retired for years, he had never stopped missing the excitement or the challenge the job offered.

"What about the baby's father? Or at least I assume one of the men was the father."

"You assume right, but he was so drunk he didn't even know his wife had been killed until after my supper break this evening. He was so out of it on the day shift that no one was able to talk to him."

"What a waste."

"It's worse than that."

"The father wasn't the one driving, right?"

"No, but he's got an arrest record a mile long."

"Poor baby."

"It doesn't stand a chance."

"Well, I'm proud of what you did, anyway."

Carly's smile was genuine. "Thanks. Coming from you, it's special."

"Has there been any more mention of a transfer?" Matt asked unexpectedly.

"No," she said more sharply than she intended. Seeing the

puzzled look on Matt's face, she softened her tone. "As far as I'm concerned it's now a dead issue."

"For your sake, I sincerely hope so."

Carly stood up. "I think I'll turn in, Unc. I've about had it."

Matt stood, also. "Oh, by the way, I'm leaving in the morning. Be gone for ten days."

"Ten days!" Carly was stunned. A confirmed homebody, her uncle hardly ever left home.

His right hand slapped the air as he glanced away. "That woman next door has talked me into taking a trip with the Autumn Club." He paused, a scowl on his face. "What's so damned funny?"

Carly quickly smothered her laughter. "Why, nothing Uncle Matt," she responded innocently. "When are you leaving?"

He watched her with skepticism. "In the morning. Six o'clock, to be exact."

"And you're just now telling me?"

"Well, I didn't want to hear your famous 'I told you so.'"

It was an effort for Carly to keep a straight face. "Oh, I understand."

"Anyway, we're leaving at six in the morning," he added gruffly. "I left a phone number in case you need me."

Carly walked over and gave him a hug. "You don't worry about a thing here. Just take care of yourself and have a good time."

"You sure you'll be all right? I mean—"

"I'll be fine. Don't worry. And have a great time."

The doorbell rang promptly at ten. As Carly placed her hand on the doorknob and turned it, her hands weren't quite steady.

"Good morning," Rance said with a rare smile.

Caught up in his unfamiliar mood, she failed to notice that he held something in his hand.

"For you," he said lightly, thrusting a bouquet of flowers at her. "From Stacy...and me."

She gazed up at him, and her heart pounded in confusion as she thought how heart-shakingly attractive he was in a blue chambray shirt, dark blue windbreaker and jeans.

"They're lovely. Thank you." Trying to regain her balance, Carly buried her nose in the fragrant blossoms. Then, looking up, she said, "Hang on, and I'll get a vase. I'll be right back."

It was only after Carly had climbed into the front seat of the Bronco and Rance had slammed the door behind her that she realized something was not quite right.

When he slid in beside her, Carly swung around, her eyes wide. "Where's Stacy?"

There no longer seemed to be enough air in the close confines

Chapter 10

Rance closed the door, but he did not start the engine immediately, nor did he answer her.

"Rance," Carly prodded, "where's Stacy?"

He was staring straight ahead. "She's already gone. Her grandmother picked her up late yesterday afternoon."

Carly's tongue felt suddenly brittle, and she had difficulty speaking. "And you didn't call?"

"Didn't even try."

"Why?" The tiny word sounded like a squeak.

He was facing her now. She could see every line in his face, see the downward slant of his mouth, feel the tautness in his body.

"I knew you wouldn't go, that's why."

There no longer seemed to be enough air in the close confines of the Bronco. Hot color flooded Carly's cheeks. Her chaotic emotions kept her sitting exactly where she was, but cold logic clamored for her to go back into the house. "You're right, I wouldn't have."

"Well, you can still change your mind," he said in a gruff, strained voice.

Her choice. The next minute, the next hour would be a gamble. Rarely did she leave anything to chance. Maybe it was time she did, even if the price was high.

She searched his face. "Do you want me to?"

"No." His voice was hoarse, but steady.

Looking at him, his dark eyes holding hers, she felt her senses stir again with the primitive feelings that only he could arouse in her. The smell of his body further assaulted her senses, locking her in the vehicle as surely as if the door on her side were bolted and chained.

"Where are we going?"

The powerful Bronco swung away from the curb onto the busy street, and after a few more minutes of silence, Carly noticed they were headed down the Crockett Highway.

Instead of answering her question, he asked one. "Are you hungry?"

She smiled ruefully. "Now that you mention it, I am."

"Me, too. I know a place up the road that serves great biscuits, the best you've ever put in your mouth."

"That's fine by me, but you still haven't told me where we're going."

"Does it matter?" he asked quietly.

The question echoed dangerously, so full of emotion that the very air seemed to tremble.

Carly didn't pretend to misunderstand him. Shrugging helplessly, she said, "No, it doesn't matter."

And it didn't. Not now. Not on this glorious fall morning with the sun shining down on them.

Even though they both knew they were playing with fire, at this point they were unwilling to pull back. Still, payday was bound to come, and they knew that, too.

Rance didn't say anything, just looked at her with those unreadable eyes before turning and concentrating on his driving. It was only after they were twenty miles down the road and seated at a table in the rear of the restaurant that he seemed to relax.

"It's not your class joint by any means, is it?"

Carly laughed with delight. "No, can't say that it is, however..." She trailed off, turning her attention to the waitress who hovered at her elbow with two cups and a pot of coffee.

"You folks ready to order?" the buxom woman asked, her smile friendly.

"Carly," Rance said, directing his attention toward her.

"Mmm, I'll have just one biscuit and honey, please."

Rance's lips twisted while his eyes slid over her trim figure. "One biscuit, huh? Whatever you say." Then he added to the waitress, "Give me the number two."

Once they were alone, Carly didn't miss the way his eyes appraised her openly, lingering a tad longer than necessary on the voluptuous swell beneath her sweater. Carly felt his gaze like a soft, insistent touch.

With trembling fingers, she placed her napkin in her lap and stared out the window beside her, breaking the contact. She wished she knew what he was thinking, what thoughts lurked behind those dark eyes.

Their food arrived shortly, and for the most part, they ate in silence.

"Well, was I right?" Rance asked, pushing his empty plate aside in a satisfied manner, his gaze resting softly on her.

He was doing it again—smiling in that way that made him appear so touchable, so human. She felt its danger, its pull.

"You were right," she said, her insides in an uproar. "That biscuit melted in my mouth." She struggled to give him a bright look.

He felt as though he were gazing at sunshine. Draining his cup quickly, he said, "Ready?"

"Whenever you are."

"Let's go. We have a lot of territory to cover."

As they walked outside, Carly was still puzzling over that statement. She still had no idea where they were going or what they were going to do after they got there.

Noting that the wind had picked up, she crossed her arms over her chest, trying to ward off a shiver.

"You're cold."

"A little. The wind wasn't blowing like this when we left."

"Come on," he said, closing his fingers around her elbow,

hurrying her to the Bronco. She shivered again, the unexpected contact sending electric sparks down her veins into her hand.

Silence as deep as a well fell between them as the Bronco covered mile after mile.

In the harsh slant of sunlight, the hard lines of Rance's profile were accentuated. It was strange how sometimes he looked so human to her, so like a man she could fall in love with and cherish forever. Then at other times he looked so inhuman that even to think of him in terms of forever was ridiculous. She shook off the thought, determined not to ruin the day by trying to analyze him.

Rance was the one who finally broke the silence. "Stacy was sorry she didn't get to see you this trip."

"I'm sorry, too," Carly said. "I was looking forward to seeing her." She cut a glance at his face. "How's...she doing?"

Rance's expression changed. "One week fine, the next one not so good."

"It's a shame she can't seem to settle down. These years should be the happiest of her life."

"I know. But Denise just can't handle her—nor does she give a damn." For a brief moment, his eyes locked with Carly's. "I'm thinking of going back to court and trying to get custody."

"That speaks very highly of you. Most men wouldn't want the responsibility."

His features remained set in grim lines. "After the way I handled that last fiasco, I'm surprised you agree."

"It's obvious you acted more out of fear than anger."

He smiled suddenly, another of those rare smiles. And if she hadn't been so surprised at her defense of him, she'd have caught her breath. The smile was off center, yet it lightened his face, made him appear young and free.

"I'll tell Stacy you approve."

"Please do."

"Thanks for the vote of confidence."

"You're welcome," she answered lightly.

Another long silence followed, and while not comfortable, it was not awkward, either.

From time to time, Rance gave Carly quick sideways glances, then concentrated on the traffic again.

He still was not able to sort out his feelings for her, but at least he was better able to cope, though one wouldn't think so if one could see the way his palms greased the wheel when she was beside him.

At times it was all he could do not to grab her and try for another taste of those soft lips. And more often than he cared to admit, he'd find himself lying awake at night, staring into the darkness, wondering what it would be like to reach out and rub a hand over her hip. With each passing day the fantasies became more frequent, draining him, yet leaving him with a raw need to possess her completely.

Suddenly remembering what he was supposed to be doing, he pulled the steering wheel hard to the right, just making the turn onto a black-topped road that was so dense with trees on either side that they blocked out the sunshine.

"We're here," he said at long last.

Carly sat up straight in the seat and surveyed her surroundings. They were on the outskirts of Crockett, a full sixty miles west of Timberland, but that was all she knew.

She licked her lips and began to fidget. "Where?"

"You'll see shortly."

Carly was all eyes as Rance reached a padlocked gate and stopped the Bronco. Beyond the fence was a huge pasture dotted with cattle. Off to the right sat a white frame house neatly trimmed with yellow shutters.

Before he could scramble out of the car, Carly stammered, "Does...does this belong to you?"

"Surprised?"

She shot him a dry glance. "You know I am."

He chuckled. "I can say one thing about you, Mitchum, you're not afraid to speak your mind." He got out then, leaving the door open behind him.

Seconds later he was back inside and was steering the Bronco past the guardrail, not stopping until they had pulled up in front of the house.

"Well, what do you think?"

"I...I think it's beautiful, but does it really belong to you?"

He placed his hand across his chest. "Scouts' honor."

She knew he was teasing her, but she didn't care. She was shocked, having never dreamed that Rance would be interested in anything other than his work, and certainly not in cattle ranching.

"Let's go inside and start some coffee brewing, then I'll show you around."

"I'm game," she said almost breathlessly, his mood having lightened once again. Why he had brought her here no longer mattered. The fact that he had was all that counted.

Yanking open the door on her side, Rance was careful not to touch her. And Carly, equally as careful, eased out of the Bronco on her own.

The inside of the house was almost as much of a shock as the outside had been. The second she crossed the threshold, the rustic charm of the interior seemed to envelop her.

"Feel free to look around," Rance said, his long legs taking him into the kitchen. "Or make yourself comfortable or whatever," he tossed over his shoulder.

Carly could hear him banging around while she ambled through the enchanting living room with its large fireplace, the two small bedrooms, one bathroom and back to the kitchen and breakfast nook. It was possibly the coziest house she had ever been in.

Having finished her tour, Carly paused in the door to the kitchen and watched Rance, watched as his hands handled the delicate china cups the same way they had handled her—with total ease. She shivered.

Rance's voice cut into her thoughts. "Are you cold?"

"Chilly," she lied. "But don't worry about me."

"Here, drink this. It'll warm you up."

As the cup changed hands, they were again careful to avoid touching each other. But nothing could stop their eyes from colliding.

Rance cleared his throat and mumbled, "I'd best get a fire started."

A few minutes later when she had regained her composure,

Carly went looking for him, and found him squatting in front of the fireplace, stacking wood.

As if sensing he was no longer alone, he stood and twisted around. "While we're outside, Big Mama here will warm this place up."

Carly rubbed her hands up and down her arms. "Even with the wind blowing, I think it's actually warmer outside than it is in here."

"You bet it is." Rance brushed the tiny specks of debris off his jeans.

"How often do you come here?" Carly asked, moving toward the front door, Rance close on her heels.

They were outside before Rance answered. "Whenever I can. I was here yesterday, in fact. Restocked my pantry."

"You've owned it a long time, then?" she pressed.

"Several years now. I'd have to stop and think exactly how many. But one thing I do know, I had to bust my buns to buy it, then to hang on to it." His tone sounded harsh, even with the strong wind. "It came on the market when I didn't have a pot to boil water in or a window to throw it out of."

"How about your family?" she asked curiously. "In addition to Stacy, I mean."

They were strolling behind the house now, and Carly could see into the distance. Beyond a cluster of tall oaks and sweet gums was a barn with a tractor and a pickup truck parked beside it. Farther to her right, she spotted a place where a garden had been. "Stacy's it," he said flatly.

"Your parents are dead?"

His eyes became distant. "My mother is," he said brutally. "Took her own life."

Carly stopped and looked up at him, stunned by the pain that twisted his features. "I...had no idea. I'm sorry."

"Don't be. It's my old man who should be sorry. He drove her to it. Couldn't hold a job or his booze. And wouldn't leave the women alone. He finally split. My mother got fed up with it all, and the rest is history, as the saying goes."

"And your father?"

"Don't know and I sure as hell don't care."

He stood in the sudden stillness, a faraway look in his eyes, his shoulders stooped. Carly wanted to comfort him, touch him, tell him it was all right to give in to the despair inside him, just as long as he didn't shut her out completely. But she was afraid to reach out. Touching him was too dangerous. Last time she hadn't wanted to let go.

"How old were you when all that happened?"

"Thirteen. And from then on I was left to battle it out with one foster parent after another."

"I know how it is to lose those you love," she said softly. "When I was only nine, I...lost my parents in an accident, then...later my husband."

"But your uncle and aunt reared you and you didn't want for anything."

Carly took umbrage at his insinuation. "Money's not everything," she said hotly.

They had stopped, and Carly was leaning against a fence post, while Rance had a boot propped on the rail.

"That's easy for you to say," Rance spit, "especially when you've always had plenty."

She batted the air in disgust. "That's not true! While I might have had everything money could buy, my aunt hated the ground I walked on. She never forgave me for interrupting her life, for coming between her and Matt."

They glared at each other for a long moment, then Rance spun around with a muttered curse. "Forget it. How the hell did we get on this subject, anyway?"

Carly pressed her hands against her thighs, feeling the brooding silence swell out of proportion.

Then she felt Rance's probing eyes on her as if he were trying to dissect her thoughts through his own brown eyes. "Did you love your husband?"

Carly caught her breath. "Did you love your wife?"

"I asked you first."

"Yes...I loved him," she admitted soberly, "but we were so young and...had so little time together that..." Her voice simply faded away. Ben was the last person she wanted to talk about.

The feelings Ben had aroused in her were sweet and innocent, nothing like what she felt when Rance touched her.

He took a deep breath and scuffed a toe against the fence post beside him. ''I guess maybe you do know what it's like to suffer.''

Her eyes had a faraway look in them. ''Yes, I do,'' she whispered.

A brief silence ensued. An uneasy silence, he thought, and wished he'd kept his mouth shut.

''What about you...and Denise?'' she asked in a throaty voice.

He ran his hand over his hair. ''Well, for one thing she hated my being a cop. She saw bad guys lurking on every darkened street after ten o'clock at night. But that wasn't the real problem.'' He snorted a humorless kind of snort. ''She didn't like not having the biggest house in town, or the best car, or the best clothes.''

He paused a minute, then went on, ''The only thing that came out of those miserable years was Stacy. That's the only reason I stayed.''

Unable to think of anything to say, Carly turned away.

''But something good did come of it,'' he continued, his tone hard. ''It taught me a lesson I'll never forget.''

''What...was that?''

''That marriage is not for me. I've been that route. No more for me, thank you.'' He paused. ''How do you feel about it?''

Was there a hint of desperation in his voice, or was she imagining it? ''I...feel just the opposite.'' She couldn't look at him. ''I want a home and a family.''

''I see.''

Her insides twisted. He didn't see, Carly thought. Couldn't see for the ambition that was driving him.

''Come on,'' Rance said abruptly, his face as sealed as a tomb. ''Let's head back toward the house.''

''What do you think of having the Bishop fund-raiser here?'' Rance asked later, as if he were in total control of his emotions. But his voice, which was a tone too low, betrayed him.

"I guess it depends on what you have in mind," Carly said, groping to put things on an even keel once again.

"A barbecue."

A smile lighted her face. "It's perfect for that."

He turned his head sideways. "So how about helping me make some plans while I grill us a steak?"

Again she wanted to touch him. Instead she took a deep breath. "What are we waiting for?"

The next few hours passed quickly, but it was only after the steaks were done and they had consumed them along with baked potatoes and salad that they had actually firmed up the plans for the shindig.

Replete from the delicious dinner, they sat on the living-room sofa, ignoring the notes strewn on the coffee table in front of them as they sipped their coffee.

"I think we've about covered everything," Rance said, watching the way the firelight flickered across her face.

He moaned silently and turned away, but not before Carly saw the naked desire in his eyes.

Carly's breathing slowed as she tried to think of something to say that would ease the building tension.

"Rance, why did you become a cop?" The minute the question passed her lips, she wished she could retract it. Work was the last thing they needed to discuss. In fact, they had gone to great lengths *not* to discuss it. Maybe that was why she'd broached the topic, to clear the air, to call a spade a spade.

Rance had edged closer to Carly until he was within touching distance of her. She pretended not to notice.

"Ego," Rance was saying. "Pure and simple. You start out thinking you can make a difference in this old world, change it for the better. Only later do you find you can't. Yet like an idiot you hang in there, keep trying. But you pay one helluva price for that ego ride, and the broken homes only scratch the surface."

"I know," she said, aware that he was watching her with a mocking twist to his lips that sent her blood pressure sky-high. Even so, she kept her tone cool and even. "Coming from a family of law officers, I learned to respect the law at an early age. For me, ego had nothing to do with it. It was like you said, I felt I could make a difference. It's—"

He interrupted with a sneer. "It's just wishful thinking mixed with sheer stupidity. Women don't belong in this profession."

Her temper flared. "Oh, spare me, please. You're way behind the times, in case you haven't noticed."

"I don't give a tinker's damn about your opinion. Women just don't have the nerves for this job. I oughtta know. I got my gut ripped open because one didn't do her job." His eyes were iced over.

Carly didn't back down an inch. "One. You said it yourself. You can't judge us all by that one bad apple. Still, I can understand why you feel that way. But *I'm* different. I like living dangerously."

His tone changed. Although it no longer had a cutting edge, it was equally as disturbing. "Maybe it's that little bit of danger that made you come with me today."

"How dare you!" she said through clenched teeth, outraged that he had cut to the heart of the matter.

Their eyes clashed for a long moment, each determined, each battle scarred, each coming from different backgrounds but having the same ambitions.

It was Rance who broke the charged silence, leaning closer. "Oh, I dare all right. Because I feel the same way." His warm breath tickled her cheek, while his face filled her vision.

She didn't turn away. Couldn't turn away, not when her mind chose that moment to play a terrible trick on her, creating an image of the two of them naked together. Naked and eager.

"Maybe...you'd better take me home," she said dully, lowering her head.

"God, Carly, I didn't mean for the evening to end like this." His voice had fallen to a hoarse whisper.

"No?" She flung her head back, more furious with herself than Rance. But she took it out on him. "Just how did you mean it to end? Were you planning to take me to bed so you could gloat to your fellow officers that you'd gotten a piece—"

Suddenly he lunged to his feet, dragging her with him, fury etched in every line on his face. "Don't you ever say anything like that again!'' His angry mouth moved closer to hers. ''No, dammit, I wasn't!''

Suddenly the fight went out of Carly, and she felt precariously close to tears. ''Please just take me home,'' she said again, backing up.

''Oh, Carly, Carly,'' he whispered thickly, reaching out and touching the side of her face with his hand.

Carly flinched. ''Don't...''

He placed his hand under her chin and slowly turned her around. ''Don't what?''

She began to tremble. ''Don't...do what you're...doing.''

''And what is that?'' His gaze never wavered.

''Touch—touching me.''

Later neither one knew quite how it happened, but the next minute they were in each other's arms, and not just holding but clutching at each other in desperation.

Her fingers dug into his back, while his hands moved down her hips to her buttocks. She moved against his hard body with mindless abandon, her mouth still fused with his, tongues meeting and tangling.

''I want you...want you...want you,'' he rasped, his hands sliding under her sweater and down her sleek back.

She heard his sharp intake of breath when he realized she wasn't wearing a bra. His hands curved around her breasts, which were wonderfully firm.

''You're beautiful, beautiful,'' he whispered, locating the zipper on her jeans and, in spite of his trembling fingers, pulling it down. He touched her then, moaning softly the instant he did.

''Oh, Rance, oh, yes,'' she murmured, touching, exploring his body the same as he was hers. ''That's wonderful...*you're* wonderful.''

He surrounded a breast, fondled and squeezed, manipulated the rigid nipple, seized by more than need, more than lust. He felt all that and something else, something more powerful, more dangerous. Abruptly he realized it was—love. God, *love.*

Suddenly, without warning, Rance wrenched himself from her arms, more scared now than he'd ever been in his entire life.

Carly stared up at him and whispered, ''Rance?''

Shaking visibly, he swore beneath his breath.

Chapter 11

Carly stood transfixed, her blue eyes wide with disbelief and pain.

He let out his breath in a rush. "It's no use, Carly, I can't go through with it. Not...when there's a chance—" He broke off, his inner turmoil getting the best of him. "Oh, what the hell!"

The passion she had unleashed in him never ceased to amaze him. But love? No way. What he felt for her *could not* be love. His mind raced. Love was impossible. He no longer believed in it. Denise had proved that the love between a man and a woman was a word that had no meaning; it was a sham.

Lust. Now that was more like it. Label it lust. Call it sex. Whatever, but that was what he needed, what he wanted. Not hearts and flowers. Not romance. And certainly not commitment.

It was Carly straightening her clothes that drew him from his tumultuous thoughts. When he looked down at her, there were tears in her eyes.

"Take me home," she whispered, looking bewildered and hurt. And embarrassed. She felt like a puppet, with Rance controlling the strings, yanking her to him, then pushing her away. But no longer. She'd had her fill.

The trip back to Timberland was a nightmare. Carly sat straight as a reed and stared ahead into the inky blackness, never once flinching under the bright headlights of oncoming cars.

Rance drove in stony silence.

When he pulled the vehicle into the circular drive in front of the rambling brick home, Carly was already gripping the door handle. The second he shoved the car in Park, she flung open the door.

"Don't bother to get out," she said over her shoulder. "I can find my own way." With that she jumped out and slammed the door behind her.

Rance bashed his palm against the steering wheel, but he didn't budge until he saw that she was safely inside the house. Then he still didn't move. He sat there cursing, calling himself every vile word he could think of.

Damn her. His unremitting state both infuriated and embarrassed him. In addition, it was damned uncomfortable.

So why hadn't he taken what had been so generously offered? Why hadn't he found out once and for all how she would feel against, above and beneath him?

Because of what he'd seen in Carly's eyes. If he had taken her, it wouldn't have been just a roll in the hay. To her it would have been more.

No, it was better to call it quits while he still could. She deserved better, and it was time she faced that and got on with her life. Letting out a deep, ragged sigh, he turned and stared out the window.

It was cold and raining. He had never been so miserable.

In spite of the damp, rainy weather, things were fairly quiet, much to Carly's relief. She couldn't remember a time when her enthusiasm for her work had been at such a low ebb. The weather didn't help; it was synonymous with her mood—dreary.

It had been two days since the disastrous episode at Rance's ranch. And for two days she had gone out of her way to avoid him and so far had succeeded, partly because she had been on midnights.

Today she had feared her good fortune might come to an end,

as she was back on days. However, for once Lady Luck had smiled on her. She'd managed to get out of the station without their paths crossing.

Now, as she cruised around town on patrol, her thoughts kept returning to that fateful evening. The only conclusion she could come to was that it was best to stay away from Rance, best to know that what never should have been was now over.

Maybe if it was a home and family she was hankering for, she should try harder to establish a relationship with Brian. So why not invite Brian to the fund-raising party this coming weekend? She'd have an escort, and he'd been wanting to see her. Just having settled that made her feel better.

Noticing that the rain was starting again, she switched on her windshield wipers and looked around. She was in a less than desirable part of town where there had been several disturbances of late.

It was while she was stopped at a red light that she saw him. Frowning, Carly increased the pace of the wipers so as to get a better view. In front of a coffee shop to her left, two men were leaning against the building, deep in conversation. There was no mistaking the taller of the two, even if she had only a side view. His red hair was a dead giveaway.

"Larry Beechum," she whispered.

When the light changed, Carly eased across the intersection and turned onto the first street that would give her access to the men without being spotted.

"What on earth could he be doing talking to that scumbag?" Again she spoke out loud, as if the sound of her voice helped give credence to what she was seeing.

On closer observation, Carly recognized Beechum's companion, who was now shaking his finger in the patrolman's face. His name was Henry Felton, a known drug pusher. Felton had been arrested numerous times, but was always cunning enough to beat the rap.

What could he and Beechum possibly have to say to each other?

Suddenly, Beechum twisted around and looked to his right, then his left, as if searching for something or someone. For a second, Carly's heart jumped in her throat and she was afraid that he might have seen her, but then he turned his attention back to Felton. Breathing a sigh of relief, Carly put the car into Drive and headed back toward the station, wondering again what Beechum was up to.

She had never liked the man, and it wasn't just because he was a constant thorn in her side. She thought he was a lousy cop. What she really thought was that he was an overgrown bully who used his badge to intimidate people. On occasion he'd been known to rough up his prisoners unnecessarily.

Her instincts warned her that Beechum was up to no good and that he bore watching. She intended to do just that.

A short time later, after answering a disturbance call, Carly headed back to the station. When she walked inside, Arley Bishop met her with a wide grin on his face.

"What's up?" Carly asked. "You look like the cat that's just swallowed the proverbial canary."

"I just talked to the captain, and he told me the fund-raiser is set for this coming weekend."

"I'm glad you're pleased," Carly said sincerely. "Is Ruth going to be up to it?"

"She may have to come in a wheelchair, but she'll be there."

Carly's smile was warm. "I'm glad."

Suddenly she realized that the time spent with Rance had not been a total loss, after all. Something good had come out of it. The smile on Arley's face and the relief in his eyes proved that.

"I know you're partly responsible," he was saying, "and I thank you..."

Carly shook her head. "Don't thank me. Thank the captain. He's the one who instigated the whole affair."

"Not according to him. He gave you a great deal of the credit."

The surprise on Carly's face was not faked. "Well, that's...uh...nice to hear," she said lamely, unable to meet his gaze.

"Hey, changing subjects, have you heard?"

Carly swung around to face him once again. "No. What?"

"The Dies kid flunked the polygraph."

"And?" Carly waited with baited breath.

"He was arrested for the murder of his father and sister."

"Well, it's about time."

Arley sighed. "Somehow I thought you'd say that."

"Well, can you blame me? When I think of the way the investigation was handled, I get mad all over again. You know yourself that if another officer had suggested the kid be questioned on the spot, he would've been." Bitterness underlined Carly's every word. "But because *I*, a female, suggested it, the idea of his guilt was blatantly ignored."

"But not for long," Arley said with a grin. "If I were you, I'd pat myself on the back."

"Thanks, I believe I will."

Arley laughed out loud.

"See you later," Carly added breezily.

So she'd been right after all about the kid. A warm glow settled around her heart, and she did indeed silently pat herself on the back. By the time she reached the squad room, she was grinning from ear to ear, wondering what Captain Knight was thinking right about now. She'd like to think he was choking on a little crow.

But when she pulled out the papers that were stuffed in her box and read the top sheet, her grin disappeared and the blood in her veins turned to ice. She blinked to clear her vision, positive her vision was playing tricks on her. No such luck.

The words "See Chief Crawford concerning transfer" had not changed.

"Come in, Officer, and have a seat," Crawford said, running a quick hand over the bald spot on the top of his head and standing.

Carly was poised on the threshold, in the process of schooling her emotions to show none of her feelings, when a movement to her left caught her attention. Her gaze shifted and was instantly filled with Rance.

Their gazes tangled for one uninterrupted moment. Looking at him, Carly felt her senses come alive once again. The reality of it galled her. She wished she could hate him.

Following Carly's eyes, Crawford muttered irritably, "Knight, quit lurking in the corner and sit down."

Carly saw Rance's jaw clench, but when he spoke his voice was cool and steady with only a hint of sarcasm. "If it's all the same to you, sir, I'd prefer to stand."

"Suit yourself," the chief bit out before refocusing his attention on Carly. "Now, young lady—" Carly cringed inwardly at his choice of words, feeling like a puppy being patted on the head "—have you had a chance to look over the transfer papers?"

Pretending that Rance was not in the room, she said, "Yes, and I'm asking you to please reconsider."

"Can't do that," Crawford said easily.

"Why not, sir?"

"For starters, I don't want to. For another, and as I've already told you, you've proved yourself, and C.I.D. can use you."

"But—" Carly began.

"Forget it, Mitchum. My mind's made up. Anyway, Knight's all for it, aren't you, Captain?"

If anything, Rance's face turned darker, more threatening, but the timbre of his voice still did not change. "Sure, anything you say, chief."

So, Carly thought to herself, the rumor had merit, after all. Crawford wasn't out to get her; he was out to get Rance. And where she hadn't been convinced before, she was now. Rance wanted the chief's job, and Crawford knew it. The chief would do anything he could to needle Rance, make his job more uncomfortable.

Too bad she had to be the one caught in the cross fire, Carly thought. Damn them.

"So," Crawford was saying, "beginning the first of the month, you'll be Detective Mitchum." He smiled, but the smile never reached his eyes. "Doesn't that have a nice ring to it?"

Carly didn't say a word. She stood stiff as a plank, seething inside.

Just as Crawford was about to say something else, the phone next to his hand rang.

Carly's tense body suddenly went weak, and as if her eyes

had a will all their own, they darted to Rance, who remained in the shadows. He was watching her.

"Can't it wait?" Crawford demanded impatiently, then added, "Oh, all right," before slamming the receiver back in its cradle.

He then walked to the door, his eyes taking in both Carly and Rance. "I gotta go." It was clear he was agitated; sweat was now dotting his upper lip. "The mayor's here to see me," he added, his eyes now on Rance exclusively. "If your men don't come up with something soon, I'm going to hand the mayor your butt, Knight, on a silver platter."

Crawford left only silence behind him.

Rance stepped out of the shadows toward her.

In order to get out of the way of Crawford's hurried stride, Carly had crossed to the window and was staring outside. Sunlight had replaced the rain. She closed her eyes against the harsh glare.

Yet she was very much aware when Rance came to a standstill in front of her. Her heart rate increased twofold, but she refused to acknowledge him.

"Just to keep the record straight," he said tersely, "I want you to know that I fought your transfer to the bitter end."

"Well, you didn't fight hard enough is all I've got to say!"

She spun around then, and when she did, he noticed the haunted look in her eyes.

A groan tore loose from his throat at the same time as he raised a finger and ran it across a deep gray circle beneath her right eye.

"My fault."

Carly looked up at him and swallowed convulsively, overwhelmingly aware of his potent attraction that left her feeling breathless.

"It's...it's nothing."

"Oh, yes, it is."

"I'm okay...really."

"God, Carly," Rance muttered, turning around. "About the other night, I need to...to explain." He could hear his breathing, shallow and fast.

"But I don't want you to."

He turned back around. "Me, neither, but we have to."

"No."

"Yes."

"Why?" Carly barely heard her own voice.

"Because we're going to be working together," he said, anguished.

"Are you saying that I'll let my personal problems interfere with my job?"

"No, dammit, that's not what I'm saying." He was trying, without much success, to hang on to his patience.

They were glaring at each other now.

"Then what are you saying?" Her stomach was heaving.

"Aren't you the least bit curious?"

Carly followed his train of thought and quickly lowered her eyes. "You don't owe me an explanation."

She hadn't been quick enough; he saw the flicker of pain, and he felt as if a giant hand had squeezed his gut.

"Look at me, Carly," he pleaded.

Unwillingly she lifted her face.

"Oh, Carly," he groaned. "What do you want me to say? That I want you? God knows I do. That I need you? That, too."

Carly's face went stark white.

Still he went on. "I wanted you so badly I hurt." His eyes were tormented as they held hers. "I wanted to bury myself deep inside you, feel your warmth surround—"

Carly began shaking her head, backing up. "No," she whispered, "you...have no right to say those...things to me."

"I have to, because I don't intend to ruin your life, or mine." He ran a hand through his hair.

Carly winced as if he'd struck her. "I don't believe you heard me ask you for anything."

He looked away. "That's just as well, because I have nothing to give."

She longed to charge into him and rake her nails across his face to make him pay for tearing down the solid foundations of her life. Instead she raised her head and squared her shoulders. "Now we know where we both stand."

"Right."

"So we can work together without any problems."

The corners of his mouth turned down. "Absolutely."

"It's settled then."

He avoided her gaze. "It's settled," he said tightly.

"Good."

He turned brooding eyes on her once again, but Carly was already at the door. "By the way," he said, stalling her, "you were right. The Dies kid was guilty as hell."

"I know," she said. "Arley just told me."

"Good work."

Carly nodded, then closed the door behind her, her victory as hollow as her stomach.

Carly, however, had no time to fret over her mind-boggling transfer or Rance and their disturbing conversation. She had been patrolling only ten minutes after she left Rance when she got the call.

A disturbance had been reported in the country club section of town. A neighbor walking by a house had heard a scream.

Carly just happened to be in the vicinity and was now on her way to the specified location. Once she found the house and pulled up in front, she immediately scanned the area. Something was wrong, even though the scene appeared peaceful and quiet.

"Two-oh-five."

"Go ahead 205."

"Ten-twenty-three. Send backup."

"Ten-four."

A minute later when Carly received no answer at the front door, she began walking slowly and cautiously around the side of the house toward the rear.

All was still quiet. Noticing that the sliding glass door to the den was open, Carly paused and looked inside. Deserted. It was only after she had stepped across the threshold that she heard the noise.

She stopped and listened. Had she heard a moan? She couldn't be sure, but instinct told her that the house was not as deserted as it seemed.

Quickly she checked the rooms downstairs. All empty. Then treading lightly, Carly began to climb the stairs. By the time she reached the first door on the right, she was more than just uneasy.

She heard the sound again.

Drawing her gun, she peered around the door.

A man was bent over a woman's prone body.

"Police!" Carly shouted. "Don't move!"

Chapter 12

Paying no heed to Carly's warning, the man lunged to his feet and bullishly charged into Carly, knocking her hard against the doorjamb and stunning her for a moment.

By the time she regained her balance and tore after him, he had bolted down the stairs and was already out the front door.

"Damn!" she cried in frustration, only to then feel a flood of relief. Two patrol cars roared up to the curb and screeched to a halt. The doors opened immediately; uniformed policemen were everywhere.

"Stop him!" Carly yelled.

The burglar, who was sprinting across the yard, stopped as if paralyzed for a split second, then twisted his head right to left. Then he spun on his heels and began to run.

"Stop!" an officer yelled. "You're surrounded."

Carly didn't wait to see handcuffs snapped on him. Turning, she dashed back in the house and climbed the stairs two at a time. She knelt beside the unconscious woman and felt for a pulse; Carly's own heart was pounding against her rib cage. Blood was seeping from the nasty gash above the woman's left temple.

"Oh, God," Carly prayed aloud, "let her be alive."

She was, but just barely. Her pulse was so faint it was almost undetectable. It was while Carly was scrambling to her feet that she saw the diamond necklace lying beside the woman's right shoulder.

Leaving it, she jumped up, ran out the door and back down the stairs, only to miss running into Sergeant Farrell by inches. By his side stood Bud May.

"Radio for an ambulance," Carly said, out of breath. "Woman unconscious."

Farrell quickly turned and barked an order to another officer coming up the sidewalk.

When Carly returned to the room with Farrell and May on her heels, she noticed for the first time that the room was torn apart. Drawers were open and their contents littered all over the carpet. The large walk-in closet had been trashed, as well, and the woman's large jewelry box had been emptied.

From that point on, things moved fast. The med tech team arrived and loaded the still unconscious woman onto a stretcher. Carly tried in vain to reach the woman's husband.

With the burglar having been caught red-handed and already in custody, there was nothing left for Carly to do but go back to the station and make her report.

"Here, Mitchum," Sergeant Farrell said, "May said to take this with you and turn it in for safekeeping until the husband can claim it." He then tossed the bagged necklace toward her.

Though Carly reached for it, the bag slipped through her fingers.

"Jeez, Mitchum, is that the best you can do?" Farrell asked as Carly bent to pick it up.

But the instant she lowered her head, the room began to spin. One knee hit the carpet, instantly supporting her; otherwise she would have fallen flat on her face. Fighting for her composure as well as her equilibrium, Carly closed her eyes and took several deep breaths.

When she finally was able to get to her feet, clutching the bag in her hand, Bud May was watching her, a strange expression on his face.

"Are you all right, Officer?" he asked.

Carly took another deep breath. "I'm...fine."

"You sure as hell don't look it," he countered, coming closer with narrowed eyes. "You look like you're about to faint. How did you get that goose egg on the side of your face?"

Carly lifted a hand to the spot Bud was pointing to and touched it. She flinched. Damn, she hadn't even realized she'd been hurt.

When she didn't respond, Bud asked, "Do you need to go to the emergency room, Officer Mitchum?"

Carly straightened her shoulders. "No...sir. I'll be fine. I surprised our thief, that's all, and in his haste to get away, he gave me a slight shove."

"Slight shove, my foot. It looks to me like he gave you a helluva shove."

"You don't need to concern yourself about me, sir." Carly was growing more uncomfortable by the minute, as well as annoyed. It wasn't from the whack on the head, either; it was from the attention she was receiving. In addition to Lieutenant May, all other eyes were on her. She knew what they were thinking, could read it in their expressions, and it made her angrier than ever at May for calling attention to her, making her yet again the object of their ridicule.

May shrugged. "Whatever you say."

Later, as Carly drove back to the station, she tried to pretend her head was not about to split in two.

It was only after she was in the report room that she asked herself what Bud May had been doing at the scene. Maybe he was just in the vicinity, or maybe he was sent there by Rance to check up on her. The latter thought set her teeth on edge and made her headache worse.

She fought the urge to put her head down on the table and let the tears inside her have free reign. She was tired, and her head ached, and her eyes felt as if they had been doused with sand.

But she could handle those problems. What she couldn't handle was the fact that soon she would be working under Rance, seeing him every day.

Twisting around, she stared out the back window. Clouds were once again blocking the sun, coloring the day as dark as her mood.

She shuddered.

"Well, well, look who just graced us with her presence."

"Knock it off, Beechum," James Long ordered. "The property room's my turf, so you best mind your manners."

The second Carly walked through the door, she wished she hadn't, but she had finished her report and now she was turning in the necklace, so she could go home. Although she'd tried to dispose of it earlier, the property room had been locked.

She would have given anything to be able to slap the smirk off Beechum's face. Instead she kept her composure and turned a pleasant face to Long. "Lieutenant May said—"

Beechum cut in, Long's warning completely lost on him. "I wish you'd take a look at this one, Lanier—Her Highness is sporting a nasty lump on her head. What d'you know about that?" All the while Beechum was talking, he was punching Lanier, who stood next to him, in the ribs.

Still favoring Carly with his undivided attention, he added, "Tut, tut, my dear, you shouldn't let a suspect do a number on you like that."

Lanier snickered.

A fourth officer was standing off to the side, drinking a cup of coffee. "Yeah, Beechum, why don't you just shut your ugly mouth for once and keep it shut."

"Aw, shucks, Mailer, don't tell me this little lady here has got you dancing to her tune, too?"

"One of these days, Beechum," Long interceded, "someone's going to knock your teeth down your throat." His face was flushed with unnatural color.

This time Carly cut in, determined to head off further confrontation. "James, Lieutenant May wants this necklace locked up."

Long nodded. "Just toss it on the table."

Carly almost said, "Are you sure?" but didn't. The long table looked like a rat's nest. No, she was positive a rat's nest would be neater.

Still without looking at Beechum or any of the others, Carly completed her task and turned to walk out. Beechum stood in front of her, blocking the door.

"Get out of my way, Beechum."

"And if I don't?"

"Then I guess we'll both just stand here for the rest of the day," Carly said calmly, her face devoid of expression.

"Dammit, Beechum," Long said, shoving back his chair and standing. "Let her by."

Suddenly the room was filled with an ominous silence that seemed to last forever.

At last Beechum stepped aside, but not before leaning over and whispering in Carly's right ear. "Later, sugar. And that's a promise."

Carly's expression did not change. "I'll see you in hell first, Larry." She smiled sweetly. "And *that's* a promise."

When Carly let herself into the house a short while later, she was still fuming. She wondered what Larry Beechum would have done if she'd slapped him. Probably slapped her back, she thought with a cynical smile, going to her room and pulling off her uniform.

She was convinced that Lanier and Beechum would end up causing the department trouble. On the way home, she had replayed in her mind the way Beechum had been cozily conversing with that dope dealer as if they were planning the deal of the century. Maybe they were, which strengthened her resolve to watch him, along with Lanier.

After slipping into a robe and swallowing two aspirin, she headed toward the telephone in the kitchen to check for messages. The housekeeper, Jessie, was always careful to write everything down.

The house was too quiet, she thought, looking around with a frown, feeling more depressed than she cared to admit. She missed Matt, though she was glad he'd gone and hoped he was having a good time. Suddenly the phone rang, unexpectedly filling the void.

Grabbing the phone as if it were a lifeline, Carly said, "Hello."

"Remember me?" The voice on the other end of the line was smooth.

"Oh, Brian," she whispered, "it's good to hear your voice." Suddenly he seemed so safe, so secure.

"Mmm, that's nice to know."

"Are you free this weekend?" Carly asked without wasting any time.

"Yes and no."

"What does that mean?" She tried to control her impatience.

"First, what did you have in mind?"

"Well, there's a fund-raising party I have to attend, and I was hoping you could go with me."

"When is it?"

"Saturday night."

He was silent for a moment. "That presents a problem. However, if we don't stay too long I think I can swing it, although I'll have to leave right after the party."

"Why on earth do you have to be back home on Sunday?"

"Several guys are working on a deal, and if it takes off, I could become a very rich man. This meeting's been set for a long time, and I can't back out now."

Carly made a face. Brian was always working on some kind of deal, most of which didn't pan out.

"I guess if that's the best you can do," she said.

Brian's tone dropped an octave. "You know your being there and my being here is crazy. We need to talk."

"I'll see you Saturday."

He sighed, as if realizing he'd been put off again. "Yeah. You'll see me sometime Saturday afternoon, I'd imagine."

"Be careful."

"Yeah. You, too."

Once the conversation was over, Carly looked down at the pad she still had in her hand. The message was from Matt. He'd left word that he was fine and that he'd see her sometime next week.

A wan smile touched her lips as she rubbed her temple, then crossed to the stove and opened the lid on the pot that was sitting on the back burner. Homemade soup. Surely a bowl of that would make her feel better.

Maybe she should have listened to Bud May and had her doctor check her over. No, the cure to what ailed her was a long, hot soak in the tub and an uninterrupted night's sleep.

Under the circumstances, she seemed to be asking for the impossible.

When Carly got out of bed the next morning and stared at herself in the mirror, she seriously considered not going to work.

"Ugh," she whispered to her reflection. Not only was her temple black, blue and yellow, so was her eye. She could pass for a battered wife with no difficulty. The only saving grace was that the swelling had gone down considerably, but only because she had put an ice pack on that side of her face.

And sore. She felt as though every muscle in her body had been stretched to the breaking point. Yet the idea of staying home alone with only her bleak thoughts for company did not appeal to her. She'd just have to wear her sunglasses to ward off any smart-mouthed comments from the troop.

The squad room was quiet, as it was so often early in the morning. Several of the officers were sitting around working on reports and drinking coffee. This was the time of day Carly liked best, and since the incident with the baby, there had been a subtle change in the attitude toward her.

Still, there were the skeptics, Beechum for one, and Rance for another. And she knew that even those who *had* accepted her would continue to scrutinize her closely.

She just wondered what her fellow officers in patrol would think when they found out she was being transferred to C.I.D., wondered what the detectives in C.I.D. were going to say. Word was probably out by now, along with wagging tongues.

Now, as she poured herself a cup of coffee, she offered a fervent prayer that she wouldn't have to start all over in Rance

Knight's department, that the men would be more tolerant of her, recognize her capabilities, give her a chance.

"Morning," Arley Bishop said, interrupting her thoughts.

Carly faced him and smiled. "Good morning."

"Damn, Mitchum, what happened to you?" Bishop was eyeing her closely, his head slanted to one side as if determined to see through her shades.

Carly lifted her hand to her face and removed her glasses. "Oh, you mean this shiner?" She gave a humorless laugh. "It's my trophy from the guy who burglarized the Ivy home and knocked Mrs. Ivy unconscious in the process."

"Heard about that, but I didn't know he'd trashed you, as well."

"Now you know."

"How do you feel?"

"Like I've been beaten with a wet rope, if you really want to know."

"Maybe you should have taken the day off."

Carly smiled again, knowing his concern was genuine. "I thought about that, but not for long. Anyway, I'm here, so I guess I'll stay. It's possible the natives will cut us a break and not be restless today."

Arley rolled his eyes. "You haven't heard?"

"Heard what?"

They were making their way toward the back of the room in order to find a seat. After speaking to the other officers seated at the next table, Arley lowered his voice.

"Another pharmacy was hit last night, and the word is, the captain is furious, not to mention the chief."

Carly sighed. "And of course the paper's having a field day."

"That I can handle," Arley said, "but what I can't handle is the rumor that cops are involved."

Carly shivered at the vision of Beechum and the drug pusher. Beechum was a creep, she'd admit that. But "dirty"? No, she couldn't believe that. Suddenly guilty for letting her imagination run wild, she looked directly at Arley and asked, "You don't think there's anything to that gossip, do you?"

"Naw, but it sure as hell can't help our image, especially when there's already so much grumbling."

Carly pursed her lips. "I couldn't agree more."

A silence fell between them as the shift sergeant got up to make his morning announcements and assign duties.

The meeting was short, and soon Carly was at the door ready to walk out.

"Officer, wait up."

Her heart skipped a beat before she slowly turned around.

Rance was standing a few feet from her, looking overwhelmingly attractive in a white shirt, tie and snug slacks that exposed the powerful muscles of his thighs. She didn't want to look at him, much less talk to him, but she had no choice, particularly as any show of reticence would work to his advantage.

"What the hell!" He stepped closer, then looked around as if to make sure the corridor was deserted.

Her dismay at seeing him again was momentarily swept aside. "First Arley, now you. I couldn't look *that* bad?"

"You sure don't look good." Then, following a muffled groan, Rance asked softly, "Did Barnes do this to you?"

Their awareness of each other seemed like a silent scream. Seconds ticked by.

"Yes," she whispered, failing to keep her voice steady.

"That sonofabitch," he muttered, the gravelly sound in his voice drawing her gaze back to him like a magnet.

A warm weakness invaded her body as his eyes fixed on her for another breathless moment.

Rance pushed long brown fingers into the thick dark hair at his nape. "Thanks to that sonofabitch," he muttered again, "the Ivy woman is barely alive." His voice had turned cold as steel and just as hard. "The same thing could've happened to you."

She stared at him. Rance concerned about her safety? Yet she knew she hadn't misunderstood him.

"I'm sorry about Mrs. Ivy." Her throat was dry. "Is that what you wanted to tell me?"

Suddenly the atmosphere changed; he changed. He glanced at her, then looked away, his jaw rigid, his face taut.

"No." His voice was as impersonal as his expression. "I want to see you in my office."

"Now?"

"Now."

"It can't wait?" she asked boldly.

Rance inhaled sharply. "No, dammit, it can't."

"Yes, sir," Carly said tightly. She didn't dare stand there another moment, or she would come apart in front of him.

On entering his office, three men rose: Detective Bud May, Sergeant Robert Farrell and a tall sandy-haired man Carly didn't know.

May and Farrell nodded at her, while she murmured a faint, "Good morning."

"Officer Mitchum," Rance said, "this is Carlton Ivy."

Ivy's smile was weak as he acknowledged Carly. "Officer."

"I'm sorry about your wife, Mr. Ivy," Carly said.

Ivy couldn't quite meet her eyes. "One reason I came here this morning was to thank you personally for your quick actions."

Carly was not only embarrassed, but puzzled. She hadn't missed the "one" in the beginning of his statement. "I appreciate your saying that, but I was just doing my job."

What was going on? Both May and Farrell looked as though they would rather have been anywhere but in the room. And Rance—well, he remained heartless and cold. Seeing him now, she found it hard to believe he'd ever held her in his arms, kissed her until she was wet...and crazy with desire....

Unable to stand on her unsteady legs another moment, Carly sank into one of the chairs in front of Rance's desk.

"Mr. Ivy," Rance was saying, "if you'll wait outside, I'll be with you in a minute. If you'd like a cup of coffee, there's some in the squad room."

Once Ivy had gone, Rance stared down at Carly from his upright position behind his desk and cut to the heart of the matter, his expression hard. "Mr. Ivy's other reason for being here is to pick up his wife's diamond pendant."

"I can understand that," Carly said, only because she felt some type of response was expected of her. "It's...it's lovely."

"It was spotted by you on the floor beside his wife, right?"

"That's correct." Out of the corner of her eye, Carly could see Bud May puffing on a cigarette as if his life depended on it. Farrell had his back to her and was staring out the window. "And I bagged it as I was told and turned it in to the property room for safekeeping," she added, still puzzled.

"Then why was that not mentioned in your report?"

Carly frowned. "Not in my report? I don't understand."

"There's nothing to understand, Officer," Rance said flatly. "You failed to put it in your report." He paused. "But that's not the problem, not at the moment, anyway."

"Then what is the problem?" Carly asked bluntly, her eyes locked with his.

His answer was equally as blunt. "The necklace is not in the property room."

"What!"

"Shortly after Mr. Ivy arrived," Rance was saying, "I sent for the envelope, and when I opened it, it was empty. Nothing."

"Well, it was in there when I left the property room," Carly said. "You can ask Long."

"Bud did, and he verified what you said. Still, I want you to retrace your steps."

"No one's accusing you," May put in, crossing to Rance's desk and perching on the edge of it.

Carly had been holding her breath, and wasn't even aware of it until May spoke up on her behalf.

"But the fact remains," Rance said, "the necklace is missing, and we have to find it."

With confidence that camouflaged her inner turmoil, Carly repeated everything that had happened except the encounter with Beechum. When she finished, no one spoke.

May finally broke the silence. "Long's going through the envelopes now, Officer. Don't worry, it'll show up somewhere in that disaster we call the property room."

His gentleness was almost Carly's undoing. She lowered her head.

"Because of the botched report, a written reprimand will be placed in your file," Rance put in.

"Yes, sir."

"For now you're free to go."

With a smile glued on like wallpaper, Carly said, "Thank you."

After her shift ended, Carly simply could not face going home to an empty house, especially not after the day she'd had. Yet the whole time she'd steered her car in the opposite direction, her mind kept conjuring up images of her bathtub filled with hot, scented water, a cup of coffee laced with Bailey's Irish Cream and the comfortable softness of her bed.

Later, she'd promised herself, and hadn't veered from her destination.

Now, as she sat across from Angie in her friend's apartment, she was glad she hadn't talked herself out of visiting the dispatcher, especially as she had just told Angie the situation concerning the necklace.

"Surely you don't think the captain's accusing you of anything," Angie said. "Or do you?"

"I sure hope not, but the necklace *is* missing."

Angie flapped her hand. "Pooh, that necklace is somewhere in that room. If you ask me, I think they ought to condemn that place."

"It just has to be there," Carly said, ignoring Angie's caustic remark. "I will admit, though, that when I pitched it on the table, I didn't pay attention to where it landed."

"I guess not with Beechum and Lanier like two dogs in heat."

Carly laughed. "Oh, God love you, Ang. I don't know what I'd do without you." Then her face sobered. "I think what ticked the...the captain off was that he was embarrassed when Ivy asked for the necklace and it wasn't there."

"That's when he should have chewed on Long instead of you."

"Well, I did goof on my report."

"So, nobody's perfect."

"Well, you can bet I'll have a very negative documentation put in my file."

Angie's eyes sparked. "The way those men act you'd think they never made mistakes."

"Why, Angie—" Carly's tone was mocking "—how can you even think such a thing. Of course they don't make mistakes."

"Like hell they don't."

Carly smiled, but Angie didn't.

"This doesn't exactly endear you to the good captain, does it?"

Carly paled and turned away, no longer able to look Angie in the eye. She longed to tell Angie about Rance; the burden was almost too heavy to bear at times. But she couldn't. Not now. Not ever.

"No...no, it doesn't," Carly answered at last.

"Why do you think Crawford transferred you?" Angie pressed.

"He said it's because he thinks I'm needed in C.I.D., which we both know is hogwash."

Angie grinned. "Scuttlebutt has it that Crawford's after Rance's hide."

"That's true. He's doing everything he can to make things tough for Knight. And I'm the one caught in the middle." Carly's tone was bitter.

Suddenly Carly's reserve energy deserted her, and she felt as if every nerve in her body were exposed. Giving Angie a wan smile, she stood. "It's been great, friend, but it's time I took myself home to bed."

Angie stood also, and glanced down at her watch. "Gosh, I didn't realize it was after eight o'clock."

Carly leaned over and gave Angie a quick hug. "Thanks again for listening. I'll keep you posted."

"Please do. Oh, by the way, are you going to the Bishop fund-raising shindig this weekend?"

Carly took a deep breath. "Yes...I am. Brian's going with me."

"Why don't you give in and marry him?" Angie asked bluntly. "Even though I think he's a little too prim and proper, what the hell—he's a good man."

"Oh, please, Ang," Carly begged, edging toward the door, "don't start on that, not now."

"Okay." Angie laughed. "But I'm reserving the right to open that can of worms again later."

Carly was also laughing as she walked out the door and closed it behind her.

A short time later, as she approached her driveway, she saw a strange, empty car sitting on the side of the road. Shrugging, she pulled into the garage and got out, thankful to be home.

She took out her key and unlocked the door, then walked into the den to build a fire before taking her bath.

The man standing indolently in front of the floor-to-ceiling window turned at the sound of her approach. Carly's initial panic quickly gave way to stinging resentment.

"How did you get in here?"

Chapter 13

For a long moment the only sound in the lamp-lighted room was the grandfather clock above the mantel and the crackling of the fire in the hearth, which Rance had taken the liberty to start.

When he didn't answer her immediately, Carly opened her mouth to repeat her question, but nothing came out.

Rance, too, was unable to get one word past his throat, a throat that was suddenly closed. All he knew was that he hadn't been able to stay away. He had to see her.

Carly was staring at him, her face so beautiful, but so terribly drawn.

Following their meeting in the hall and the confrontation in his office, he'd had to see for himself that she was indeed all right. That goose egg on her temple had shaken him more than he cared to admit. And then there'd been the incident with the missing necklace.

After leaving the station, he was not only frustrated, he was at loose ends, as well. He'd gotten into his car and begun driving, forcing his mind to stay on business. The investigation into the pharmacy heist was progressing with all the speed of warm tar moving uphill. As a result, he and Bud, along with the other detectives, were baffled and angry.

But the problems at work had been only part of the reason for the burgeoning pressure inside him, and he'd known that. Only one person could alleviate that—Carly—he had to make love to her, bury himself deep inside her until they were both satisfied and weary.

It was then that he'd whipped the car around and headed toward the Armstrong house, having no idea what he was going to do or say when he got there.

Now, as his brown eyes continued to search her wide blue ones, Rance moved uneasily, realizing again how insane it was for him to have come.

"How...how did you get in?" Carly asked again, feeling her lower lip tremble. She bit down on it.

"Your housekeeper was kind enough to do the honors," he said after clearing his throat loudly. "She said you were probably working late and that Matt was out of town."

Carly frowned while clutching her keys to her chest as if to shield herself from his potent allure. "Jessie? But...how...I mean...she should have been long gone...." Her voice trailed off.

Rance expelled a breath. "Apparently she forgot something, because when I walked up the drive, she was getting out of her car. In a few minutes she came back outside clutching a sack. That's when I approached her. But it was only after I showed her my badge that she agreed to let me in to wait for you."

Carly laughed, but without amusement. "And you always get what you want, right?"

"Wrong." His eyes burned into hers. "And I think you know that as well as I do."

Carly inhaled sharply, resenting that veiled insinuation. And she resented *him*, resented his being here.

"What do you want, Rance?" she asked, beginning to squirm under his dark appraisal.

For the longest time, he didn't answer. Couldn't answer. He was conscious that her nipples had hardened during their exchange and were now perfectly outlined against her blouse, cutting off his train of thought, tempting him. With another inward groan, he dragged his eyes back level with hers.

"The necklace. I suppose you've come to tell me there's going to be an investigation," she added, giving him a simmering glare.

"No, there isn't going to be an investigation."

"Well, you weren't acting that sure this morning when you were raking me over the coals."

"I wasn't raking you over the coals," he stressed, his lips white.

Her eyes widened in pained reproof. "Oh. You sure could have fooled me."

"That's your own paranoia talking, and you know it." He rubbed the bridge of his nose. "Bud told you no one was accusing you of anything."

"Has the necklace been found?"

"No, but it'll show up. Long is in the process of going through the evidence."

"And until it does, I'm suspect."

"No, dammit, you're not. But you're too stubborn to—" He broke off in midsentence and turned his back.

For a long minute, the silence was stifling.

"Then...why...?" she whispered, unconsciously moving toward him, feeling her anger drain away.

He turned around slowly and held her eyes with his. "Like I said, I wanted to see if you were all right." A strained smile appeared on his lips. "But again the joke's on me, isn't it? I'm the one who's in bad shape."

Carly heard his labored breathing, while the scent of his heated body filled her nostrils. "Tell me what you want." Her voice was a tormented whisper.

"Oh, God, Carly!" Her name came out on a note of desperation.

Taking advantage of his momentary weakness, she asked again, "Tell me, damn you."

"I just did," Rance said between his teeth, unable to look at her.

"Liar."

The word was so softly spoken and unexpected that Rance thought he'd imagined it.

"What?"

"You heard me."

His heart was in his mouth and his mouth was dry. Positive he was hearing something that wasn't there, he began moving toward the door. If he stayed another second, he'd pull her into his arms and to hell with the consequences.

Without giving herself time to consider her actions, Carly reached toward him and whispered, "Don't go."

Rance froze, Carly's face only inches from his. "Do you know what you're saying?"

For a heartrending moment, neither moved nor said a word. A heady burst of excitement overwhelmed Carly as she stared at him, her eyes revealing her innermost emotions.

Rance finally found enough air to drag through his lungs, his eyes falling from Carly's flushed face to the steady rise and fall of her chest. His lips parted involuntarily, and a moan slipped through them.

"Are you sure?" he asked, his thoughts spinning.

"Yes...I'm sure."

She had never been more sure of anything in her life. She was asking him to make love to her; there was no sense in kidding herself any longer. She ached for him and knew the feeling was mutual. Their desire for each other was ripping them to pieces. Although she couldn't get him to admit it, deep down she knew that was why he'd come.

Anyway, she had no choice, not if they were going to have any type of workable relationship on the job. Her physical craving could no longer be suppressed.

Still afraid to hope, Rance was incapable of moving. "Are you...sure?" he asked again, his senses drugged with longing.

Carly didn't hesitate. "Yes."

That was all Rance needed. His hands curled around her nape and drew her toward him. He kissed her gently, a lover's kiss that seemed to reach to her very soul. When they could no longer breathe, he removed his mouth from hers and rained moist kisses on her nose, her eyes, her forehead, then her mouth again.

Carly responded to the touches and kisses that she'd dreamed about for so long. When at last he raised his eyes, they were smoldering. "Oh, God," he whispered hoarsely, "tell me this is real, that I'm not dreaming."

"You're not dreaming," Carly whispered, the tip of her tongue tracing his upper lip.

Their need was suddenly all-consuming, a culmination of weeks of unfulfilled desire and secret yearnings.

As he bent his head to her again, she met him halfway, her breath sweet and intoxicating on his mouth. "You taste so good," he whispered. "Don't ever stop kissing...me."

Their hands moved over each other, seeking, probing, touching, trying to make up for lost time. When merely touching was no longer enough—they sought for more, much more.

"I want you, *need* you," he whispered again, kissing her mouth, her ears, her neck, her soft white throat, feeling the pulsing life beat under his lips.

She sagged against him and clung. "Oh, Rance..."

"You're...lovely. I want to kiss you all over." He stood back then and began unbuttoning her blouse. With Carly's help, her clothes were soon disposed of. She stood before him in naked splendor. He was so mesmerized by the sight of her round, white breasts, full and firm, that he could barely breathe.

Watching his eyes devour her, Carly stood in trembling need.

"You're perfect," he whispered, touching a nipple, feeling it turn rigid under his fingers. By the time he put his arms around her, Carly was so weak she couldn't stand, especially when he ducked his head and placed his mouth on the sweet, moist flesh.

"Oh, Rance...oh...oh...please..."

"I know, my darling, I know."

"I...want you."

"And you shall have me."

He turned her loose then, and she watched while he stepped back, watched while he stripped off his clothes and flung them aside. Carly could feel the heat rise from his body as his face came closer once again. His eyes fluttered shut at the same time as his mouth covered hers. Holding her fast, his large hand molded a breast, then touched her stomach, her navel...between her legs to her moist center.

Clenching handfuls of his hair, Carly moaned and let her head fall back.

"Where?" he asked, dropping his arm under her knees and lifting her as she buried her head against his shoulder.

"In there," she murmured, pointing toward her bedroom.

He stood her on her feet and yanked back the covers. Then, pulling her back into his arms, they fell onto the bed with an urgency and need that came from being denied for too long.

His smoldering eyes held hers. "You feel so good," he whispered close to her ear.

She shifted in his arms and moaned softly, her lips brushing his. "You, too."

He traced her mouth with his tongue, licking and nibbling and then kissing hotly. Her body molded with his, enjoying the sensation of flesh against flesh. He lay between her thighs, rubbing against her, and without thinking, she began to move against his hot loins.

"Now, Rance, now. I want you inside me."

He surged forward, and in one sundering stroke penetrated her fully, bringing him a pleasure so exquisite that it blotted out Carly's cry.

She had never been so totally, so completely filled.

"Oh, Rance," she cried wildly, clutching his hips, locking her legs around them, lifting herself to meet him thrust for thrust. Her body strained against his, and she moaned in shameless abandon, falling into a well of pleasure so intense, she thought she'd surely die.

He felt her hand digging into his buttocks, and with her cries drowning in his, Rance spilled into her and collapsed on her breasts.

She held him and cried.

Her tears stirred something inside him. Tenderly he gathered her to him. He murmured soft, soothing sounds into her hair, afraid he had hurt her, calling himself all kinds of ugly names.

The fact that they were forbidden to each other no longer made a whit of difference. He could stop breathing easier than he could let her go.

"Did I hurt you?" he whispered, rolling to his side and bringing her with him.

She sniffled and snuggled against his chest, her tears falling on his throat. "No...you didn't."

"Then why the tears?"

"It...was so wonderful."

He sighed as his finger trailed down her back. "It was, wasn't it?"

"Are you...sure? I mean, you sound upset."

"Well, I fought like hell not to give in, but..."

She pulled back so she could see him. "Your lust overcame your sound judgment."

"I guess that about sums it up."

"I'm glad," she said, smiling.

He gave a low moan, tugging on a nipple. "It's been a while since you've made love, hasn't it?"

"There hasn't been anyone since Ben," she whispered against his arm.

He was astonished. "No one?"

"Well, there is someone...sort of."

His hand stilled on her breast; his whole body stiffened. For a moment she was afraid she'd made him mad, but when he finally spoke, he sounded more dejected than anything. "But he hasn't touched you, right?"

"No, he hasn't," she said, flushing. "But how did you know?"

"You're so very tight inside," he murmured, "so virgin-like."

"Oh, please," she whispered.

"And very hot," he added, ignoring her agony.

"You...make me crazy when you say things like that."

"Good."

They were quiet for a long moment.

Then Rance said, "Why?"

Her voice was dazed. "Why what?"

"Why haven't you let..." He paused as if waiting for her to supply a name.

"Brian, Brian Calhoun," she responded, a tremor in her voice. She didn't want to talk about Brian, not with her body still linked with Rance's.

"Why haven't you let him make love to you?" he went on in a strangled tone.

"He's...just a friend."

His heart soared, and the emotion that rushed through him felt like happiness.

He put his hand on her throat and tilted her head back. Her lips parted. "You have a lovely mouth," he whispered, brushing his lips against hers.

She reached up and outlined his with an unsteady finger. "I kinda like yours, too."

"I like the way you kiss," he said, trapping her finger in his mouth and sucking on it.

She squirmed against the heat building inside her.

"And your breasts. Ah, they're perfect. I've never touched anything softer. They remind me of velvet."

Color surged in her cheeks as she lowered her head. "I always thought they were too large."

"Never. They fit my hand completely. See." He covered a breast with his hand, squeezed and then replaced it with his mouth.

"Ah, that feels, oh...so good."

"You feel good all over. And for now you belong to me."

Carly wished she had the nerve to tell him that she would belong to him forever—all he had to do was say the word. Instead she twisted in his arms and met his moist, questing lips.

Suddenly his mouth was everywhere on her. She felt on fire, kindled by mouth and fingertips. She was lifting her hips to meet his mouth, but suddenly she stopped.

"Please," she whispered with glazed eyes. "I want you to be satisfied, too."

"Oh, Carly, Carly," he whispered in turn, "will you never cease to amaze me?" Then, honoring her request, he eased her over him, rising warm and hard into the core of her body.

Before he could draw her mouth down to his, her head fell back with a muted cry as he began to move under her. Their timing was simultaneous and perfect—a first for him. He wondered in one last lucid moment if it was for her, too.

They fell sideways, still joined, and lay panting, breathing in the air from each other's lungs.

"You're…"

Carly pressed a finger to his lips, silencing him. Utterly spent, but aware of his inactive but solid presence still within her, she said, "Shh, don't say anything, not a word. Don't spoil it."

"Whatever you say, my love."

My love. Had he said "my love"? Those words echoed again and again as they both fell into a deep, exhausted sleep.

"Carly?"

"Mmm." She inched closer against his chest.

"Are you awake?"

"Are you?"

"Barely."

"Why are we talking then?"

He chuckled. "A good question."

"What time is it?"

"Nearly six." His tone was sober again.

"Time…to go."

He drew in a harsh breath. "Yes."

Suddenly she felt a lump in the back of her throat.

"Carly."

She rolled over on her back and looked up at Rance. The moonlight was still streaming through the window, allowing her to see him clearly. She then sank her fingers into the thick, coarse mat on his chest and began to massage the solid muscles.

Rance covered her small hand with his large one. She saw the uncertainty then, the fear in his eyes, and her heart sank. The one thing they had not discussed, had been so careful to avoid discussing was their work. Instinct told Carly that was about to change.

He avoided looking at her by simply turning his head.

Voicing her thoughts, she asked, "You're sorry, aren't you?"

"Are you?"

"I...asked you first."

"No...I'm not sorry, but..."

"But...what?" Her lower lip trembled.

"Our...being together...this is going to make things more difficult."

"For you or me."

"For us both."

"No one knows."

"They will."

"I promise not to tell if you don't."

Her attempt at humor fell flat. Rance didn't smile.

"So what are you getting at, Rance?" Numbness settled over her, and she felt as if she were withering and dying inside.

"Nothing, except we don't need to make the situation any more complicated than it already is."

"What are you suggesting?" Her face was the color of chalk.

"The best solution would be—"

"To leave me alone," she finished for him.

"Yes," he said tersely. "Only..."

"I couldn't agree with you more," she said quickly, her heart feeling as if he'd stepped on it. "I guess I...we both went a little crazy. But it's over and done with now. No regrets."

The grooves around his mouth deepened. "No regrets. After all, we're both cops, which is more important than a relationship."

"Right," she said, forcing a laugh. "You have your sights set on the chief's job, and nothing must interfere."

"And you're determined to be the only female to advance in the department."

"Right."

"So no problem."

"No problem."

Rance was the first to disengage himself, rolling off the bed in a swift, jerky motion. "I guess that settles it then," he said, stamping out of the room.

"I guess it does," she said to his back.

A minute later, he stood in the door, his eyes hooded. "I'm...leaving now."

She fiddled with the sheet. "So long."

"Goodbye." His voice was raspy. "Carly...?"

"I think you can find your way out."

It was only after she heard the front door slam that she released the tears.

Chapter 14

The first day of November, the day of the fund-raiser, dawned bright and clear, though with a biting chill in the air. As Carly listened to the weather report, she became sure that by party time the weather would be on the mild side.

That was hardly a consolation. She was miserable. For one thing she had awakened with a splitting headache, a holdover, she suspected, from the whack on the head. That, and Rance.

She thanked God she was off today and tomorrow. By Monday, if she survived the party, she would have herself together enough to return to work.

She'd known she was playing with fire, living dangerously when she'd encouraged him to make love to her, so she had no one to blame but herself. Still, it hurt.

Now, as Carly padded into the kitchen to pour herself a healthy cup of coffee, she wished she could do the same. Following a deep sigh, she took a long sip, thinking how much she missed Matt.

The big house was empty without him. And she was no longer comfortable with just herself for company.

She headed into her bedroom and was about to slip into her

sweats and head for the jogging track, when the phone rang. Plopping down on the side of the bed, she reached for it.

"Hello."

"Carly, Brian."

"I know who it is, silly." She cast a sidelong glance toward the brass clock on the wall and frowned. "Shouldn't you be on your way?"

His sigh filtered loud and clear through the line. "Yes, but—"

"You can't come," Carly interrupted, her heart plunging.

"Dammit, babe, it just isn't going to work out as I planned."

"But Brian, you promised," Carly pointed out, her knuckles turning white as she clutched the receiver.

"I know, and believe me I hate like hell to let you down, but there's been a snag in the deal and I can't leave. I'm at the office now, working."

Carly wanted to scream at him, beg him to come if necessary, but she knew it wouldn't do any good. Nothing she could say or do would change his mind.

"Carly, please try to understand," Brian pleaded, a whiny tone to his voice. "I need this deal, not just for me but for us."

"Don't bring me into it," Carly rasped, furious with him for letting her down and furious with herself because she had depended on him.

"I know you're upset," Brian told her soothingly. "And on one hand I don't blame you, but on the other, I don't get it. You sound...oh, I don't know..." He paused as if searching for the right word. "You sound as if you're more concerned about having an escort to the party than seeing me. What's going on?"

Carly's face burned. "Nothing," she lied, feeling awful.

He didn't sound convinced. "Well, as soon as this deal is cemented, I'll call and we'll get together. And this time, we're going to get some things straight."

"I don't take well to ultimatums, Brian."

Brian sighed again, this time deeper and longer than before. "Look, Carly, I'm going to hang up before we both end up saying things we shouldn't. I'll be in touch."

"Goodbye, Brian."

Fighting back the tears, Carly donned her sweats and Reeboks and bolted out of the house as though it were on fire.

"I'm so glad you thought to call," Angie said.

Carly smiled as Angie continued to navigate the car smoothly down the highway toward Rance's place. It was five-thirty, and they were almost there.

"Me, too. But since Brian isn't coming, it was foolish for both of us to go alone."

Angie flashed her an impish grin. "Actually, I was thinking about calling and seeing if I could bum a ride with you and your banker."

"Well, you would've certainly been welcome." Carly frowned. "By the way, he's not my—" she stressed the word "—banker."

Angie lifted a brow. "Oh, since when?"

"Since never."

"Does he know that?"

Carly flushed. "No."

"Sounds to me like you got a problem."

"That's just one of many."

Angie didn't miss the dejected note in Carly's voice. She shot her a glance. "Hey, how about leveling with me. What's really bugging you?"

Carly licked her lips, but before she could say anything, Angie went on.

"You're pale as a ghost and if I'm not mistaken, you've lost weight. Is it the transfer?"

Carly seized on that subject like a lifeline. "Mostly," she said.

"Think it's going to be that bad, huh, working under the hunk?"

"Don't call him that," Carly said tautly, instantly regretting her quick response. Angie was far too perceptive. She'd have to be more careful or Angie would have her baring her soul any minute now. And to make things worse, Carly wished she could. Maybe it would help to lessen the ache inside her.

Angie laughed. "You're right. The mood he's been in the

past two days does make him less than hunk material. Everyone is steering clear of him.''

While discussing Rance definitely made Carly uncomfortable, it also did her heart good to know that he wasn't as immune as he'd made himself out to be.

"Look, do you mind if we...we talk about something else," Carly said at length. "Someone else. It's...it's bad enough that I have to work with him without..." Carly's voice faded, but Angie got the message.

"We're nearly there, anyway, aren't we?" Angie asked lightly, slowing down and peering straight ahead.

Carly pretended to study the written directions that Angie had given her, but she didn't need to. The way to the ranch was committed to memory, as was everything else about that entire day.

"That we are," Carly responded, taking a deep breath. "In fact, at the next blacktop road, you need to hook a right."

Angie grinned. "By now the place ought to be rocking. Can't wait.''

Carly forced an answering grin. "Me, neither."

Angie was right. When she steered her car across the cattle guard, cars were everywhere. In the distance Carly could hear the band bellowing out a Kenny Rogers tune, and the air was rich with the tantalizing aroma of barbecue.

She'd have to hand it to Rance, Carly thought. He'd done an amazing job of putting this fund-raiser together, and in record time, too. When they had laid the groundwork, she had agreed to help him decorate his patio and grounds. So much for plans gone sour, she thought, her lips twitching bitterly.

"Hey, everybody, look who's here," Arley Bishop cried, ambling toward them, a grin splattered across his face and an apron tied around his waist.

Carly felt instantly self-conscious, but smiled nevertheless, as several of the men and their wives turned in her direction and waved and spoke good-naturedly.

Before she turned her attention back to Arley, her eyes swept the premises. Her gaze landed on Lanier and Beechum, who, with several other officers, were off to themselves drinking beer. She pretended not to notice them and caught Bud May's eye. He was standing with his wife, both wearing aprons, behind the steam tables. Bud grinned and waved. Carly waved back.

Their host was nowhere to be seen.

"I'd about decided you two weren't coming."

Carly switched her attention back to Arley, pleased to see him looking so happy, so hopeful. "You know better than that, Arley. I wouldn't have missed this for anything."

Angie had already spotted a couple of the other female dispatchers and was off in their direction. "See you two later," she called over her shoulder.

"Come on," Arley said, "Ruth wants to thank you again for the buttermilk pie."

Carly smiled. "You mean she got a piece?"

Arley frowned in jest. "Now do I look like the type of fellow who would deprive his wife of something?"

"You sure as hell do," a deep voice said from behind, almost causing Carly's heart to jump out of her chest.

Arley spun around the same time as Rance slapped him on the back. "Hey, Captain, I was just telling Carly how much we enjoyed the pie she sent us."

"Hello...Mitchum."

For a moment his gaze was naked, and Carly saw the sizzling desire there. Her knees almost buckled under her. Finally she dragged her eyes away and composed herself enough to speak. "Hello, Captain. Nice party," she added lamely.

"Yeah, isn't it, though," Arley chimed in, as if totally oblivious to the tension in the air. "Hey, by the way, where've you been? Bud was looking for you a second ago."

"In the house making sure the beer was holding out."

Arley grinned from ear to ear. "Don't doubt that, especially with this bunch of drunks. And speaking of drunks, I promised to bring May a cool one." He turned to Carly. "You comin'?"

Carly's relief was instantaneous. "Yes."

It was Rance who interrupted this time. "You go ahead, Bishop. I want to talk to Mitchum a second."

Arley shrugged. "Sure. I'll catch you both later."

Looking up at Rance proved to be disastrous. She was dismayed to feel tears stinging her eyes, and blinked furiously in an effort to keep them from running down her cheeks.

"Carly, I..." he began, looking as if he'd been hit in the solar plexus.

She forced her eyes back to his. "Please...just go away. I...we don't have anything to say to each other. We said it all the other night."

He didn't move.

Though he didn't touch her, he might just as well have. His gaze was as clinging as a caress. His eyes swept from the top of her silky curls to the denim long-sleeved jumpsuit, to the toes of her boots. Then it moved up again, loitering on her breasts, which were enticingly shadowed under the fabric.

Nervous, she raised her hand and fiddled with the diamond pendant at the base of her neck. "I need to speak to Ruth," she said for lack of anything better.

"God, Carly," Rance said in a strangled tone, "I thought it would be easier to walk away, not see you...not touch you, but..."

"Don't Rance," she said fiercely, trying to keep her desperation from showing, especially as he was so near. In spite of everything, she yearned to touch him.

"Carly," he said again.

But the agonized use of her name fell on deaf ears. Carly had already turned her back and was walking away.

"Now what do you suppose our captain and Ms. Astor were discussing?"

Beechum and Lanier were alone now, sitting on the ground, using a huge oak tree to brace their backs. With several beers under their belts, they were relaxed and feeling no pain, yet Beechum's words had come out sounding like a sneer.

Lanier shrugged. "Who knows, but whatever it was, neither one looked too happy."

"Maybe they were having a lovers' tiff." He snickered. Then his expression changed, turning evil. "Or maybe they were discussing me."

Lanier jerked his head up and narrowed his eyes to beady slits. "Now just why in the hell would they be discussing you?"

"I think Mitchum spotted me talking to Felton the other night." Beechum rubbed his chin with his index finger. "In fact, I know she did."

"That's great, Larry. Just great."

"Well, don't get yourself all steamed up. Even if she did, she's too stupid to put two and two together and come up with four."

Lanier snorted. "That's where you're wrong, my friend. She's plenty smart, and besides that, she'd like nothing better than to see you hanging from the short end of a long rope."

Beechum's eyes glittered dangerously. "Yeah. And people in hell want ice water, too."

"Don't get cute with me," Lanier bit out furiously. "What if she was telling Knight that you were with Felton and Knight starts thinking that maybe the rumors about dirty cops flying around town have some merit?" Lanier smiled a humorless smile. "You certainly can't say that Felton's tippin' off the captain."

"Hell, Hal, you worry too much."

"Yeah. And you don't worry enough. You're too goddamned sure of yourself. Everything could blow up in our faces."

"Well, if it does, it won't be because Mitchum tattled."

"I think we'd better cool it for a while."

"Not until we've knocked off those two new pharmacies, one at a time, of course. Felton already has the buyer for the drugs lined up. This will be the biggest haul yet, and if you want to bow out then—" Beechum lifted his shoulders "—that's your prerogative."

"I just think it's time. I got more money now than I can spend."

Beechum's mouth twisted. "Well, I don't, not with that wife of mine. She gets more greedy by the goddamned minute."

"That's your problem," Lanier snapped. "Mine is protecting my ass. And if there's the slightest chance that Mitchum—"

"Forget Mitchum!" Beechum spoke in a harsh whisper.

"When the time comes I'll handle her." His eyes turned cruel.
"I've been waiting a long time to do just that."

The remainder of the evening passed in a blur for Carly. As
if programmed, she laughed at the right times, said the right
things and even managed to swallow a few bites of the succulent
beef, though it tasted like sawdust when she tried to chew it.

For once the majority of the officers put aside their long-
standing mistrust of her and in the presence of their wives joked
about lining Carly's locker with lipstick and greasing her steering wheel with lard. Carly took the tales in stride, even managed
to laugh.

Through it all, she was conscious of Rance. Though he never
said another word to her, she felt his eyes tracking her movements. Once she'd considered approaching Angie and asking
her to leave, but she didn't have the heart, as Angie seemed to
be having such a good time.

Finally, when the money had been counted and turned over
to the Bishops, a smiling Arley and a tearful Ruth, many of the
officers and guests began departing.

When Angie indicated that she was ready to leave, Carly ex-
cused herself and made her way inside the house to use the
bathroom. The second she cleared the side door, she pulled up
short.

Rance was in the kitchen, talking on the phone. As if aware
that he was no longer alone, he twisted around and stared at
her. His face was devoid of color. Carly, unable to move,
watched as he turned and slammed the phone down, then drew
in a harsh breath.

"Rance?" She bit her lip nervously.

He didn't say a word; he seemed to look through her.

"Rance, what's wrong?" This time there was an urgent edge
to her voice.

His features were a stony mask. "It's…Stacy. She…she's had
a wreck."

His words struck her like a thunderbolt. "Oh, my God,"
Carly wheezed, her hand flying to her mouth. "Is…is she hurt?"

"Yes, but they're not sure how bad."

"Is there anything I can do?" Carly asked lamely, knowing there wasn't, but she had to ask, anyway.

He didn't hesitate. "Yes. You can go with me. Now."

"But...but...I'm with Angie." Carly's eyes were wide as she stared at him in stunned amazement.

"I'll pick you up after she drops you off. Bud can wrap things up here."

This time it was Carly who didn't hesitate. "I'll be ready."

As the Bronco headed toward Lufkin, Rance kept his eyes on the road ahead, but he was aware of Carly sitting beside him with every nerve in his body. Though he longed to say something, he didn't.

Fear and guilt could do strange things to a person. He ought to know; at the moment both were gnawing at his insides. His life was a mess. *He* was a mess, and so was his daughter.

If only he had let her come to Timberland this weekend, she wouldn't be lying in the hospital, hurt and possibly maimed for life. He'd never forgive himself for this.

No way could he fault Denise for neglecting her daughter when he'd been guilty of the same thing. He'd been so wrapped up in Carly Mitchum, in satisfying his lust for her, that he, too, had neglected his daughter.

But he'd been unable to help himself. He'd intended to leave her alone, to stay away. Then, when he couldn't, he'd been so sure that once he'd tasted her delectable body he would no longer be interested. After all, wasn't part of the fascination supposed to be the chase?

His theory had backfired. Once he'd acquainted himself with the secrets of Carly's lush body, he'd wanted her more than ever.

It was Rance's ragged sigh that drew Carly's eyes back to him. Though the details of his profile were blurry in the dim interior, she knew his jaw was set in a tense line.

Suddenly he glanced at her. "Thanks for coming."

"You're...welcome."

"I would've understood had you told me to go to hell."

Carly swallowed. "I... To be honest, that thought never crossed my mind."

For a moment their eyes locked in the semidarkness.

"I'm glad," he said softly. He took one hand off the wheel and massaged the back of his neck.

"She's going to be all right, Rance," Carly said, torn by the ravaged expression on his face. "I just know she is."

"God, I hope so." His breath rattled in his chest.

"Do you know any details?" she prodded gently.

"Only that she was alone and ran into a telephone pole."

Carly was wild-eyed. "You mean she was driving?"

"She's just gotten her license."

"Bless her sweet heart."

"And wouldn't you know it, Denise is out of town." His tone was bitter.

"Stacy was staying with a friend," Carly said more to herself than to Rance.

"Dammit, Stacy called and wanted to stay with me, but I had this party and...so much on my mind that I told her it wasn't a good time." He paused. "If only she'd told me her mother was going out of town..."

Without thinking, Carly reached over and laid her hand on his arm. "You have to have faith that she's going to be all right and that you'll get the chance to make it up to her."

"It seems that all I do lately is correct my damned mistakes with my own kid."

Pacing back and forth in the waiting room, Carly repeated first one prayer, then another and another. When they had arrived over an hour ago, Rance had dashed through the emergency room door, and he had not come out as yet. By now Carly's nerves were frayed.

She paused at the nearest window and gazed outside at the multitude of stars, but their beauty hardly registered. Her thoughts were with Stacy and Rance.

"Carly."

She spun around. Rance was standing behind her, a weary but relieved expression on his face.

"She's...going to be fine," he said. "No internal injuries. But her arm's broken, and she has a mild concussion."

Carly covered her face with her hands and whispered, "Thank God it wasn't more serious."

"And it very well could have been, too," Rance said.

"What happened? Did she tell you?"

"Yeah. Said a car ran a red light, and when she swerved to miss it, she lost control and slammed into a telephone pole."

Carly shivered. "It's a wonder she came out of it as well as she did."

"And the sonofabitch who caused it didn't even stop."

"That figures."

"Would you like to see her?" Rance asked unexpectedly. "I told her you were with me, and she asked to see you."

She scanned his face, but his eyes were dark and unreadable. "Do you...mind?"

"Come with me."

When Carly walked in the room and saw Stacy lying against the white sheets and looking so bruised and battered, a lump rose in her throat.

"Hi, Carly."

Carly leaned over and kissed her on the forehead. "Hi yourself."

"Thanks...for coming with Daddy."

"Anytime," Carly whispered. "You just concentrate on getting well."

Stacy tried to smile. "I hear you." Then she turned to Rance, who was standing close beside Carly, and said, "Don't worry about me, Daddy. I'm going to be fine."

Rance's hand trembled as he stroked his daughter's hair. "You bet you are, sweetheart. I'm going to see to it." He smiled into her eyes.

"Does Mom know?"

Rance tensed. "Your mother's on her way back home. She should be here shortly."

"What about you?"

"I'm going to take Carly home. You rest while I'm gone, and I promise I'll be back before you wake up."

Stacy nodded, then closed her eyes, cradling her cheek in Rance's palm. He stared down at her for the longest time before bending over and kissing her cheek.

When he stood and withdrew his hand, his cheeks were wet with tears.

In that moment Carly realized she loved him.

Chapter 15

They had made the trip home in silence. Carly couldn't have said anything sane if her life had depended on it.

Now, as they sat in front of her house, she felt his eyes on her.

"I guess I'd better let you go," he said.

"I guess you'd better."

He made no move to get out of the car. Instead they continued to look at each other.

"Where are you going?"

"I don't know." His lean features constricted. "Back to the hospital, most likely. I...don't think I can stand myself for company."

Carly wet her lips. "Then don't."

Suddenly time seemed to stop.

"What do you mean?" His voice sounded disembodied.

When she answered, it was in a whisper. "Stay...with me."

"Oh, Carly," he said, reaching across and pulling her against him, her sweet-smelling hair brushing his chin. "God help me, but you're making an offer I can't pass up."

She awoke to the aroma of coffee. With a sigh, she flopped over on her back, trying to recapture the dream. Then she remembered, and shot up in the bed. The space beside her was empty.

Rance had stayed, and they hadn't been able to restrain themselves. The minute they'd walked into the bedroom and disrobed, they'd come together on the bed.

"Carly, I can't wait. I need you so...desperately. All day, all evening I've been thinking about you...wanting you...."

"Me, too," she said urgently, tightening her arms around him.

His invasion was sharp and piercing and wonderful. When it was over, he slowly eased his weight against her, still sheathed within her.

"Was it lousy for you?" he whispered, kissing her lips. "I couldn't wait. I'm sorry."

She gave him an amused smile. "Don't be sorry. It was what I wanted and it was perfect."

He continued to lie on top of her, finding her unbearably beautiful.

"You're beautiful," he rasped, "and wild and hot and bright and soft and so many things—everything."

Carly reached up and tenderly traced a finger over his face as if to commit it to memory. She wanted to say, "I love you," but she knew it would shatter this rare intimacy, so she kissed the base of his throat, and felt him tremble. If only time would stop, she thought, now, with them joined together.

But nothing was forever. Soon she'd have to start building her life over again. Only for this coveted moment did he belong to her. Her arms tightened around him even more, and she held him, eager to bear his weight.

"Hold me," she pleaded, her eyes closed. "Hold me hard! I'm so frightened."

"I know," he murmured. "So am I."

They had twisted and turned and made love into the night until they'd fallen into an exhausted sleep.

Now it was morning—five o'clock to be exact.

Carly found Rance in the kitchen. "Good morning," she said, standing on the threshold, uncertainty edging her voice.

He looked up and smiled.

Carly caught her breath. It was so seldom he smiled that it never failed to shake her. She walked to the table where he was sitting with a cup of coffee in his hand.

"Good morning," he finally said, standing, his eyes intense as they studied her face. "Want some coffee?"

"I'll get it," Carly said nervously.

Once they both were sitting, a moment of silence followed. Then Rance said softly, "I have to go."

"To the hospital?"

He nodded. "I told Stacy I'd be there when she woke up."

"Did you call the hospital?"

"Just got through. The floor nurse told me she had a good night, but was still sleeping."

Carly's tense muscles relaxed. "That's good news."

"I wish I could say the same for work."

She frowned. "I thought you were off."

"I'm supposed to be. But another pharmacy was ripped off last night."

"Great."

Rance sipped on his coffee. "I suppose you've heard the rumor."

Carly picked up on his train of thought. "You mean about cops being involved?"

"That's exactly what I mean."

Surprised that he had even broached the subject, Carly spoke with caution.

"I suppose everyone's heard," she answered slowly, "though no one's talking about it, at least not to me. But, then, they wouldn't."

"Do you think it has merit?" he asked, ignoring her bitterness.

Carly raised her brows. "Are you asking my opinion?" She was so shocked, she didn't think to mask the sarcasm.

"I asked, didn't I?"

The mood had changed. Gazing at him now from under thick

lashes, Carly saw the hard, brooding Rance of old. Gone was the tenderness, the warmth. He was all cop now.

Carly rubbed her temple. One cop did not rat on another, and he damn well knew that, so what was he fishing for?

"I guess anything's possible," she said, trying to erase the image of Larry Beechum on the street late at night, too late at night.

"Just the thought of a dirty cop being in our department makes me want to puke." Rance was standing now, his eyes narrowed in naked fury.

"I couldn't agree more. Uncle Matt has always said a man who takes advantage of his badge is the scum of the earth."

"Well, if there is one, you can bet I'll find him and nail his butt to the wall."

Carly's footsteps echoed against the kitchen walls as she got up and carried their cups to the sink. She stood a moment and looked out the window, no doubts in her mind that Rance spoke the truth.

She didn't have to turn around to know that he was behind her. The clean, soapy smell of his body filled her nostrils. She felt her legs wobble when he placed his hand on her shoulders and turned her around.

"Carly, Carly."

Thrilling to the sound of her name on his lips, she stood on her tiptoes and met his lips as they claimed hers in desperation, holding her, devouring her mouth and her will.

"I'm not sorry for last night," he groaned when they moved apart.

"I don't want you to be."

He smoothed her hair back. "I have to go," he said again.

"I know."

"What about you?"

"I have to work mids tonight."

He was quiet for a moment, then said brusquely, "Well, be careful, for heaven's sake."

By the time Carly recovered enough to speak, Rance was already out the door and in his car.

The next two days, Carly was positive her feet never touched the ground. Yet soon she would have to face the reality that while Rance might care for her, caring was not the same as loving. Deep down she knew she was spinning daydreams out of air.

Now, as she walked into the station, back on days, the first person she saw was Rance. He was making his way down the hall toward her.

Although she hadn't seen him since he'd left to return to the hospital, she had talked to him on the phone twice.

When Rance stopped in front of her, Carly's heart beat out of control.

"Hello," he said, and though he spoke in a cool tone, his eyes were anything but cool. Peering down at Carly, they sparked with unsuppressed passion.

"Hi," Carly answered quietly.

"I was looking for you."

Carly blinked. "You were?"

"Uh-huh."

"It's not Stacy, is it?"

Rance shook his head. "No, it has nothing to do with Stacy. She's doing just great. I took her home from the hospital yesterday and she thanks you for the flowers. You'll be hearing from her." He looked at her more intently. "Actually, I have a surprise for you."

"Oh?" It was only then that she realized he was holding something in his hand. "What is it?" she asked, her brows drawn together in a perplexed frown.

"Look familiar?" he asked, pulling out a dazzling diamond pendant and dangling it in front of her.

Her blue eyes widened. "Is that whose I think it is?"

"One and the same. It's Mrs. Ivy's."

Carly raised a trembling hand to her heart. "Thank God for small favors," she said. "I guess Long finally found it in that mess."

"Nope."

"Then where?"

"In court."

Carly looked baffled. "Court?"

"That's right. Apparently when you tossed the envelope on the table, the necklace slipped out of it and into another one. Long, of course, sealed all the envelopes and filed them in the bin."

"And when the evidence was presented at an unrelated trial, the necklace appeared out of nowhere."

"You got it."

"So now I'm fully vindicated?"

"You could say that, only you were never under investigation."

"Well, thanks...thanks for telling me."

"Anytime."

They were staring at each other. The connective force of their gaze was powerful, so powerful that they didn't hear the approaching footsteps.

"Hey, Mitchum, what the hell are you doing? Get the lead out, will ya? You're holding up the meeting."

Startled at the sound of Farrell's strident voice, Carly whipped around. Rance stiffened and turned also, but more slowly.

"Uh...sorry, Captain." Farrell's face was red from the neck up. "I didn't realize it was you she was talking to," he spluttered.

"Obviously." Rance's tone was as sarcastic as it was clipped.

Farrell began backing up, as if knowing he'd put his foot in his mouth.

"However," Rance added, "Mitchum and I have concluded our business." Then, switching a bland face to Carly once again, he added, "You can go now, Officer."

"Thanks...sir," Carly managed, before spinning and following Farrell into the squad room, wondering how much longer she and Rance could keep their liaison a secret.

When Carly got off duty and started home, she was plunged into the depths of depression. She missed Rance; at this point phone calls were simply not enough. She wanted to touch him, hold him.

But his commitments were elsewhere. She couldn't fault him

for spending time with his daughter, nor could she fault him for working overtime to solve the pharmacy burglaries.

She knew he would come to her when he could. With that she had to be content.

She opened the door to the sound of the fireplace crackling and someone singing. Her mouth widened into a grin.

"Uncle Matt," she cried, dashing into the kitchen, "is that you?"

"Of course it's me, girl. Who the hell else would it be?" Though his voice was gruff, as usual, there was a grin on his face as Carly fell into his arms.

Stepping back after a fierce hug, Carly scrutinized him. "Well, I must say that this vacation agreed with you. You look as fit as I've ever seen you."

Matt grimaced. "I wish I could say the same for you. You look like a killdeer, you're so poor. You're working too hard."

Carly gave him another hug. "Now, now, calm down. I'm just fine." As the lie rolled off her lips, she couldn't quite meet his eyes. "I've just been working such crazy hours that sleep has been impossible."

Although Matt looked as if he wanted to argue, he didn't. Instead he pointed at the newspapers strewn across the table. "I see they haven't made any arrests in the pharmacy burglaries."

Carly sighed and eased herself down into the nearest chair. "And everyone's walking on eggshells around the department, from the chief on down."

Matt was silent while he poured Carly a cup of coffee and brought it to her, then eased himself into the nearest chair. "I guess I'm going to have to go down there and show 'em how it's supposed to be done."

Carly smiled. "Come on, I know you wouldn't trade the good life for the world of work again, no matter what you say."

"Well, you might be right." His grin was sheepish. "But, then, if that woman next door doesn't leave me alone, I just might change my mind."

"Speaking of Martha, how did she make the trip?"

"Fine."

"Well, did you have as good a time as your postcards indicated?"

"Guess so. The leaves in New England were 'bout the prettiest things I've ever seen."

Carly smiled. "I'm glad you enjoyed yourself, but I'm also glad you're back. This place has been like a tomb."

Suddenly Matt squirmed in his chair and shifted his eyes. "I'm afraid that won't be for long."

Carly's face puckered. "What won't be for long?"

"Oh, damn, I might as well spit it out. Martha and I are..." He paused and wiped his upper lip. "I guess what I'm trying to say is that Martha has asked me to marry her and I've said yes."

Carly's mouth gaped.

"Shut your mouth! I know it's a shock. Hell, how do you think I feel?"

Carly sprang to her feet, circled the table and flung her arms around Matt. "It's about time, and I couldn't be happier."

Matt returned the hug. "You sure you don't mind?" His expression was troubled.

"Why on earth would I mind? If anyone deserves to be happy, it's you. You've more than paid your dues."

His gaze was penetrating. "And so have you, my dear. After all, you gave up your job to come here and look after me."

"So."

"So now I have Martha...."

"And I'm free to leave. Is that what you're saying?"

"Yeah," Matt growled. "I guess it is. And I feel guilty as hell because you came in the first place."

Carly reached out and squeezed the hand lying on the table. "Don't say it. Don't even think it. As it is, I'll never be able to repay you for all you've done for me."

Matt waved a hand. "I doubt that. But that's not the issue right now."

"What is then?"

His voice gentled. "You'll be free to leave, return to Dallas."

It took a second for his words to soak in, trapping her breath in her lungs. Leave Timberland?

Matt leaned his head to one side and went on, "And then you won't have to work under Rance Knight. I know how much you hate even the thought."

Suddenly Carly came to her senses, forcing down a feeling of panic. "Oh, please tell me that's not why you're marrying Martha."

"Of course it isn't," Matt snapped. "But you'll have to admit it'll relieve you of the responsibility of me."

"Oh, Uncle Matt," Carly cried with tears in her eyes, "when are you going to get it through your thick skull that I don't think of you as a responsibility?"

"Well, anyway, you can get on with your life, marry Brian if you're so inclined."

Carly drained the last of her coffee and set the cup firmly on the table. "Well, I'm not so inclined. Nor am I interested in returning to Dallas."

"What if Crawford forces your transfer?"

Carly averted her gaze. "He already has."

"Why that bas—"

In spite of herself, Carly laughed. "Don't worry, Unc, I can handle it." It amazed her how easily the little white lies spilled from her lips.

"Are you sure?" he asked sharply, though he looked relieved.

"I'm sure."

"Well, this house is yours for as long as you want it to be. We plan to live in Martha's."

"You'll do no such thing. I'll get an apartment."

"No." Matt's eyebrows jutted over narrowed eyes.

"Yes."

"Now, listen here, girl,"

"No, you listen. I *want* to get an apartment." Then, seeing the hurt expression on his face, she hurried to qualify her statement. "Don't get me wrong, I've loved living here, but at the same time I've missed having my own place. Surely you can understand that."

"Of course I can," Matt said, backing down. "Don't pay any attention to me."

"Now that we've got that settled, when's the big day?"

"Soon."

"How soon?"

"Next weekend."

"Next weekend!"

Matt flashed her a lascivious grin and lowered his voice. "Says she can't wait to get me to herself."

Carly laughed out loud. "Why, you dirty old man."

"I suggest you watch your mouth, young lady."

Carly gave him a mock salute. "Yes, sir. Now how about getting Martha over here so we can celebrate?"

And celebrate they did until eleven o'clock that night. It was only after Carly took a shower and fell into bed that she realized how drained she was. And furious. Furious with herself for the jealousy she'd felt when she'd seen Matt and Martha looking at each other with such profound love in their eyes.

Now, as she peered up at the ceiling, listening to the rain beating against the windowpane, she had never felt such a keen sense of loneliness. Was it possible for her and Rance to have the same thing? Or was she again dreaming the impossible dream?

Determined to block out the offensive questions that had no answers, she closed her eyes tightly and placed her hands over her ears. Hence she didn't hear the phone on the first ring.

Finally realizing that the tingling sound was not due to the pressure on her ears, she bolted upright in the bed and reached blindly for the phone, wondering who could be calling at this time of night. Brian, most likely, she thought with tumultuous sigh.

"Hello." She barely breathed the word.

"Were you asleep?"

At the sound of the deep voice, Carly's palm turned moist against the receiver. "No...no, I wasn't."

Rance didn't sound convinced. "Are you sure?"

"I'm...sure."

A short silence followed her breathy admission.

"I've missed you," Rance muttered thickly.

His unexpected confession rendered her speechless and brought fresh tears to her eyes.

"Carly—"

"Oh, Rance, I've missed you, too," she whispered.

"What were you doing?"

"Getting ready for bed."

"Are you there now?" His tone was husky, intimate.

"Yes."

He groaned. "What if I came over and crawled in beside you?"

"Oh, Rance...you—" she began.

He interrupted. "What are you wearing?"

"Now?"

"Yes, now."

Carly ran a tongue over her upper lip. "Noth-nothing."

He groaned again. "Do you know what the thought of you lying there naked does to me?"

"I...can imagine."

"Oh, no, baby, you can't. I'm so hot right now, I'm about to combust."

"Oh, Rance..."

"You've got to let me come over," he said in a strangled voice. "Now."

"No, don't!" she cried.

"Why?"

"Uncle Matt came home today, that's why."

"Damn!"

She sniffled. Tears of frustration made their way down her face.

"Don't do that. Don't cry." Carly heard him struggling to get his breath. "I'll have to see you soon or go crazy."

"Is that a promise?" she whispered.

"You'd better know it."

"Are...you all right?" Carly asked, reluctant to let him go.

"You know I'm not," he ground out harshly. "But I'll survive."

Carly swiped at the tears on her cheeks with her free hand. "Where are you?"

"At the office."

"You should be at home."

"I wouldn't be able to sleep."

"I have the same problem."

His voice dropped. "Soon, my darling, soon."

For the first time since Rance had become part of her life, Carly fell asleep with hope burning bright in her heart.

Chapter 16

Carly's day started off at a hectic pace with Martha asking her to help her with the wedding plans, even though the affair was going to be short and unpretentious. That took the morning and part of the afternoon. As a result Carly had to rush to get to the station by two-thirty.

By the time she was getting ready to go off duty, things had quieted down. It was while she was making a final swing through the downtown area, using her spotlight, that she noticed the open door. Immediately she slowed down, pulled over to the nearest curb and reached for the microphone.

"Two-oh-five."

"Go ahead 205," the dispatcher said.

"I'm in the alley behind Dave's Appliance Center. The door to that particular store is standing slightly ajar."

"Ten-four."

"Request backup."

"Ten-four, 205."

Once the microphone was back in place, Carly waited and watched in the rearview mirror until another patrol car rolled up behind her. But when she identified the two officers that got out, her heart sank. Beechum and Lanier. What had she done to deserve those jerks?

Suppressing a sigh, Carly unbuckled her seat belt, opened her car door and met them halfway.

"Hiya, sugar," Beechum said with a grin, not bothering to mask the contempt in his voice.

"Not now, Larry," Hal Lanier snapped.

Pretending Beechum didn't exist, Carly turned to Lanier and said, "Let's go check it out."

"Let's go."

With guns in hand, they approached the building and, after taking the necessary precautions, entered it. Minutes later the premises were cleared; the place had indeed been burglarized.

"I'll report it," Carly said, slipping her walkie-talkie from her belt."

"Think you're up to it, sugar?" Beechum sneered.

Carly countered with syrupy sweetness, "Oh, I'm up to it all right. But, then, I know exactly what my job is."

"Are you saying I don't?" There was a menacing curl to Beechum's lips.

"You figure it out," Carly responded curtly, though she knew she should have kept her mouth shut.

"At least I don't kiss up to make points."

Carly was taken aback. "What does that mean?"

"Aha, now the shoe's on the other foot." Beechum laughed, jabbing Lanier in the arm.

Furious with herself for letting Beechum goad her into playing his game, she gave a nonchalant shrug. "Drop it, Beechum. We have work to do."

Beechum wasn't about to drop it. "Don't think I haven't seen the way you and the capt—"

Blind panic forced Carly to cut him short and counterattack. "What about you and Felton? What about the way you two were sidled up to each other in shantytown?" Again Carly knew she should control her tongue, but the need to put this man in his place forced her hand. "What were you doing, sealing a drug deal?"

"Why, you little..."

Beechum was looming over her, and it was an effort for Carly not to strike the heavy-jowled officer. She wondered what he'd do if he knew she had considered telling Rance she'd seen him consorting with the pusher. She'd bet that would take him down a peg or two. Rance wouldn't take any flack from Beechum, and Beechum knew it.

"Stay away from me, Beechum," Carly warned, backing up.

White-faced and white-lipped, Lanier chimed in, "Dammit, Larry, knock it off!"

Beechum ignored him, having eyes only for Carly. "I'm not through with you yet, bitch," he snarled.

Proud of her control, Carly merely turned and walked to the opposite side of the room. There she lifted the walkie-talkie and reported the burglary, asking that the owner be notified. Though Beechum kept his distance and his mouth closed, she nevertheless felt his eyes boring into her back. A short while later the sound of a door opening and closing behind her drew Carly's attention. She whipped around. A short, rather nondescript-looking man had entered the store, his features pinched in an angry frown.

"I'm Dave Holt, the owner," he said tersely, his eyes encompassing the three officers.

Once the introductions were out of the way, Carly lifted her notebook and said, "I'd like you to tell me as best you can what's missing."

"All right," Holt said with a deep sigh, indicating that Carly should precede him. "Let's start at the back and work forward."

The second Carly and Holt were out of sight, Beechum faced Lanier and whispered, "Dammit, I was right. She saw me."

Lanier looked sick. "What the hell are we going to do? What if she goes to Knight?"

"She won't."

"How do you know?"

"I got an idea."

Lanier looked desperate. "What?"

"Are you willing to help me fix Mitchum once and for all?"

"Yes," Lanier spit, "if it means protecting my rear."

"Good. Then this is what we'll do...."

When Carly and Holt returned to the front to continue taking inventory, Beechum unfurled his body from against a wall and spoke directly to the owner.

"Mr. Holt, I noticed there's a blank space on this shelf behind me."

Holt's eyes narrowed as he rushed forward. "A minicam recorder was there." His eyes were filled with despair. "I'd like to see whoever did this rot in hell."

Throwing a malicious look in Carly's direction, Beechum said, "If you'll come with me, sir, I'd like to show you something." Then, motioning to Carly, he added, "You, too, Officer."

As they all followed him out the door and started to approach Carly's squad car, she angled her way past Holt and Lanier to stand in front of Beechum. "What do you think you're doing?" she demanded angrily.

"You'll see" was Beechum's caustic reply as he jammed his master key into the lock and twisted it open.

"Beechum, I'm—" Carly began.

Beechum continued, overriding Carly's words, "Mr. Holt, if you'll look on the floorboard, I think you'll see why I brought you out here." Beechum's gaze was triumphant.

Carly gasped.

Holt's face turned ashen; Lanier said nothing.

With his jaw slack, Holt focused his attention on Beechum and asked, "What's going on here, Officer?"

Beechum answered the question with another of his own. "Does this belong to you?"

"You know it does," Holt bit out.

"Well, then, I think you should ask Officer Mitchum. Before you arrived on the scene, looks like she helped herself to that minicam."

All eyes shifted to Carly, and for a moment no one said a word. But Carly was very much aware of the evil glint in Beechum's eyes.

Dave Holt finally broke the silence. Pinning Carly with a

hostile gaze, he demanded, "Officer Mitchum, what do you have to say for yourself?"

"Officer Mitchum, we're waiting to hear your side of the story."

And they were—waiting to pounce on her like buzzards on a dead animal. Crawford. Detective May. Sergeant Farrell. And Rance. When she'd walked into the room at eight o'clock the next morning, he was the first person she saw. For an instant she feared her heart would literally stop beating. What was he thinking? she asked herself, letting her eyes linger on him for only a heartbeat. His expression gave nothing away, but his expression reminded her of carved granite.

Concentrating on a point beyond Crawford's shoulder, Carly sucked in a deep breath, forcing much needed air through her deprived lungs. But it did nothing to quiet her hammering heart or dampen the anger raging inside her. By sheer willpower, she kept her face impassive.

"Well, Mitchum," Crawford said again.

Carly straightened her shoulders. "I'm innocent of the charge brought against me."

"Are you saying officers Beechum and Lanier lied?"

"Yes, sir, I am. I never touched that recorder."

"How do you explain its being in your car."

Carly's lips thinned. "I...don't know, sir. I just know I didn't put it there."

Rance was standing close enough that she was aware of him with every fiber of her being. She swallowed, then stiffened. Somehow she had to dredge up the strength to get through this ordeal.

"Is that all you have to say for yourself, Officer?" Crawford asked.

"Yes, sir."

"There will be a full investigation into this matter, Mitchum. In the meantime I'm assigning you to desk duty."

"Yes...sir," she managed to say.

Crawford nodded toward Rance. "I.A. will investigate. From

now on Captain Knight will be in charge. It's all yours, Captain. Take it away."

Not Rance! Carly cried silently. Then, unable to stop herself, Carly looked at him.

His eyes, as they linked with hers, were cold and empty.

"Be in my office first thing in the morning, Mitchum."

She nodded, then walked out of the room with her head held high. She might have lost this battle, but not the war.

Rance had quit counting the number of cigarettes he'd smoked since he'd left the chief's office and came back to his.

There was no doubt in his mind that Carly was innocent. And God knows he'd wanted to come to her defense. More than that, he'd wanted to storm out of the room and confront Beechum, beat the bloody hell out of him, force him to tell the truth. He hadn't, of course. He'd simply stood there and stared into Carly's eyes, seeing both confusion and pain, and cursed vehemently.

Rance guessed that Carly had probably turned Beechum down a time or two, and so Beechum decided to set her up. Or was there something more? If Beechum was out to get her, which certainly looked to be the case, Carly could be in danger.

He'd had his own doubts about Beechum and Lanier for a while now, Beechum in particular. And if his informant was right, he had every reason to be. The problem was proving it.

Suddenly he ground the cigarette butt into an ashtray already overflowing with them and swore.

"Shall I leave and come back later?"

Rance's head popped up. "Dammit, May, don't you ever knock?"

"Your door was open."

"So what?" Rance's tone was terse. "Learn to knock anyway."

"No problem," Bud said without offense, sauntering farther into the room. "Want me to back out and knock?"

"Cute."

The detective shrugged.

"Hell, now that you're here, you might as well shut the door and take the load off your feet."

"Consider it done," Bud said lightly.

Moments later, Rance was still standing. Bud was grooming his mustache and watching his boss with an eagle eye. Rance, uncomfortable under such scrutiny, thrust another cigarette between his lips and lighted it.

"When did you start chain-smoking again?" Bud asked bluntly.

"This morning," Rance said with equal bluntness.

"Mitchum?"

"Right. The whole thing stinks."

"I couldn't agree more." Bud shook his head. "But why would Beechum risk his career, everything, to set her up?"

Rance's eyes turned as cold as chips of ice. "That's what I aim to find out."

Bud sat down and, tilting his head to one side, said, "You know me, Rance, know that I speak my mind and call a spade a spade."

"What the hell you getting at, Bud?"

"Is there something between you and Carly Mitchum?"

A cold mask slipped over Rance's face. "Where'd you get a cockamamy idea like that?"

"Hell, Rance, gimme a break. I didn't just fall off a watermelon truck."

"I didn't say you had."

"I saw the way you two looked at each other."

Rance didn't say anything.

"You're playing a dangerous game."

Rance's voice was razor sharp. "Dammit, don't you think I know that? But—"

"But you can't leave her alone. Is that it?"

"That's it in a nutshell."

"You poor bastard. What are you going to do?

Rance expelled a harsh sigh. "I wish to hell I knew."

The first thing Carly did when she got home that afternoon was to head for the bathroom, determined to soak in a hot tub until she figured out her next course of action.

It had been one of the longest days of her life as she'd fought to distance herself from the mixture of sympathetic and unsympathetic stares that had come her way.

As she discarded her clothes and quickly filled the tub with hot water, she was glad that Matt and Martha were out and she had the house to herself.

"What a mess," she groaned, easing down into the sweet-smelling water and placing her head on the back of the tub. Tears ran down her face.

Not only had Rance broken her heart, but her integrity and her career were both facing annihilation. Everything was in his hands. Still, she wasn't about to give up without a fight. She had been a fighter all her life and now that the stakes were high was no time to back down. Somehow, she vowed, she would prove her innocence, with or without Rance's help.

Later, when the doorbell chimed, she had felt that her composure was back in place, only to lose it again at the sight of Brian on the other side of the threshold.

"What...what are you doing here?" Carly stammered in astonishment. He couldn't have picked a worse time to show up on her doorstep.

"If that's not a helluva greeting, I don't know what is."

Before Carly could diffuse his anger, Brian grabbed her and planted a firm kiss on her parted lips. But just as soon as he withdrew his lips, Carly pushed him away, thoroughly repulsed.

His face turned the color of chalk. "I take it you're not glad to see me."

"Of course I am," Carly said lamely. "It's just that I wasn't expecting you, that's all."

Brian tried to smile, but failed. "I just decided to take off from work this morning and drive down here. I called, and Matt told me you were working days." He paused. "Apparently I made a mistake."

Carly reddened. "Please, come in and sit down. Do you want something to drink? Coffee?"

"Not now, thanks. Maybe later."

There was an awkward silence as they both finally sat on the couch and examined each other.

"How've you been?" Brian asked with his most charming smile, seeming to have recovered his self-assurance.

A dark cloud passed over Carly's face. "Oh, Brian, let's just cut the small talk, shall we. It's been a terrible day, and I'm not in the best of moods."

"Care to tell me about it?"

"No...not really."

His cheek twitched. "I see."

"Oh, Brian..." Carly began, knowing that she was doing this all wrong. She didn't want to hurt him; that was the last thing she wanted to do. But at the moment, she didn't see any way around it.

The minute she'd flung open the door and had seen him standing there, she'd known she didn't love him, had never loved him, could never love him. God help her, in spite of Rance's betrayal, she still loved him. And the thought of Brian or any other man touching her turned her stomach.

"Marry me, Carly. Now."

Carly stared at him. "What?"

Brian was looking at her, meeting her stunned blue eyes with his angry green ones. "You heard me. Give up this crazy job of yours and marry me."

Carly lunged to her feet. "I can't do that and you know it."

"Can't do what, marry me or give up your job?"

"What about your job, Brian? What if I asked you to give it up? I feel the same way about—"

Brian cut her off with a sneer. "Always the job. And what a lousy one it is, too, especially for a woman. I just can't hack it anymore, Carly. There's no way I could handle my wife charging out of the house at the most ungodly hours, facing Lord knows what, and not knowing if she'll come back home."

Carly shook her head in disgust. "Don't you think you're being a little melodramatic?"

"I sure as hell don't. In fact, I want you to choose now—the job or me."

Her temper snapped, but peering down at him, she kept her

voice neutral. "That's absurd and you know it. What if I demanded you choose between me and your job?"

"That's not the same," he countered.

"I beg to differ with you. Anyway, I happen to take great pride in my job and I won't have you belittling it or me." She couldn't believe she was arguing with him like this, wasting her time and his, when she couldn't care less what he thought about her or her job. Her shoulders slumped suddenly, and she turned her back on what she knew was a good friend.

"Carly, listen to me!"

"No, Brian, you listen," she said, staring out the window. "We both know it would never work between us. Perhaps I should have told you my feelings, my doubts a long time ago."

"Hell, Carly," he said, grabbing her and forcing her to look at him. "You're not making any sense."

Abruptly, she instinctively knew that deep down he agreed with her. "Oh, yes, I am and you know it."

"All right, Carly," he said after a moment, "I won't argue with you." He shifted his feet. "But if you ever change your mind..."

Her features gentled. "I won't, but thanks, anyway."

He nodded, then turned and made his way to the door. Silently Carly followed him outside to the porch. When he reached the bottom step, he turned to her. "Guess, I'll see you around."

"Guess so."

Carly was so intent on watching Brian climb behind the wheel of his silver Mercedes that she was unaware of the other car creeping up the drive. It was only after she heard a door slam that she spun around.

Rance was standing beside his Bronco, arms folded across his chest.

Carly closed her eyes, stifling a gasp.

"Who the hell was that?" Rance asked, stopping on the bottom step, his eyes piercing.

Carly shivered, but not from the cold.

Chapter 17

"Who was that?" Rance repeated.

Carly lifted her head defiantly. "I don't see how it's any of your business, but it was Brian Calhoun."

"Your banker friend."

She nodded, trying in vain to control her runaway heart. Rance was the last person she expected to see tonight, and she wondered how much more torture she would have to endure.

Standing in front of her, he looked so big, so strong, so handsome. Instead of exchanging harsh words, she longed to pitch forward into his arms and beg him to hold her, to say "I love you," to say, "I believe in you."

But she knew he wouldn't say either. As head of Internal Affairs, he was her enemy.

Rance raked a hand through his already tousled hair. "What did he want?"

"He asked me to marry him." She said it to shock him, to get back at him for hurting her, and it gave her great pleasure to see that she had.

Rance put her thoughts into words. "Is this how you're plan-

ning on paying me back?'' His features were sharp; his eyes
were hard. ''If it is, you're succeeding.''

They stared at each other while the seconds seemed to pass
slowly. The wind whistling through the treetops was the only
identifiable sound around them. But for Carly, it was somehow
a comfortable sound, something familiar in a world that was
suddenly coming undone.

''I don't know what you're talking about,'' she said innocently.

''Oh, I think you do.'' His response was savage.

''What do you want, Rance?'' Carly asked in a cracked whisper, knowing that she was perilously close to the breaking point.

''I want to talk.''

''Talk.'' Her hand went to her throat, and she kept staring at
him. ''There's nothing left to be said.''

''Look,'' Rance muttered hoarsely, ''I know what you're
thinking, and I—''

Carly took a step backward. ''I seriously doubt that.''

''Dammit, woman, will you just listen to me a minute?'' With
the help of the porch light, Carly could see the stern, tense lines
around Rance's eyes and mouth.

''You're going ahead with the investigation, right?'' she
asked, her teeth beginning to chatter.

''You know I am, but—''

''Then I'm not interested in anything you have to say.'' She
tipped her chin up. ''Anyway, you...you shouldn't be here.''

''Are you alone?'' he asked suddenly, catching her off guard.
She paused. ''Why?''

''For one thing, it's damned cold out here, and for another,
this is no place to sort out our differences.''

Carly locked her arms around her chest as if for protection
and stepped backward. ''Well, I'm...sorry. Uncle Matt's here.''
As the lie slid off her lips, she asked the Lord to forgive her.
She couldn't let Rance come in.

''Then let's go somewhere, for a ride, anywhere.''

Carly steeled her heart against the desperation punctuating
each word. ''Please...Rance...just go away.''

For the longest time Rance didn't move a muscle; he just

looked at her. "All right, Carly, I'll leave. But before I go, I'm going to say what I came to say, and you can take it for what it's worth. I don't think you stole that damned recorder, and with or without your help, I intend to prove it."

With that he whipped around, and while Carly was reeling in shock, he was slamming the door shut on his Bronco.

"Oh, God, I'm sorry," she whispered. "Please...come back."

But it was too late. The wind merely flung her words back in her face. She stood in a stupor and watched as the taillights of Rance's car winked at her from afar.

The next day when Carly had reported for desk duty, she did not see Rance. However, shortly thereafter she was called into Rance's office, only Rance was not there. Bud May, who had been handpicked by Rance to work the I.A. stint with him, was behind Rance's desk. May questioned her at length, and again she repeated everything that had transpired at Bob's Appliance Center.

But she hadn't minded, especially since Rance believed in her. She just wished she'd been able to swallow her pride and approach him, tell him she'd gladly accept his help. For certain she was going to need it. Still, she walked with a spring in her steps, even though she hadn't been exonerated by the department.

Now that she'd finally whittled down the mountain of paperwork, she stood and stretched her aching muscles.

"Tired?"

Carly turned around with a colorless smile and looked into Arley Bishop's concerned eyes.

"Hello, Arley," she said calmly.

He shifted uncomfortably. "I just want you to know that I'm behind you one hundred percent and so are most of the other men."

Carly swallowed against the sudden lump that rose in her throat. "You're a good friend, Arley, and I appreciate it."

He scoffed. "Friendship has nothing to do with it. Beechum's walking a tightrope, and I think he knows it."

"I wish that were true."

"In my opinion, he's a bastard and shouldn't be allowed to wear a badge."

"I couldn't agree more, but right now my opinion doesn't count for much."

Arley was quiet for a moment. "If there's anything I can do, you'll holler, won't you?"

Carly smiled again, this time with more conviction. "Thanks, I appreciate your support."

The second Arley ambled off, the smile on Carly's face disappeared. Bracing her shoulders, she walked out of the room and came face to face with Rance.

Caught unawares, they both pulled up short. For a moment, neither moved. Carly could hear his breathing as well as her own. With so much to say, for an instant they found themselves out of words.

Then Rance cleared his throat and asked, "Do you have a minute?"

Her heart beat in confused alarm. "Of...course."

"Has Beechum said anything to you?"

"No."

"How about you? Have you said anything to him?"

Carly bristled. "No, why?"

"I just want to caution you not to. After all, there is an investigation going on."

It wasn't what he said but the way he said it that rankled. Either way, he'd insinuated that she didn't have enough sense to stay clear of Beechum on her own. So much for Rance's help, she thought, pressing her lips together.

"Look, I have to go," she said, her tone as cold as the glint in her eyes.

"Dammit, Carly, I'm trying to help you. But you sure as hell don't make it easy." He looked around, then lowered his voice. "Just stay away from Beechum. That's an order. I'll handle him." He looked at her a bit more sharply. "I want you to think hard. Is there any reason Beechum would want to get back at you, other than the fact that you wouldn't sleep with him?"

Carly's mouth twisted into a humorless, lopsided smile. "One thing never changes—the department grapevine is forever live and well.''

"Dammit, Carly," he said again. "Answer me. He's out to hang you, for God's sake."

Carly took a moment to respond. "A while back, I saw Beechum talking to Felton." She pulled in her lowered lip. "And he knows I saw him."

Rance's eyes widened. "You mean you actually saw him with that weasel?''

"You're on to something, aren't you?"

"You bet I am."

"Captain."

They both jumped at the intrusion.

Rance spun around. "What? Can't you see I'm busy?"

"That call you've been waiting on has come through."

"Tell him I'll be right there," Rance said. Turning back to Carly, he added, "Don't go away."

Carly waited until Rance was out of sight, then she made her way down the hall, all the while damning Rance for treating her like an imbecile. Damning Beechum for putting her in this mess. And damning herself for letting them both get away with it.

Her thoughts remained in turmoil for the next hour as she did some paperwork Chief Crawford's secretary didn't have time for. Suddenly feeling the urge to take a walk before she screamed—stuffing files was *not* where her talent lay—she stood. With a muttered excuse thrown the secretary's way, Carly walked out of the room.

Larry Beechum had just stepped out of the men's room.

"Well, well," he said, a cynical grin plastered on his fat face.

Carly felt something inside her snap. Rance be damned. Career be damned. She'd take matters into her own hands. She might not accomplish anything by confronting this creep, but she'd let him know she wasn't going to roll over and play dead, that she was going to fight him to the end.

"You and I need to have a talk," she said, her eyes flashing.

If anything, his grin became more obnoxious, more leering. "I'm for that, sugar. But not here. Come on."

He pivoted on his heels and walked away, leaving her to

follow. It was a moment before Carly realized that Beechum was heading toward Forensics; the department was normally closed at this hour.

Well, that was just fine with her. What she had to say to him was not meant for an audience.

"In here," Beechum ordered, opening the door and flipping on the light.

So intent were they on what they were going to say to each other, neither one noticed the red In Use light that shone above the connecting darkroom door.

Taking a stance in the middle of the room, Beechum folded his arms across his chest and grinned. "All right, sugar, let's have it. Whatcha got on your mind?"

"I just want you to know," Carly said evenly, refusing to stoop to his level, "that you won't get away with framing me."

He raised his eyebrows. "Framing you? Why, I don't know what you're talking about, sugar."

An unreasoning rage gripped Carly, a rage such as she'd never known before. "Oh, yes, you do. And sooner or later, you'll get what's coming to you. I'll see to it. Also, you might keep in mind that you haven't won yet. The investigation isn't over."

"Ah, that's where you're wrong, sugar. It's cut-and-dried. Dave Holt's not about to drop those charges, especially not after seeing the recorder in your car."

She gave him a frozen glare. "I wasn't talking about Dave Holt."

"Well, no matter. You have about as much chance as a snowball in hell of shaking this rap, unless—" He broke off and stroked his chin. "Unless you were willing to make a little deal, such as trading a few nights in the sack to—"

"Forget it, Beechum," Carly snapped. "Hell will freeze over before I let you lay a finger on me."

"I wouldn't be too sure of that." His voice was an icy sneer.

"Oh, I would," she argued breezily. "But at the moment, that's beside the point. What I think you ought to know is that I told the captain I saw you talking to Felton. And I'll just bet he's real anxious to hear what you two talked about."

Beechum took a step closer, his face darkening and taking on a sinister glint. "You little bitch. You'll pay for that."

Suddenly she laughed. "Why, Officer Beechum, I do believe I got your attention."

His nostrils flared. "You're pushing it, sugar."

Carly was on a roll and not about to back off now. "As sorry as you are, I wouldn't put it past you and your pusher buddy to be involved in those drugstore burglaries."

He smiled a wide, self-confident smile. "So what? So I did tap a couple of pharmacies. But remember, sugar, it's your butt that's in a sling, not mine."

Carly couldn't believe her ears. "How does it work? Does Felton peddle the pills you rip off?"

"Right again," Beechum said in a low, mocking tone. Before Carly was aware of his intentions, he reached out and trailed a beefy finger around a breast.

Carly glared at him, her face rigid. "Get your filthy hand off me, you piece of garbage."

He laughed and went on, "But proving I had anything to do with the burglaries is gonna be the real bitch."

"Maybe not as much of a bitch as we once thought," Rance said, ambling out of the darkroom.

The slamming door behind him had the same effect as a bullet hitting a tin can. Carly winced in shock, while Beechum turned a sickly green color.

"Carly, read this sonofabitch his rights."

It had been three o'clock the following morning before Carly got home and crawled into bed. To say she was exhausted was an understatement, yet she couldn't have been happier.

The moment the news had broken about Beechum's and Lanier's arrest, pandemonium erupted at the station. Even though the hour had been late, television and newspaper reporters had shown up in force. Carly, Rance and Crawford had all been interviewed at length.

Still, each time Carly had rehashed the facts and listened to Rance do the same, she had found it hard to believe that Rance had been in the darkroom. But no one had questioned it, least of all Carly.

But what had been equally as shocking was that Rance, through expert police work involving a tip-off, had already linked Beechum and Lanier with the pharmacy holdups.

She couldn't have been prouder, for herself and for Rance. Congratulations had come from everyone.

"Way to go, Mitchum," Arley had said.

"Yeah, friend," Angie had chimed in, "we're all proud of you."

But as far as Carly was concerned, the only praise that counted had come from Rance. On her way to the parking lot she had been hailed from behind. She had paused and slowly turned around, her heart in her mouth.

"What's your hurry?" he'd asked, finally catching up with her.

In spite of her exhaustion, her lips twitched. "I can't imagine, since it's only three a.m."

He laughed out loud, and her legs almost caved in. "Damn, is it that late?"

Under the muted lights of the parking lot, he looked tired, but his eyes still held a gleam. Carly found herself clenching her fingers to keep from reaching out and touching him. It seemed like forever since she'd felt the fiery touch of his hands and mouth on her body.

Rance's eyes narrowed to slits, and he muttered thickly, "Don't. Don't look at me like that."

"I can't help it," she murmured before she could stop herself. Their passion for each other flared anew.

He moaned like a lost soul. "Are you aware that it's all I can do not to grab you and kiss you?"

"Oh, Rance," she whispered.

His arousal was instantaneous and painful, and he was desperate to get himself under control. "I'd better let you get home before I do something we'll both be sorry for."

She licked her lips. "I...know."

Yet he didn't move, merely continued to lose himself in her

eyes. "I guess I don't need to tell you what a good job you did and that I'm proud of you, but—"

"Yes, you do need to tell me," Carly cut in. "I've waited a long time to hear it from you, Rance Knight."

"Hey, you didn't let me finish." His voice was husky.

She smiled. "Okay, finish."

"What I was about to say is that while I'm proud of you, I'm fighting the urge to throttle you for taking matters into your own hands."

"I could've messed up your investigation, right?"

His eyes burned into her. "That, too. But more important, I didn't want Beechum to hurt you...."

Time suddenly seemed to stand still.

"If I remember correctly," he went on in a whisper, "I owe you a promise."

"And do you always pay your debts?"

"You can count on it."

Now, as she arrived at the station later that same morning, their meeting was very much on her mind and heart.

Even though she still had no idea what the future held for her and Rance, or if they even had a future, it didn't matter. Only the here and now was important. Rance wanted to be with her and she with him.

"What on earth are you doing here? I thought the chief gave you the day off?" Angie had opened the glass partition in the dispatcher's office and was leaning out, her eyebrows raised.

Carly sighed. "He did, but as I didn't get through with my paperwork, here I am."

Angie grinned and looked at Carly with a strange light in her eyes.

"What's with you?" Carly asked. "You look like the proverbial cat who just swallowed the canary."

Angie shook her head. "I can't believe you don't know."

"Know what?"

"Surely you've heard."

"Angie!"

"Oh, all right. I won't keep you in suspense any longer. But I would've sworn someone had called you."

"Angie," Carly said again.

Angie's grin was truly spectacular now. "Crawford's retiring."

"You're kidding!"

"Nope. Announced it this morning."

"I'm...in shock," Carly whispered.

"But you're glad, aren't you?"

"Of course. He should've called it quits a long time ago."

"But that's not all."

"Oh?"

"Guess who he recommended to replace him, which is the shock of the decade?"

Carly's breath caught sharply. "Who?"

"Rance Knight."

Chapter 18

One couldn't have asked for a lovelier afternoon. The sun was shining through the leafless trees, spreading its warmth on every living thing, but as Carly slowly followed the creek that wound through the woods at the back of her uncle's house, she was scarcely aware of the weather.

In fact, she was scarcely aware of anything, except that after much soul searching, she had finally reached a decision. She was going to tell Rance it was over, that she couldn't see him anymore.

She had no choice. Immediately after Angie had made her startling announcement, reality had hit her like a slap in the face. At the time her heart had ceased to function; it was as if that once vital organ were no longer part of her body.

She had managed to escape Angie's sharp, piercing gaze before she made a complete fool of herself. Opting to catch up on her work at another time, she had left the station and had driven for miles, trying to sort through the mess that her life had become.

But nothing had been settled until she'd returned home and

begun her trek through the same woods that had been her sanctuary so long ago following her aunt's severe tongue-lashings.

It was over between her and Rance. Their time had run out. To continue their affair would be sheer folly, even if Rance were willing. The chief's job was what Rance lived for, and now that it was within reach, she wasn't about to be the cause of him losing it.

In addition, and whether she wanted to admit it or not, a lasting relationship between her and Rance was not meant to be. The sooner she faced the facts and got on with her life, the better off she'd be.

Rance's promotion was giving her that opportunity. But God, it hurt. Just the idea of seeing him everyday and not being able to touch him or have him touch her, made her physically sick.

Pausing in her tormented thoughts, she drew in a deep breath and leaned against a tree, turning her eyes up to the cloudless sky. *How am I going to stand it?*

It was then that she heard the sound. Stiffening, she jerked her head around.

"I didn't mean to scare you," Rance said softly.

Carly could find no order for her thoughts. "How...how did you find me?"

"Your housekeeper," he said with a husky tremor.

Knowing that it was only a matter of seconds before she would be in his arms, Carly took a step backward and made herself smile. "I hear congratulations are in order."

"What's wrong?" Rance asked, completely ignoring her felicitations.

The strained note in his voice shook her resolve for a moment, but then she recovered. "I think...you know."

"Like hell I do!"

"It's over between us, Rance," she said dully.

"Just like that." His face was white, and the muscles of his jaw were bunched.

"Yes, just like that," she replied, her voice soft, but unsteady. "In case it hasn't dawned on you yet, you're going to be the chief of police."

"What if I decided not to take it?"

For a moment her heart charged to life, only to die again just as quickly. "Don't be absurd," she snapped. "Of course you're going to take it. That's what you've always wanted."

"Any suggestions as to how we can solve our problem?"

A tiny shudder rippled through her. She wanted to shout, *Yes. If only you loved me, I'd gladly find work elsewhere.* But he didn't love her, so what she said was "No...no, I can't."

"I see."

Although he sounded as if he'd just been punched hard in the chest, Carly knew better, knew that she was again listening with her heart instead of her head.

"It's really over, then?"

"It's really over," she said, hiding her anguish.

A soft and strange expression flickered across his face, some emotion she couldn't read, maybe pain, maybe something deeper than pain.

"You mean it, don't you?"

"Yes," she whispered in a voice that sounded like someone else's.

He took a lurching step toward her. Light from the sun splashed on his forehead, but it did nothing to soften his features. "Damn you to hell, Carly Mitchum."

Then, before she could suck enough air through her lungs to speak, he was gone.

It had been five days since Rance had stormed out of her life, and not once during that time had she laid eyes on him.

The reason—she hadn't been to work in five days, except for the few minutes this morning, when she'd made a mad dash to the station to see Crawford. But that hadn't counted, because the minute she and the chief had concluded their business, she had disappeared out the side door.

Two of her five days off were planned; the others were not. She'd been ill—sick to her stomach. But she hadn't worried, positive it was nerves or a stomach virus.

Now, as she rambled around in the den of her uncle's house and paused at the window to look outside, she wasn't so sure. She was going to have to face the fact sooner or later that she was more than likely pregnant with Rance's child. Always, without exception, her monthly cycle had been on time. This month it had not. Today she was two weeks late.

If she was indeed pregnant, Carly had no one to blame but herself for not taking precautions, especially since she'd known Rance hadn't. But she'd been so crazy to make love with him that all else had fled her mind.

Whether she was pregnant or not, it would be impossible to continue to work in the same station with him, much less *for* him. She had finally come to terms with the cruel truth.

Still, it hurt. The pain was almost as unbearable as the memories. Lying in bed at night, she summoned up the pressure of his mouth on hers, the greedy probing of his tongue...

The only bright spot during these days had been her uncle's wedding. The ceremony had taken place on her first day off, and it had been lovely. Her uncle seemed so happy, happier than she'd ever seen him.

Yet she knew her mood had cast a dark cloud over what would otherwise have been a perfect day for him. She was sorry, but she couldn't seem to brighten her spirits.

There was Angie, as well. The dispatcher had been to see her, had known something was wrong, had in fact tried to pry it out of her, but Carly hadn't budged. She'd kept her pain locked inside her heart, except where her uncle was concerned.

She'd finally broken down and confided in him, told him about her and Rance, as well as the decision she'd been forced to make. The only thing she hadn't told him was that she might be carrying Rance's child.

While Matt had been stunned and just a little piqued that she hadn't told him before, he was also supportive, holding her, encouraging her to release her pent-up tears.

Carly closed her eyes suddenly and placed a hand across her still flat stomach, envisioning her abdomen swollen with the seed from Rance's loins. No matter what, she wanted this baby more than she'd ever wanted anything, except Rance.

Realizing her face was wet, she dipped into the pocket of her warm-up pants and pulled out a tissue. Just as she dabbed at the tears, she heard the front door slam. She straightened and tried to compose her features.

"Carly, where are you?"

"In the den, Uncle Matt." Turning her back to the window, she watched as he strode into the room.

"Why are you in the dark?" he asked, his eyes sharp with concern.

"Busy feeling sorry for myself, I guess." Her voice was low and flat.

"I take it you went through with it."

"Yes," Carly whispered, "I did it. I resigned, effective immediately."

Matt was silent as he crossed to the hearth, where he began fiddling with the wood that was on the grate. Seconds later, a healthy fire brightened the room.

"Come on, honey," Matt said at last, motioning toward the couch, "let's talk."

Once they were both seated, Matt spoke gently. "You know you can change your mind, that nothing is cast in stone."

Carly shook her head. "No, I can't. It would be impossible to work with...Rance now, after—" Her voice broke on a sob.

"Shh, don't cry," Matt pleaded, awkwardly patting the top of her cold hand. "I understand. It's just that now that I know you'll be going back to Dallas, I can't stand the thought. Nothing like a fickle old man."

"You're not fickle, and Big D's not that far away," Carly told him, clinging to his hand like a lifeline.

"I know. It's just that I've gotten so used to having you around."

"But now you've got Martha."

"That's not the same, honey. You...you're just like a daughter to me." His face was noticeably pale. "Why the hell did he have to get offered that chief's job?"

"Oh, Uncle Matt, don't begrudge him that position. It's what he's always wanted, and that's what I want him to have. Anyway, he...was up-front with me all along."

"Still, I'd like to—"

"No, don't say that, either," Carly cried, jumping up and going to stand in front of the fireplace.

For a moment there was silence in the room while Carly warmed her hands. When she turned back around, Matt was standing.

"I'm sorry, girl. I didn't mean to upset you." He paused. "You know how much I love you and want you to be happy."

Carly smiled through her tears. "I know, and I love you, too." Then, taking a deep breath, she added, "Now don't you think you'd best give me a big hug and be on your way. That plane won't wait. Tell Martha again how much I love her. And you two have a great time."

The newlyweds were about to depart on a ten-day Caribbean cruise that wouldn't bring them back home until a few days before Thanksgiving.

Matt looked troubled. "I don't know. I sure hate like hell to go off and leave you, especially now. Martha does, too. Maybe—"

"No. Absolutely not. I won't hear of it. By the time you get back, I'll have found an apartment in Dallas and will be in the process of packing. I'll even cook Thanksgiving dinner for you."

Matt looked dubious, but he didn't argue. "Guess a fellow can't beat a deal like that."

Before Carly could say anything else, he walked over and gave her a loving hug. "You take care of yourself now, you hear?" he told her roughly.

"You, too," Carly whispered. "Now go on, get out of here."

After she heard the door slam, Carly sank back down on the couch, put her head back and closed her eyes, challenging herself to rest.

Having apparently dozed off for a few minutes, it took a minute for her to realize that the jarring sound was the doorbell. She shook her head to clear it and stood. Thinking that Angie had decided to drop by again, Carly reluctantly made her way to the door.

"Carly! Carly, are you there?"

The painfully familiar voice turned her bones to liquid and

forced her to pause and lean against the nearest wall to steady herself. She was half-inclined to believe she was hallucinating.

With trembling fingers she unlocked and opened the door.

The air was thick with tense silence as Carly stepped aside. He moved over the threshold, and when she closed the door and faced him, she felt drained.

"Hello."

"Hello."

"What...what are you doing here?"

His bronzed face was grim. "Explain this," he said tersely, shoving a piece of paper at her.

Carly's heart sank. "I...it's self-explanatory." Trying to talk now was synonymous with battling an undertow, especially when she brought her gaze back up to meet his and caught him staring at the plunging neckline of her robe. Thinking that she was going to be alone for the evening, she'd dressed for comfort.

Rance swallowed hard. "Why did you do it? Why did you resign?"

Why did he have to probe like a doctor who cared nothing about pain? "You...know why."

"I can't let you do that."

"It's...already done."

"It can be undone just as easily."

Rance was staring at her mouth the way he used to before...

"No," she said.

"Yes."

Carly didn't know how to respond. She could only stare at him, which is what she'd longed to do from the moment he'd walked in, stare at the changes just five days had made in his appearance.

He looked not only haggard, but exhausted, as well. Her gaze dropped compulsively down the length of his lean body. He had lost weight, a fact that his thick jeans and bulky sweater could not hide. It was ironic that her waistline had expanded while his had decreased.

The moments passed in stillness, her eyes locked on the pro-

truding swell in his jeans. She tried in vain to curb the heat that
was gathering at the apex of her thighs.

Unable to stand his scrutiny another moment, she turned on
weak and trembly legs and walked to the hearth. There she clung
to the mantel for support.

"*Carly!*"

She didn't have to look behind her to know he was there. She
could feel his presence like a second skin. Before she could
speak, he reached out and slowly untied the sash that held her
robe together. Then slowly he turned her around to face him.

The same tormented desire that was in her eyes was mirrored
in his.

"Why," she whispered, "why are you really here?"

Groaning, he lowered his head and laid it against her breasts,
convinced his body would explode for want of her as he felt
her softness against him. "I...couldn't stay away."

Devastating emotions caused her eyes to close for a moment.
"Sex. Is...that all you want from me?"

"Oh, God," he ground out hoarsely. "I'm sorry, so sorry
I've led you to believe that."

"Then why?" she cried again.

"I came to tell you that I'm willing to give up the chief's job
if you..." His hands spread across her back, aligning her body
perfectly with his.

"If I what?" she gasped, as the contact of his mouth with
her nipple threw her insides out of kilter.

"You're going to make me say it?"

"Yes."

"If you promise you won't leave me."

"Oh, Rance, all I've ever wanted is to be with you."

"Carly, Carly," he murmured incoherently.

"Rance," she echoed, "please convince me you're not a mirage, that you're real." Her hands traced the shadows in his face
to prove her point.

He wanted to squeeze her, bite chunks out of her soft, vibrant,
sweet-smelling flesh. "I'm no mirage, my darling, and I intend
to prove it."

Dared she hope, dared she hope that the tangible emotion she saw in his eyes, heard in his voice was love?

Then he was kissing her, hungry, devouring kisses that left their mouths damp and wanting. She bit his lower lip, sucking it into her mouth.

She never knew how she got to the bedroom. She never knew how she got undressed. The only thing that was real to her was the ecstasy of his body against hers.

"Oh, Carly, my Carly, I've missed you, missed this," Rance whispered, descending into her in stages, while she held her breath for the moment of shared rapture. In a state close to unconsciousness, she cried his name until her mind slipped into the void of perfect peace.

Through the haze of his own pleasure, he savored hers, responding to her every movement with a rapture so encompassing, he felt he owned the world.

Later, as the sun barely peeped over the horizon, her head lay against his chest.

"Rance," she whispered urgently, drowsily, reaching up and touching his face. It was wet. She sat up and leaned on her elbow and peered down at him, then lowered her trembling lips to his.

"I love you, Carly," he breathed into her mouth. "I was afraid that it was really and truly over, that you wouldn't see me anymore. I didn't know what to do."

She thrilled to his words, having ached to hear them for so long, but never believing she would. "And I love you," she responded, trapping his tears with her fingers until they were gone.

"Will you marry me?" His hand closed fast around hers.

"I...can't believe I'm hearing those words."

"And I never thought I'd be saying them again, but from the first moment you rammed into me, I was caught."

"But, oh, how you did fight."

"But, oh, how you enjoyed watching me squirm."

She grinned impishly. "Well..."

"You're enchanting," he whispered, and turned so that they

lay facing each other, laughing. He nuzzled her neck, tongued her ear, kissed her nose in a kind of frantic joy.

"I'm asking you one more time, will you marry me?"

"Only if you won't give up the chief's job," she whispered, staring up at him.

Something inside him let go. "What about you?"

"What about me?"

His eyes locked on her mouth, which had been thoroughly kissed. "It's not any more fair for you to give up your job than it is for me to give up mine."

She smiled tremulously. "Yeah, but yours pays more."

He chuckled and tweaked her on the nose. "Ah, so it does."

"Even though I have enough money that we won't have to worry," she hastily assured him. "I know—"

"You're exactly right, I wouldn't. I intend to support my wife."

"So we have to be practical, right?"

"Right."

"So I can get a job anywhere around here should I choose to do so."

"So can I. I've been offered a security job and I'm willing to take—"

"No," she cut in, shaking her head adamantly. "Timberland P.D. is where you belong."

"You know what that means, don't you?"

"No," she said, running her fingers through his hair.

"It means we're never going to work together."

"Thank God for small favors."

He raised his eyebrows. "Why, you mean you weren't looking forward to working for me?"

"Not in the least." She flashed him a saucy grin.

With fingers of iron, he clasped the back of her neck and pulled her to him. He kissed her hard, hungrily. "That's too bad, because I was looking forward to working with you."

When she was coherent enough to speak again, she slapped playfully at his arm. "That's a lie, Captain Knight, and you know it."

"That's where you're wrong, woman. You made a believer out of me. I'd trust you at my back anytime."

She looked up at him, her eyes glazed with wonder. "Oh, Rance, I didn't think I'd ever hear you say that."

He grinned. "To tell you the truth, me neither. And it's a damn shame husband and wife aren't allowed to work on the same force. We'd make one helluva team."

"Yeah, wouldn't we? But the city fathers aren't about to change the rules just for us."

He grinned and shook his head. "Well, again that's a shame. I sure was looking forward to pinching your backside and not getting slapped for it."

"Oh, you're bad." She wiggled beneath him, her moist belly rubbing his. Feeling him thickening against her, she rolled on top of him.

"Oh, yes!" he groaned, as she took him inside her and began moving slowly, exquisitely.

Later, sated, they lay entwined, watching the shadows dance across the ceiling.

"Rance?"

"Um, darling?"

"Do...you think Stacy will mind about us?"

"She'll love it. You know how she feels about you."

"I hope you're right. Are you still going to try to get custody of her?"

He hesitated. "Do you still feel the same way? I mean, you once told me you thought it would be a good idea, but if you've changed—"

"I wouldn't have it any other way."

"You're amazing, you know that?" he whispered.

She gave him a quick kiss. "So are you."

"What about Matt? How's he going to feel?"

Carly ran her hands over his chest, threading her fingers through the coarse hair. "You don't worry about Uncle Matt. I'll take care of him. Anyway, he only wants me to be happy."

"And are you?"

Carly now folded her arms on his chest and propped her chin on them to watch his face. "I've never been happier."

"Ah, Carly, my beloved Carly," he murmured, rolling over onto his side, taking her with him. "I do love you."

"There's something else I have to ask you," she confessed.

"Anything love. Ask me anything."

"How...how do you feel about having more children?"

He pulled back and looked at her in astonishment. "Well, I've never really thought about it."

"Well," she said huskily, "I think you'd better."

His eyes darkened. "Are you trying to tell me something?"

"I think I'm...we're going to have a baby."

Rance sat up and stared at her incredulously. "A baby," he repeated softly.

Carly nodded.

"And would you have told me?" he asked, pain in his eyes.

"I...don't know," she answered honestly.

He caressed her fingers with his lips.

"You won't be sorry if...if I am?"

"Sorry? Dear Lord, what a question. But you—do you want it? I know how important your career is, how much you want to work."

She pressed a finger against his lips. "It's important, I won't deny that, but you and our baby are more important."

"Oh, Carly," he began on a strangled tone.

"For now and always," she added, drawing him down into the golden enchantment of her arms, circling him with her strength.

"Dying is the only end for us, my love."

*   *   *   *   *

This April
DEBBIE
MACOMBER

takes readers to the Big Sky and beyond...

MONTANA

At her grandfather's request, Molly packs up her kids and returns to his ranch in Sweetgrass, Montana.

But when she arrives, she finds a stranger, Sam Dakota, working there. Molly has questions: What exactly is he doing there? Why doesn't the sheriff trust him? Just *who* is Sam Dakota? These questions become all the more critical when her grandfather tries to push them into marriage....

Moving to the state of Montana is one thing; entering the state of matrimony is quite another!

Available in April 1998 wherever books are sold.

MIRA

MDM434

Take 4 bestselling love stories FREE

Plus get a FREE surprise gift!

Special Limited-time Offer

Mail to Silhouette Reader Service™

P.O. Box 609
Fort Erie, Ontario
L2A 5X3

YES! Please send me 4 free Silhouette Intimate Moments® novels and my free surprise gift. Then send me 6 brand-new novels every month, which I will receive months before they appear in bookstores. Bill me at the low price of $3.96 each plus 25¢ delivery and GST*. That's the complete price and a savings of over 10% off the cover prices—quite a bargain! I understand that accepting the books and gift places me under no obligation ever to buy any books. I can always return a shipment and cancel at any time. Even if I never buy another book from Silhouette, the 4 free books and the surprise gift are mine to keep forever.

345 SEN CF2W

Name	(PLEASE PRINT)
Address	Apt. No.
City	Province Postal Code

This offer is limited to one order per household and not valid to present Silhouette Intimate Moments® subscribers. *Terms and prices are subject to change without notice.
Canadian residents will be charged applicable provincial taxes and GST.

CMOM-696   ©1990 Harlequin Enterprises Limited

23191139304117

Catch more great

◆ HARLEQUIN™ Movies
featured on the movie channel ™

Premiering April 11th
Hard to Forget
based on the novel by bestselling
Harlequin Superromance® author
Evelyn A. Crowe

Don't miss next month's movie!
Premiering May 9th
The Awakening
starring Cynthia Geary and David Beecroft
based on the novel by Patricia Coughlin

If you are not currently a subscriber to
The Movie Channel, simply call your
local cable or satellite provider for more
details. Call today, and don't miss out
on the romance!

the movie channel ™
100% pure movies.
100% pure fun.

◆ HARLEQUIN™
™ *Makes any time special™*

Looking For More Romance?

Visit Romance.net

Check in daily for these and other exciting features:

Hot off the press

View all current titles, and purchase them on-line.

What do the stars have in store for you?

Horoscope

Hot deals

Exclusive offers available only at Romance.net

Plus, don't miss our interactive quizzes, contests and bonus gifts.

PWEB

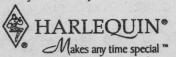